STELE PROPHECY PENTALOGY
PREQUEL 4

IRON
IN THE
SCEPTER

T0273497

RANDY C. DOCKENS

Carpenter's Son Publishing

Iron in the Scepter

©2020 by Randy C. Dockens

Published by Carpenter's Son Publishing, Franklin, Tennessee

Published in association with Larry Carpenter of Christian Book Services, LLC
www.christianbookservices.com

Cover and Interior Design by Suzanne Lawing

Edited by Robert Irvin

Printed in the United States of America

978-1-946889-71-3

CHAPTER 1

Look away, Janet. He's a farmer.

She tried to listen to her common sense by focusing on her delicious three-cheese and spinach lasagna, taking the last couple of bites. Studying her electronic tablet, she sipped her tea and tried to concentrate on a book she started the night before. After reading the same paragraph for the third time, she sighed and put the tablet down. Why was something so engaging the previous night not able to keep her attention now?

The waiter came by. Dinner came with complimentary cheesecake for guests with a birthday. How pathetic was it to spend her twenty-fifth birthday alone? *Just like last year.* Well, at least she was consistent. She stared at the slice of cake. *Leave it, Janet. Walk out now.* She almost did. Instead, she picked up her fork.

She heard him laugh. *Don't look over at him.* She glanced his way. He had all the qualities on her "perfect man" list: square jaw, dimples, engaging smile, and, most importantly, muscles. He had on a long-sleeved shirt, but when he bent his arm, it looked as if the fabric would burst at its seam. His hair had strong red highlights, somewhat disheveled, but that made him all the more intriguing in her eyes.

She looked away and shook her head. *Why did I look? I should leave.* She didn't. *You're a loner, Janet.* That's the way she had always worked. That's why she became a commodities analyst, so she could avoid entanglements. She should leave this farmer to his wheat and antigravity harvester. That's the way it had to be. But against her better judgment, she glanced at him again.

This time he glanced back. Their eyes made contact. The glance was brief but not so brief before he smiled at her. Trying to act nonchalant, she picked up her tablet again and pretended to read. His glancing rate increased, and soon he was looking at her nonstop, even when talking to his friends.

They stood. *Are they leaving? Good.* Soon all of this would be behind her.

He patted the shoulder of one of the others and headed her way. She now tried to ignore him completely. That became impossible when he was standing next to her table.

She repressed the urge to look up. "Can I help you?"

"That depends." He sat down across from her.

She took a glance. He had his chin in his palm with an arm propped on the table, displaying an adorable smile.

She put down her tablet and forced herself to remain expressionless. "Upon what?"

"Whether you go out with me or not."

"And why would I do that?"

He shifted in his seat, letting go of his chin, and placed both elbows on the table to lean forward, dimples now in full force.

"Let's turn this into a challenge," he said.

Janet's eyebrows went up. She didn't say anything. The guy's smile broadened, if that was even possible.

"If I get you to smile in, say, the next three minutes, you go out with me."

"Oh, that's the challenge, is it?" Janet kept her matter-of-fact tone.

The man nodded.

"I must warn you. Better men have tried."

"Other."

Janet scrunched her brow. "Excuse me?"

"Other men. Other men have tried. Not better."

Janet set back. "Oh, confident are we?" She nodded toward a table on the other side of the restaurant. "See that lady over there?"

The man turned his head and looked to where Janet nodded. The woman diverted her attention back to her salad.

"She's been staring at you the whole time, eating her salad very slowly trying to get your eye. Maybe you'd have better luck with her."

The man shook his head. "I'm more of a three-cheese lasagna man myself."

Janet almost smiled, but she caught herself. *Careful, Janet. If you let him win, social entanglements will only complicate things.*

The man's eyebrows raised, but she ignored him.

Janet looked at her T-band, a thin bracelet around her wrist displaying the time when touched, and then back at the man. "I believe you have only two more minutes."

"All right then." He cleared his throat. "Four men walked into a restaurant. Which one left with the prettiest lady there?"

Janet rolled her eyes and crossed her arms. "That's it? That's the puzzle you want me to solve?"

The man nodded, dimples glaring.

"Well. Let me ponder this a moment. The depth of this puzzle is so vast."

"Yes, but your pondering is eating away my minutes."

Janet unfolded her arms, putting her hand to her chest. "Oh, sorry. Yes, I wouldn't want to win on a technicality." Janet thought for a moment. "I'm going to assume this is a hypothetical question and not what is currently happening. OK?"

The man shrugged. "Sure. OK."

Janet squinted her eyebrows together. *What is he up to?* She really had no idea how to answer his question. There was no information to come up with a logical solution, so there probably wasn't one. "Sorry. I have no idea how to answer that."

The man leaned farther in. "The one who asked her."

Their eyes met for several seconds. His with a twinkle in them, hers trying not to give into his. In spite of herself, and against all internal reservations, a smile swept across her face. Shaking her head, she chuckled. "That has to be the stupidest question and answer in the world."

The man sat up and chuckled along with her. "Yes, but effective." He held out his hand. "Hi. I'm Bruce. Bruce O'Brien. It's my honor to meet the most beautiful woman here."

Janet took his hand. "Hi, Bruce. I'm Janet." She was hesitant to give out her last name. While adorable, if he didn't work out—or she didn't want the social entanglement to work out— she didn't want him knowing how to reach her.

"Janet." The way he said her name made it sound like hers was the most beautiful he had ever heard. He held her hand a couple of seconds longer before letting go.

He is certainly the smooth operator. Stay on your guard, Janet. But if he hugs me with those arms . . . I may just melt and pool on the floor. Without meaning to, she was now staring at his biceps.

"Shall I pick you up at nineteen hundred tomorrow evening?"

"What?" She slightly shook her head, coming out of her trance. "Oh, yes. That will be fine. I admit my defeat and accept the consequences."

Bruce held his head back and gave a hearty laugh. "I certainly hope you find our time together to be good consequences."

Janet displayed a smile but kept her tone matter-of-fact to hide delight. "We shall see."

Bruce returned her smile, displaying his dimples again. He stood and planted a kiss on the back of her hand. "Until tomorrow night, Janet. I'll meet you in the hotel lobby?"

Janet nodded. He turned and walked back to his friends, who had waited to see if he would be successful. They each patted him on his shoulder or back as they left the restaurant and headed to the hotel.

Janet leaned back and let out a long breath while taking her napkin and fanning herself. As she thought through the experience again, she smiled. Her smile slowly faded, though. *What did you do, Janet?* What could a city girl and a farmer find in common? *After all, you came from farming territory to Chicago vowing never to return.* Could any good come from this? *Come on, Janet. It's a date, not a lifelong commitment.* Her smile slowly returned.

Yes, it would likely be a good consequence after all.

She validated the check to her hotel room with her thumbprint, gathered her things, and headed back to her room. Either sleep would be hard to come by or she'd have very pleasant dreams.

CHAPTER 2

J anet left the hotel lobby and waited for the company antigravity accelerator. In a matter of minutes, a turquoise-colored, two-seater AGA pulled up. The car hovered as the door lifted. Janet got in and pressed her thumb on the pad on the dash which scanned her thumbprint as the door closed.

"Hello, Ms. Singleton." The mechanical voice sounded melodic. "Corporate office or satellite office?"

"Corporate office, please."

"Your travel time will be eleven minutes."

The AGA pulled off without a sound. Janet had an unobstructed view as the roof was also clear glass. She loved being in the city. The combination of high-rises, parks, and sculptures peppered throughout made great views as the car traveled through the city.

Once at the corporate office, Janet took the floating elevator to the fifteenth floor. Some found the optical illusion disconcerting, but she loved the effect. From ground level, the view looked as if the elevator was totally disconnected from the building.

The entire fifteenth floor was the commodities office. At a cobalt-colored glass desk sat a woman in her early twenties, her brown hair pulled to the side in a French braid.

"Hi, Molly. Is Edgar ready for me?"

Molly gave a bright smile. "Hello, Janet. He'll be with you shortly. He's finishing up a call."

While waiting, Janet pulled up the files on her tablet that she would need for her meeting; she reviewed them briefly.

"Janet. Come in."

Edgar gave her a big smile and shook her hand. Although not very muscular, he had a strong grip. He held the glass door open as she entered his office and directed her to the small conference table that had an oversized monitor at the other end.

"Have a seat. You said you have some exciting news."

Janet laughed. "Well, *I* think so. I guess you'll have to tell me if you agree."

Edgar raised his eyebrows. "It's hard to imagine something more surprising than your previous ingenious finding. Understanding the pattern of crop consumption in various places around the world helped increase our long-range teleporter efficiency for crop distribution by 73 percent. Even Tiberius was impressed."

Janet's mouth fell open. "Professor Tiberius of the Jerusalem Science Center?"

Edgar nodded.

"I had no idea he was involved."

"He's always had an interest in the teleporters. I've heard he was involved in their installation in the early days. He was the one who calculated the increased efficiency. They were able to better predict the timing of crop shipments using the long-range teleporters."

"I'm honored."

"And you're going to impress again today?"

"Well, I hope so," Janet said, smiling.

Edgar gestured toward her. "OK. Show me what you've got."

Janet turned on her tablet and flicked the files onto the large monitor. She pointed to what was showing onscreen. "The picture on the left shows, in color-coded fashion, the crops produced in each section of the world. As we talked before, we now know, and continue to track, when each area uses each of these crops."

Edgar nodded. "And what is the one on the right?"

"Let me enlarge the picture for you. You can see the animation better."

Janet enlarged both maps to each fill half the monitor. She then tapped a button so the maps would animate.

"This shows what main crops are consumed in each part of the world over the course of a year," she said. "Now, if you compare the two maps, where the crops are grown are not necessarily where they are consumed the most."

Edgar rubbed his chin. "That's very interesting, Janet." He looked at her. "But I'm not sure I see the impact you want me to see."

"Most areas grow two main crops a year. If we have the crops grown where most eaten, then we can gain even more efficiency on the long-range teleporters. Less crops would have to be teleported to the areas of consumption."

Edgar's eyebrows rose. "Ah, that is impressive."

"As you know, the King has prescribed that crops must be grown for only six years, and the seventh year the land left fallow."

Edgar nodded.

"I've measured soil content in all areas over the earth where the major crops currently grow, and I've devised a crop rotation schedule which fits into this paradigm so nutrients needed for the next crop are always replenished by the previous crop."

"Wow, Janet. You've really done your homework."

Janet laughed. "Thanks. Not to brag, but this crop rotation schedule was hard to come by and took me almost five years to get all the details worked out."

"Now that I understand what I'm seeing, play the video back for me again," Edgar asked. "I think I can appreciate your animation better now."

Janet felt proud of herself and hoped more accolades would be coming. Still, watching Edgar's face as he watched the animated map a second time made her concerned. He was no longer smiling.

"What's the matter, Edgar?"

Edgar pointed at Africa. "You have crops growing in Africa."

Janet nodded. "Yes, the ground there is important to the entire delicate balance as its soil has a higher density for some critical nutrients other places need. Seeds from crops grown there used in other places will help keep the correct soil nutrient ratio everywhere."

Edgar shook his head. "I don't think this is going to work, Janet."

Janet furrowed her brow. "What? What makes you say that?"

"There's a reason we don't grow crops in Africa. The King has declared the area be left untouched."

"Yes, but—"

Edgar held up his hand. "There is no 'but,' Janet. You know that. This was the King's decree. There is no rebuttal."

Janet took a deep breath and let it out slowly. "Perhaps if the Administrator showed him these data, he would change his mind."

Edgar shook his head more vigorously this time. "There is no way I can present this to the Administrator. I would get shot down in a second. I don't want her to think we're trying to usurp the King's decrees."

Janet bit her bottom lip as Edgar talked. "Edgar, no disrespect, but you've just dismissed five years of work in a few seconds."

Edgar put his hand on her shoulder. "Janet, I can see a lot of logic went into your plans, but Africa has to be off-limits. The King leads a safari to Africa every Sabbath Year. The area has to be a pristine place."

Janet drummed her fingers on the table. Her breathing was short and shallow as she tried to stay calm.

"Why not rework some things and see if there's another alternative?" Edgar queried.

Janet nodded with lips pressed together. There was no use trying to argue her point. She picked up her tablet and turned to leave.

"Janet, I'm sorry. I'm sure you can find another approach."

Janet walked out of Edgar's office without a reply. She went to her temporary office two doors down from Edgar's and plopped into her desk chair. How could Edgar dismiss her hard work so easily?

It also irritated her the King made decisions seemingly for no apparent reason. Shouldn't her logic override the need for a safari? Doesn't he want to increase efficiency, she asked herself, and shouldn't that be more important than him wanting to indulge his whims?

Janet shook her head and sighed. *What a waste of time and effort.* There was no need to look over her work again. It wasn't as if she had brought Africa into the picture because she wanted to do so. Unless the King would change his requirements for only six years of growing crops, there would be no way, without Africa in the mix, to work out a proper schedule to keep the right nutrient ratio for all crops grown near their area of consumption. As far as she could see, there was no other way to increase teleporter efficiency regarding crop shipments.

Janet sighed again and leaned back in her chair while crossing her arms. What if she went over Edgar's head and talked to the Commodities Administrator herself? She shook her head. No, that would be career suicide. Janet leaned forward and propped her head in her hand, elbow on her desk, and looked out the window. The beauty of the city brought her calmness. Maybe she should move from the satellite office on the outskirts of the city to the city itself. Would they allow her to work here on a permanent basis? After all, she wasn't asking for more space. This temporary office looked not much larger than her current office.

Her office door opened and Administrator Billingsley walked in.

Janet's eyes widened and she stood instinctively.

"Administrator Billingsley."

"Call me Beth, Janet." She motioned for Janet to sit. "Please. Please, have a seat."

Janet motioned for Beth to sit as she sat herself. Why would an Administrator be coming to her office? Would this be the time to mention her idea? If she did, she would have to make Edgar the good guy in the scenario.

As Beth sat in the clear Plexiglas chair, Janet noticed the entire chair glowed from the brightness of Beth's skin resonating from her glorified body.

"Janet, I came by because I didn't want you to be discouraged about the rejection of your idea." Beth gave a reassuring smile.

Janet's jaw went slack and her lips parted. "Uh, I didn't know you knew that." She shook her head lightly and turned her brow. "How *did* you know that?"

"The King has reasons for everything he does. I wanted to stop by and say not to take any of this personally. He values your deductive reasoning skills. You have had brilliant ideas in the past, and I'm sure you will continue to do so." Beth smiled. "One day, I'm sure your children will be blessed with obtaining such life skills from you in this area."

Janet sat, immovable, not knowing what to say.

After a few awkward moments of silence, Beth tapped her knees with her palms. "Well, I should be getting back to my office."

She stood. Janet did also.

"Janet, you are a valued employee. Keep up the excellent work." Beth smiled, turned, and left Janet's office.

Janet sat with a thud. *Edgar.* He had to be the one who told Beth. Janet puckered her mouth and breathed out hard through her nose. *How could he do that?* She drummed her fingers trying to decide whether to let the incident slide or to confront him. *No, he had no right.*

Janet passed Molly without saying a word and walked into Edgar's office unannounced. Edgar looked up from his reading. His eyebrows raised.

"Janet?"

Janet stood with arms on hips and stared at him.

Edgar cocked his head slightly and squinted. "Are you OK? Anything wrong?"

"How could you?"

He shook his head slightly. "How could I what?"

"Tell Administrator Billingsley about my idea."

Edgar stood and came around the side of his desk. "What are you talking about, Janet? I haven't talked to anyone since you left my office."

Janet's tone remained agitated. "Well, neither have I." She pointed toward the door. "Yet, lo and behold, Administrator Billingsley came to my office and said I shouldn't be disappointed about my rejection, and then said I was a valued employee." She took a couple of steps toward Edgar. "So, how would she know about you nixing my idea?"

Edgar shrugged. "I don't know, Janet. I guess from the King. You know the tight psychic connection those with glorified bodies have with the King."

"And how would the King know about my work?"

Edgar narrowed his eyes. "Really? The King knows everything about everything."

Janet wanted to roll her eyes but thought better of it. Apparently, Edgar bought into the King-being-omniscient thing. "Well, I'm sure the King has better things to occupy his time than my crop rotation schedule."

Janet turned and opened the door, then paused. "Just talk to me before you talk to anyone else."

"Janet—"

She stepped out without waiting for Edgar's reply.

She went to her office, picked up her tablet, and left the building. Working in the park across the street would be better than staying and talking to anyone else. A bench near one of the fountains seemed to call to her. As she closed her eyes for a couple of minutes, the sound of trickling water relaxed her muscles. The breeze brought a scent of lilacs from somewhere behind her. When she turned, several large lilac bushes stood grouped together. *Ah*, she thought. *The perfect spot.*

After working for another hour, she decided to head back to her hotel.

Could the King really know what she did at all times? How could others think that comforting? The thought sounded a bit creepy to her. So, the King gives her no privacy, appreciates her logic, but essentially says, "Still, my wishes trump your logic."

None of that sat right with Janet.

CHAPTER 3

When Janet arrived at her hotel room, she immediately went to the kitchenette and prepared some tea. Taking the cup to the balcony, she sat in one of the two lounge chairs, her favorite spot. This semicircular balcony with its fieldstone floor, potted shrubbery, and small fountain in the corner always made the troubles of the day seem not so overwhelming. After taking a few sips of her tea, she leaned her head back and closed her eyes.

Bruce. She sat up in a flash. Her date had completely slipped her mind. According to her T-band, she had two hours to prepare. A sigh of relief calmed her adrenaline surge. That was just enough time to get ready. After showering and putting her hair in a French twist, she tried to decide what to wear. Normally, Janet was a decisive person. But for some reason, the thought of this man put her mind into a giddy panic. She wanted to impress but not go overboard. And for all she knew, he could be wearing overalls when he came to pick her up. She gave a suppressed chuckle. Well, that would make an easy decision for her.

After changing outfits four times, she finally decided on a carnelian-colored backless dress. The strap came from the bodice, went around her neck, and back to the bodice. She then donned a black choker with a single white teardrop pearl and put on earrings to match. She did a quick turn in the mirror and felt satisfied. Hopefully, this was dressy enough without being over the top. The clock on the wall told her she had completed her ensemble with five minutes to spare. She breathed deeply and headed for the door.

Reaching the lobby, Janet looked around. Not seeing Bruce, she headed to one of the plush chairs facing the hotel entrance, but then saw him enter. She stood in place and watched him approach. He was a little less dressy than she, but still looked stylish in a smoke-colored pullover with a mock collar, black dress pants, and a matching sport coat with thin lines of burgundy. *Very tasteful,* she thought.

He gave her a slight hug and a light kiss on her cheek. "Janet, you look stunning."

She smiled and replied, "Thanks, Bruce. You look nice as well."

"I feel a little underdressed compared to you, but thanks." He held out his elbow. "Shall we go?"

She took his arm and could feel his bicep, which seemed massive. She was tempted to squeeze, but resisted the urge.

Once outside, a hotel AGA was waiting. After helping her in one side, Bruce got in on the other and then placed his thumb on the dash scanner. A melodic mechanical voice came on as the doors closed. "Hello, Mr. O'Brien. Where shall I take you this evening? Address or point of interest?"

"Point of interest. O'Brien's restaurant."

"Very good, Mr. O'Brien. Your travel time will be fifteen minutes."

Bruce sat back as the AGA accelerated silently.

"Wow," Janet said. "It's hard to consider this a consequence for losing your riddle. O'Brien's is an elegant place."

Bruce smiled. "Well, I did say I wanted you to enjoy your consequence."

"I think I'm going to be able to endure it."

Bruce looked at her and laughed. "Making me work tonight, are you?"

"As all men should."

Bruce raised an eyebrow. She laughed.

"What made you chose O'Brien's? Are you related to the owner?"

Bruce laughed. "If I am, I'm not getting any of the proceeds. That part is a coincidence. An elegant lady deserves an elegant dinner."

Janet raised her eyebrows. "I like how my consequences are starting out."

Bruce smiled. Janet saw his cheeks redden as he fiddled with his collar.

The restaurant was on the top floor of a building not far from where Janet worked. The maître d' sat them right away, and at a table next to the window overlooking the city. The other high-rises were silhouetted in golds and reds produced by the setting sun.

The waiter came by, poured water, informed them of the specials, and took their order.

Janet sat back and gave a short sigh.

"Everything OK?"

She smiled and nodded. "Yes, everything's OK—now."

"Bad day?"

Janet chuckled. "You can say that."

"What happened?"

Janet tried to wave it off with a flick of her wrist. "Oh, you don't want to hear about that."

Bruce leaned forward. "I'm interested in everything about you."

Janet cocked her head and smiled. "Well, I was excited this morning. I had figured out how to further increase the efficiency of the long-range teleporters in regard to crop shipments."

Bruce's head jerked back slightly. "Really? What kind of job do you have?"

"I'm a commodities analyst."

Bruce's jaw dropped a bit. "Wow. You're just an onion of impressiveness."

Janet almost choked on a drink of water as she couldn't hold in her laugh.

"You have quite the way with words," she said with a playful smile.

Bruce smiled. "One of my many charms." He turned more serious. "So what happened?"

Janet sighed. "Well, the details are a little complicated. Let's just say that growing crops in Africa was essential to my plan. I was informed that was against the King's decree."

"Oh, because of the Sabbath Year safaris?"

Janet nodded and sighed. "My boss nixed five years of work in about two seconds. Quite the Friday."

Bruce took Janet's hand and looked into her eyes. "I'm sorry, Janet."

She looked down at her hand and then back at him. *He's sweet.*

The waiter returned with their first course and added freshly ground parmesan cheese and pepper to their salads.

Bruce picked up his fork and looked out the window. "So where is your office?"

Janet looked out the window, swallowing her bite of salad as she pointed with her fork. "If you look straight ahead, and then two buildings over."

"You mean the one with the floating elevator?"

Janet nodded.

"I saw that the other day. The view was impressive. I couldn't see the elevator connected anywhere. How did they do that?"

Janet chuckled. "It's awesome to ride in as well." She took a drink of water. "I'm no engineer, but I'm told they used anti-gravity technology to help the elevator go up and down and light-dispersing technology to make the elevator look like it's totally floating from ground level."

"So how do you get on the elevator?"

Janet smiled. "Actually, the same way you get on any elevator."

Bruce turned up his brow. "Really? How?"

"There's a glass bridge at every floor that goes out to the elevator. Somehow, the light is made to go around these bridges when observed from the ground. It's an optical illusion."

"I have to say, the building is very impressive."

Bruce picked up a roll and tore it open. The yeasty aroma tantalized Janet's senses and she wanted one as well but decided to hold off.

"So what do you do there?" Bruce asked.

"I look at all the crops that are grown around the world and see how to increase efficiency in production, distribution, and consumption."

Bruce smiled with a twinkle in his eyes. "That means we have something in common."

Janet's eyebrows went up. "Oh?"

Bruce nodded. "I farm, and you tell me how. Sounds like a good combination to me."

Janet laughed. "You *want me* telling you what to do?"

"You know, there are some people you don't mind getting that from," he said.

Janet felt heat rush to her cheeks. He really knew how to say the right things at the right time.

"So what about you, Bruce? What makes you tick?"

Bruce laughed. "I'm pretty simple and uncomplicated. I farm. I like to farm." He paused. "No, I love to farm."

"What you see is what you get. Is that it?"

"Pretty much." A smirky grin unfolded across his face. "Do you like what you see?"

Janet smiled. *If he only knew.* She felt warm but resisted the urge to fan herself.

Luckily, the waiter came with their entrées, which gave Janet time to recover.

"When do you have to go back home, Bruce?"

He looked down at his plate and pushed a few peas around. He glanced back at her. "Unfortunately, sometime after Sabbath. The conference ended today, and I do have to get back to my farm."

"Oh." Janet gave a small shrug. "Well, I have to get back home as well."

Bruce took a bite of his tricolored tortellini. "You must live far away if you stay in a hotel when you visit. Where's your office located?"

Janet shook her head. "No, not really. I work out of a satellite office not far from here."

Bruce displayed a confused look. "So, if you work nearby, what makes you stay at a hotel when your home is not that far away?"

Janet smiled as she swallowed a mouthful of linguini. "I just love being in the city. I need to come to the corporate office about every other month. I stay at the hotel so I can enjoy the city." She scrunched her nose. "Wasteful, I know. But a perk I'm allowed."

Bruce laughed. "Why not just move here and work at the corporate office?"

"I'm working on it."

"Always been a city girl?"

Janet laughed and shook her head. "Actually, my family are farmers. Not too far southwest from here."

Bruce sat up. "Oh. Shepherd Randall's territory?"

Janet nodded. "How did you know?"

"Oh, Shepherd Morgan talks about him sometimes. I live in the next territory down."

Janet nodded again. *How close is he to these Shepherds?* She wanted to ask but felt the question too personal since she didn't know him that well.

"So, how did you go from farm to city?" Bruce asked.

Janet took a drink of water. "Oh, I grew up on the farm but always adored the city. Dad made me learn about farming, so I took that knowledge and went into commodities." She laughed and put a loose strand of hair behind her ear. "He still has a plot of land waiting for me. I think he hopes I'll move back." She shook her head. "I don't think so, though."

"You strike me as pretty independent. I could see you running a farm."

"Dressed like this?"

Bruce laughed. "I said running a farm. Not necessarily working on one."

Janet raised her eyebrows. "You don't think I can work on a farm?"

Bruce raised his hands. "Whoa! Stop the train and let me off. I don't want to go there."

Janet laughed. "I love your comebacks. Most men are intimidated by my comments."

"I'm up to a challenge." Bruce's eyes were smiling. "Especially if it's something worth fighting for."

Their eyes met for a few brief moments. Janet felt her cheeks warm. She looked down and took the last bite of her entree.

The waiter returned, took their plates, and left a dessert menu. They ordered the geometric sorbet and shared it. Three selections came on a rectangular plate: lemon as a sphere, raspberry as a cube, and boysenberry as a cone. They were set in a thin layer of white chocolate with tiny streaks of dark chocolate interspersed. The amount was just enough to enjoy and top off the delicious meal.

"Thank you, Bruce," Janet said. "That was so delicious. Almost too beautiful to eat." She smiled. "But I'm glad we did."

Bruce laughed. "So, you suffered through the consequences OK?"

"I hardly suffered at all." She took her napkin and dabbed her lips. "Would you pardon me a moment?"

"Meet me at the entrance when you're done, and I'll take you on your next consequence."

Janet cocked her head. "Are you serious?"

"Oh, your suffering has only begun."

Janet grinned and stood, and Bruce rose as well. She headed to the restroom.

She found the restroom occupied, so Janet stood next to a nearby window and looked at the city below. All the lights were mesmerizing. There was a couple not far from where she stood. She didn't try to eavesdrop but did hear some of their conversation.

"Jack, think about it. Total freedom. Isn't that what you want? Isn't that what everyone wants?"

Janet continued to look out the window as if she was oblivious to this couple only a few meters from where she stood. Yet her ears were straining to hear more. *Total freedom?* Yes, that's exactly what she wanted.

"I don't know, Amanda. I can't go against the King. He's done so much."

"Except allow you to think for yourself. He doesn't allow anyone to have a thought different from his."

Exactly, Janet thought. She never knew others thought these things like she did. She had to give this Amanda woman credit for being willing to say these things out loud. How could she find out more information? She couldn't just walk up and admit what she had heard. Janet glanced at the two. In the chair next to Amanda was the most exquisite purse she had ever seen, white with numerous clear beads all over it. A few of the beads, however, were colored. Yet periodically, another bead would turn a color while a colored one would turn back to clear. The change was subtle and not frequent enough to be distracting, only intriguing. Maybe that was the inroad she needed.

Janet approached the table. "Excuse me. I'm sorry for interrupting."

Amanda looked at her with a questioning look. Jack looked as if he wanted to bolt.

"I was admiring your purse. It's very unique. May I ask where you got it?"

Amanda smiled. "I made it. I have my own clothing boutique." She stuck out her hand. "I'm Amanda. Amanda Story."

Janet shook her hand. "Hi, Amanda. It's a pleasure to meet you. I don't want to further disturb your dinner. Do you have a card?"

Amanda's eyes lit up. "Oh yes. Absolutely." She opened her purse and handed Janet a business card:

Amanda Story. Let my clothes tell your story.

"Oh, how intriguing. Thank you. I'll let the two of you get back to your dinner." Janet stepped back. "Thank you again, Amanda."

"Bye. Please stop by soon. I have a lot to show you."

Janet waved, turned, and walked back to the restroom. As she turned, she saw the expression on Jack's face change to one of relief.

At the entrance, Bruce was waiting. He stuck out his elbow and she took it.

"Your chariot awaits, Mademoiselle."

Janet gave Bruce a side glance and shook her head. "What are you up to?"

He said nothing but pressed the button on the elevator for the ground level. Once they reached street level, he pointed to the full-size AGA that was waiting.

Janet's eyes widened. "You have a manual AGA?"

"I just rented it for the night." He opened the door and helped her into the passenger side. He bounded around to the driver's side, climbed in, pressed the accelerator, and they were off.

"You never cease to amaze me. Where are we going?"

Bruce gave a slightly wicked grin. "To your final consequence."

Janet shook her head, leaned back, and enjoyed the view. After about fifteen minutes, Bruce pulled up to an overlook area of the lake and city and parked the AGA.

"Here we are."

Janet sat up. "Here where?" Before them, but a bit to the left, was the city, its lights reflected off the lake, which looked totally black during the night.

"Oh, and check this out." Bruce pressed a button and the top rolled away.

Janet's jaw dropped. "A convertible?" She gave a satisfied sigh. "You're amazing."

"That's what I wanted to hear."

Janet laughed. "So, what now?"

He jumped out of the car, came to her side, and opened her door. He helped her out and then opened the door to the back seat, helping her back in. He then jumped in the other side.

"That was a long walk. I'm exhausted," Janet said, smiling.

He returned her smile, removed his sport coat, and held up his arm, meaning for her to draw closer so he could put his arm around her. She obliged. They sat in silence for a while as they looked at the city in the distance, its lights twinkling on the water and across the ripples. The view was mesmerizing.

It wasn't long before Janet put her head on his chest, and Bruce put his arms around her more tightly. Running her hand over his arm, this time she couldn't resist the temptation. She squeezed his bicep. Bruce said nothing but did give a small chuckle.

Before she knew it, she was so relaxed she drifted into a restful sleep.

CHAPTER 4

Something tickled Janet's nose. As she opened her eyes, a butterfly flew away as she began to sit up.

Where . . . where am I? Slowly, remembrance came back to her. She was still in Bruce's arms. Still at the overlook. All night? She sat up a bit farther, causing Bruce's arm to fall onto the seat. He too began to wake.

He stretched, yawned, and slowly smiled. "Good morning," he said.

"You realize we've been here all night?"

Bruce gave a smirk. "Believe it or not, I deduced that when I opened my eyes."

Janet slapped his arm. "You know what I mean."

Bruce laughed, cleared his throat, and rubbed his hand across his face and hair. "Care to get some breakfast after we go back and change?"

"Sure. I don't have to work today, so I'm in no rush."

Once back at the hotel, Janet showered and changed into jeans and a white pullover. Bruce met her in the lobby and handed her a cup of yogurt and granola. He was in jeans and a cornflower blue pullover. Once again, Janet had to force herself not to stare at how his arms stretched his shirt.

"I thought we could eat and explore together," Bruce said.

As they ate their yogurt, they walked, chitchatted about various things, and would stop and admire various sculptures throughout the city. Before Janet knew it, they were at her favorite park, which was directly across from her office building. They stopped and sat near an abstract sculpture that looked like large flames independent at the base but intertwined at the top of the sculpture.

Bruce pointed to her office building. "I'm still intrigued by the elevator to your building. It looks like it just hangs there in space at the fifth floor."

Janet glanced at the building and back to Bruce. "Want to ride in it?"

Bruce's eyes widened. "Can I?" He glanced at his watch. "Tomorrow?"

Janet looked from Bruce's watch to his eyes and responded hesitantly. "Sure. Something wrong?"

Bruce grimaced. "I have to meet my conference leader before I go back home."

Janet scrunched her brow.

He gave an apologetic look. "I promised I'd provide ideas for next year's conference. We're supposed to go over ideas over Sabbath dinner."

He planted a kiss on her cheek, smiled, and then pointed at the elevator. "I really want to see that tomorrow. Can I meet you back here in the morning?"

Janet smiled. "OK. I'll bring the yogurt."

Bruce laughed as he walked away. "How can I turn down an offer like that?"

The next morning, Janet arrived at the park bench across from her office with yogurt in hand. No sooner had she sat than she saw Bruce approach. She stood and held out his yogurt with a smile.

"True to your word, I see."

"Your consequence has begun."

Bruce laughed and shook his head.

"Too much?" Janet's smile turned into a grin.

Bruce simply gestured toward the building. "Shall we?"

The building was open; the elevator was considered a tourist attraction. No one was in the building at the time, however. Janet took Bruce to the elevator and pointed out the glass walkway that went out a couple of meters from the building to the elevator.

Bruce looked up and around. "I can't believe this. You can't see any of this from the street."

Janet smiled and pressed the button to summon the elevator, which then descended. Its glass doors sequenced with the walkway's glass doors and both opened simultaneously.

Bruce looked up and pointed. "Look, you can see the other walkways extending from the building."

Janet chuckled. "You sound like a typical tourist."

Bruce looked at Janet and laughed. "Today, I am."

Janet had the option of pressing the top button for a ride in the elevator as all visitors could. Yet she had it scan her thumbprint and pressed the fifteenth floor.

Bruce raised his eyebrows. "Where are we going?"

"To my office. You mind?"

Bruce shook his head.

"I want to get your opinion on what I shared with my boss." She really liked Bruce but somehow had to get his feeling about the King if she was going to continue seeing him. She had to know now before she got too attached.

Once they stepped off the elevator, they were in the receptionist area.

"Wow." Bruce looked around and nodded. "I can see why you want to work here. It all looks so unique with the walls clear glass and every glass desk a different color." He walked over for a closer look at the receptionist's desk. "Hmm. The edge of the desk is on a light source which travels throughout the desk." He looked back at Janet. "Impressive."

"It only looks like this when the office light is off," she said. They walked into Janet's temporary office. The office light went on and the desk light turned off.

Janet sat behind her desk and motioned for Bruce to take a seat in the clear Plexiglas chair.

"I want to show you what I presented to Edgar, my boss, and get your take on it."

"OK. But why?"

"Well, I think my logic is sound, but you, an actual farmer, may see something I'm missing." Seeing Bruce turn up his brow, she sighed. "I want to see if there's another reason the King doesn't want me to pursue this."

Bruce shrugged. "OK."

Janet took a few minutes to briefly explain everything she had presented to Edgar before she showed Bruce the actual slides.

"Do you need your computer?" he asked.

Janet shook her head. "I uploaded it to the nebula drive, so I can access it anywhere." After a few moments, the map displayed and animated on the oversized monitor at the end of her desk.

"So, what do you think?"

Bruce sat there rubbing his chin and then looked at Janet, giving her a smile. "Your idea is really ingenious." Shifting in his seat, he asked, "How did your idea get shot down?"

"Administrator Billingsley sat right there in the chair you're sitting in and said not to get discouraged because my idea was rejected."

"So, your boss talked to her without you being present to give a rebuttal?"

Janet shook her head.

"Your boss didn't talk to her?"

"According to him."

"So, the Administrator received a message from the King through his Spirit, Ruach HaKadosh?"

Janet's eyes narrowed. "Do you believe in that myth?"

Bruce raised an eyebrow. "According to Shepherd Morgan, it happens all the time. He says Scripture supports the idea."

Have I gone too far? Janet wondered. Well, there was only one way to find out. "Is that what you believe?" she asked.

Bruce shrugged. "I try not to get involved in debates. But . . . " He let the sentence hang.

"But what?"

"Well, from how Shepherd Morgan explained it in one of his lessons some time ago, it explains why Administrators have glorified bodies and appear to glow somehow—because they died before the Refreshing and came back with the King when he returned."

Janet pointed. "There. Did you hear what you just said?"

Bruce shook his head slightly. "What? What did I say?"

"Death. I just don't get that. Have you ever heard of anyone dying?"

Bruce shook his head. "Except—"

Janet waved a hand quickly. "Yes, yes, I know. Not since the Refreshing." She looked at Bruce with lips pursed. "And who controls all those records explaining how death used to happen? The King and his Administrators. That's who." Janet became even more emphatic. "We both have relatives who are centuries old. How do we know the Refreshing, where 'all was made new,' is an actual event, or one that was made up to explain the King's legitimacy?"

Bruce laughed. "I'm sorry, Janet. I see this topic gets you worked up."

"Well, I choose to look at reality and use my senses. My senses tell me death is a myth."

Bruce smiled as he pantomimed tipping a hat in her direction. "To each his own."

That made Janet chuckle. "Sorry. I guess I get a little passionate sometimes." She pointed to the monitor. "So, what about my proposal?"

Bruce sat back. "Oh, I think you have a remarkable brain." He smiled. "Among other things."

Janet felt her cheeks warm once more. She smiled and placed a stray hair behind her ear. "But . . . did I miss anything? In my proposal?"

"Well, I can understand why people wouldn't want to go on a safari and see people farming when they would see that at most places around the world."

Janet's shoulders drooped. She had hoped Bruce would be more supportive.

"Yet there is one additional variable that might need considering."

Janet sat up. "Oh. What's that?"

"Farm equipment."

Janet froze for a second while trying to process the statement. She let out a sigh, shaking her head. "Farm equipment. Why didn't I think of that? If I put farm equipment in my model, the soil can be repurposed better without necessarily having to go elsewhere for a different crop." She stood and walked to the side of her desk. "I'm impressed."

Bruce grinned and stood. "I said I was simple. Not a simpleton."

She slapped his shoulder lightly and stood eye to eye with him. "I never implied that."

Bruce smiled. "No. No, you didn't."

Their eyes locked. Janet remained motionless. Bruce wrapped his arms around her as he leaned in for a kiss. Their lips touched and her body went weak. His strong arms held her steady, however, and this caused her to go even weaker. No man had ever affected her like this. After a few seconds, their lips parted.

Bruce whispered. "Janet, I've known you only a short time, but I think I'm falling for you."

"But how can we make this work?"

Bruce gave a small grin. "Teleporters make a lot of things possible."

"Maybe." Janet asked herself why she was so hesitant about this. *What's holding me back?*

"Well, just think about it this week. Can I come back and see you next weekend?"

Janet nodded. "I'll meet you in the hotel lobby. Say, for brunch around ten thirty?"

Bruce turned up an eyebrow. "I thought you were going back home."

"Oh, I am. But this gives me another reason to come back to the city."

Bruce laughed and shook his head. "You're definitely a city girl." He suddenly stopped as though a realization had hit him, letting his arms fall to his side and his shoulders droop. "Oh, I see."

"See what?"

"Why you hesitated. You can't see a relationship developing."

"I . . . uh . . . don't know." She turned and took a couple of steps toward her desk and turned back, making circles on the desk with her index finger. "I just don't want to get my hopes up."

Bruce walked back to Janet and took her hands in his. "You take your time and leave the rest to me." He kissed her forehead.

She gave him a hug. This should be an easy decision. *Why am I making it so hard? Maybe he's right. Time.* That's what she needed.

"Just be cautious, Janet."

"What do you mean?"

"Not everyone will accept negative comments about the King." Bruce paused. "Some . . . some have been taken."

"Taken?" She shook her head slightly. "I don't understand."

"Shepherd Morgan tells us that is part of the King's iron scepter. Rebellion will be dealt with swiftly. I've heard of some being called rebellious and just disappearing. No one has seen them since."

Janet's eyes widened. "What? They were taken for just having a different opinion?"

"For various reasons, I've heard." He paused. "Just be careful."

Janet turned and paced. "That's what makes me so upset with the King. Why is he allowed to be the one who defines what anyone can do?"

35

Bruce grabbed her and stopped her from pacing. He rubbed her shoulders. "Calm down, Janet. If I knew you would get so upset, I wouldn't have said anything. But I care about you and don't want anything to happen to you."

Janet gave a weak smile. "I'm sorry. I guess I get a little too independent sometimes."

He leaned in and gave her a quick kiss. "I don't mind a spirit of independence." He smiled. "Of course, not everyone is like me."

He had a point there. Not many men she had met was anything like him.

"I have to leave, Janet. You think about us this week, and we'll pick up where we left off next weekend. OK?"

She nodded. He kissed her on the cheek and walked from her office.

She sat at her desk and watched him leave. *Uh-oh.* She knew she was in trouble.

He wasn't even at the elevator and she missed him already.

CHAPTER 5

Janet stayed at her desk until well past midnight; she was determined to go through all her previous findings after considering the things Bruce had said. She researched the farming equipment needed for planting and harvesting each crop and correlated which crops utilized each piece of equipment. Next she researched which soils had the closest nutrient density to African soil. Maybe close would be good enough, she told herself. Especially if the farm equipment could be used to help prepare the soil.

Pulling up her mapping program, she took Africa out of the program's choices and made farm equipment another variable for the program to be optimized. She then reran the program to optimize crop production with the new variable inputs while still keeping individual fields fallow every seventh year, growing seed crops in nutrient-rich areas, and utilizing some crops to replenish nutrients other crops took from the soil.

While the program ran, she leaned back in her chair and stretched. Although extremely tired, she had to know the results before she left. Standing, she rubbed her neck and then walked through the reception area to stretch her legs. *Why am I so driven?* Maybe it was to prove everyone wrong. Revenge for being rejected? She looked around, tried to clear her head.

Bruce was right. This place was beautiful during off hours. With each desk glowing a different color, it was like being in a rainbow. She had to work here. Maybe this new information would be the leverage to get her transferred to this building. Well, there was only one way to find out.

Janet went back to her desk. The simulation completed. She brought the map up on the monitor, bit her top lip, and put her bottom lip over it as she intently watched the animation. As she watched, she rocked her head back and forth. It wasn't as strong as the scenario she had presented to Edgar the day before, but it was still an improvement in teleporter efficiency. Would it be enough to impress Edgar? She hoped so.

She put her head down on her arm, formed a pillow for her head on her desktop, and ran the animation again . . .

"Janet. Janet." She felt herself being shaken.

Janet sat up slowly and stretched. "Edgar?" She jerked upright. "What time is it?"

"Have you been here all night? And . . . why?"

Janet perked up. "Edgar, can I show you something again?"

Edgar used his thumb and first two fingers to cup his forehead as he shook his head. "Janet, if this is about your map animation, we've already gone over that." He gave her a hard look. "The decision was final."

"No, no . . . I mean, yes." Janet sighed. "I have redone the simulation. Would you please sit down and watch it?"

Edgar breathed through his nose forcefully. "All right, Janet." He took a seat as Janet restarted the animation.

Janet saw him go from a look of indifference to one of interest to leaning forward to watch the monitor more closely.

He glanced her way. "I thought you said Africa had to be in the mix."

Janet smiled. "That was before I realized there was a variable I overlooked."

He looked back at the screen. "This is impressive. Any idea how much efficiency is gained?"

"Well, not as much as before. I'm guessing about another 50 percent."

Edgar looked at Janet with raised eyebrows. "If that's the case, the teleporter efficiency increases to above 85 percent." He stood. "Janet, that's . . . that's unbelievable."

Janet smiled. "I still need to verify a few things, but I do think it would improve that much."

Edgar rubbed his chin as he paced back and forth. He stopped and looked her way. "Janet, would you be willing to work here at the corporate office permanently?" He held up his palms. "I know this is spur of the moment. I think I could even get you a permanent spot at the hotel where you like to stay." He spread his hands a little wider. "If you want, that is."

Janet wanted to jump up and down but forced herself to remain calm. "Well, I do love the city. So, yes, I think I would like that."

"OK, consider yourself transferred. Go back and get some rest. I'll run this by Administrator Billingsley and follow up with you tomorrow."

Janet gathered her things, said hello to a few folks briefly, then walked out of the office—tired but exhilarated. Rather than going straight to the hotel, she stopped at the park across the street. It was always such a tranquil place, and she wanted to feel the warmth of the sun for a while, so she sat on the bench near the lilacs and closed her eyes, enjoying their fragrant aroma.

She smiled to herself. She had done it. She got what she wanted: justification in spite of the rejection. And she had done it by herself. Well . . . with the help of Bruce. Rather than just flatly rejecting her previous scenario, couldn't they have said that she needed to consider farming equipment? After all, didn't the Administrator say the King knew everything? Didn't he want her to succeed?

Janet felt the sun blocked and the temperature on her face decrease as if the sun had gone behind a cloud; she then realized her arm was still feeling the sun's heat. Opening her eyes, Administrator Billingsley, standing in front of her, came into focus. Janet sat up in an instant. "Administrator!"

Beth gave a warm smile. "Hi, Janet. Mind if I sit down?"

Janet shook her head and slid over to the edge of the bench. *What is this all about?* Was she now in trouble for trying to outsmart them?

Beth sat down and leaned back on the bench. "I come here often as well. I too find it a place of solitude." She looked at Janet and smiled. "Yet my reason is probably different from yours. It brings back a lot of memories."

Janet tried to figure out why the Administrator was here. Those thoughts, though, caused her to not really focus on what Beth was actually saying. "Oh?"

"Janet, I know you love this city. I do, too." Her expression slackened and seemed to reflect her reminiscing. "I appreciate it even more today. Before the Refreshing, the city was noisy and full of pollution. Today, it has neither of those things. A lot of thought went into the city's preparation post-Refreshing." She glanced at Janet. "All the things you like about this city—the buildings, the sculptures, the parks—they all have a reason. Have you noticed the art has a purpose?"

Janet hadn't thought about this, just that she enjoyed everything so much. "Well, art is fairly subjective and means different things to different people," she said.

Beth nodded. "That's true. And that is usually why artists don't give away their why behind their art form. Yet each artist has a reason for what they do."

"That makes sense," Janet said.

"I feel you need to know the purpose of this park, this sculpture, and this building." Beth turned on the bench to face Janet directly. "Every Administrator in this city had a part in its design. This . . . "—she spread her hands widely—" . . . was what I contributed."

Janet's eyes widened. Beth had a creative side? *How surprising.* She had always seemed so businesslike.

Beth chuckled. "Not that I physically created these, but I had a part in their design, and in their cohesive nature." Beth's eyes twinkled. "Have you noticed a cohesive nature to them?"

Janet gave a blank stare. "To some extent, I guess. I like them a lot but have never thought about what the original artist had in mind."

Beth nodded. "That's OK. I just want you to understand, as I think it may help you in your understanding of our King."

Janet looked at Beth; she was unsure how to respond. She had no idea where Beth was going with all this.

"This sculpture: two independent flames which intertwine at the top. Why?"

Janet turned and looked at the sculpture. She found it magnificent. It seemed to flow and flicker even though it was one solid piece. Turning back to Beth, she shook her head. "Why? I don't know. But I find it intriguing as it seems alive, and yet it's not."

Beth smiled. "That's a great description. A lot of the credit for that goes to the artist who created it for me." She pointed toward its foundation. "If you look at the base, it states, 'Acts Chapter 2'. That is the inspiration for the piece. The tongues of fire in this passage of Scripture represent the giving of Ruach HaKadosh."

Janet's eyebrows raised. "Oh, I never made that connection."

Beth pointed to the building. "The floating elevator. This is a symbol of the work of Ruach HaKadosh: tangible things accomplished through invisible action."

Janet looked at Beth with lips parted. *Interesting concept. Who would have thought?*

"And the floor we are on. The desks glow at night. It makes great conversation for visitors to the building. But if you look above the entrance to our floor, it states, 'John 1:5'. Scripture states, 'The light shines in the darkness, but the darkness has not understood it.' Ruach HaKadosh helps us shine for our King." Beth turned back to Janet. "So, you see, a cohesive message. Actually, you can find such cohesion with all the sculptures and buildings they are in front of. The whole city is full of such messages in praise to our King."

"I never would have put all that together."

Beth smiled. "Many don't—and that's OK. Yet our King has given us many things to explore, behold, and contemplate." Beth put her hand on Janet's shoulder. "And he did not tell you how to solve your crop dilemma or what to consider to solve it. He knew you would have more joy in its solution if you solved the issue on your own. He—and we all—are thrilled with what you have achieved."

Janet gave a weak smile. "Thank you."

"And just so you know, I have approved Edgar's request for you to stay and work here in the city."

"Again, thank you."

Beth stood. "Well, I need to be getting back to work." She smiled. "And you need to get some rest. I'll see you in the morning."

Janet nodded.

Beth turned to leave but then suddenly turned back. "Janet, a certain amount of pride is important. But don't let it consume you."

Janet was unsure how to respond to that statement, or what Beth actually meant. Beth didn't wait for a response but turned and walked toward the building. Janet sat there a little longer.

She looked at the sculpture again and then at the building. Beth's story was a cohesive one, and maybe it explained the original intent. But art could mean many things to many different people. She had stood many times on the other side of the park and visually aligned the flame sculpture with the elevator and envisioned the heat causing the elevator to rise like heat waves would a paper lantern or hot air balloon. Yes, one interpretation was spiritual and one scientific. Beth saw the scientific supporting the spiritual, where she saw just the scientific. Who is to say one is right and the other wrong? Isn't art supposed to be personal? Be something different in the eye of each beholder?

And that last statement. What was that supposed to mean? *I should be proud but not too proud?* Isn't that also subjective? Well, she was certainly proud of herself and her achievement. Was the King really the one who should be praised for what she found? Wasn't she the one—with Bruce's help, of course—who put it all together? Yes, she probably put it together faster because of her earlier rejection, but she wasn't going to admit that was the King's plan all along. Anyone could make such an argument after the fact. No, there would have to be more to put her squarely on the side of the King.

She stood and headed down the street toward home. *Home.* A smile came to her face. The place she always came to stay would now truly be home. *Won't Bruce be surprised?*

She couldn't wait to tell him. So much had happened since she met him. Maybe he was her good luck charm. She giggled. *Charming is a good word to describe him.*

Both fortunate and puzzled feelings came to her simultaneously. Now that she knew Beth's ideas about the park and building, would she be able to enjoy it the same way? Was that now ruined? Her mind was too tired to think straight. She would have to ponder all this tomorrow.

CHAPTER 6

When Janet arrived at the office the next morning, she was greeted by an overly enthusiastic Molly.

"Oh, Janet, I'm so happy you're going to be with us from now on."

"Thanks, Molly. I'm glad too."

Molly handed her a packet and gave her a short grimace. "Sorry, but there is some paperwork to fill out. You can do it all online. These are just the instructions. Try and do it as soon as possible. There are also some options about what to do with your previous apartment."

Janet nodded. "OK. Thanks, Molly. I'll get to it as soon as possible."

Molly smiled. "We've made your temporary office your permanent office. Since it's centrally located, I thought you would prefer it."

"That's perfect. Thanks." Janet headed toward her new office.

"Janet?"

Janet stopped and turned.

"I want to take you to lunch to say welcome. Do you have time for that?"

Being sociable wasn't Janet's forte, but having Molly as an office ally would be helpful.

Janet returned Molly's smile. "I'll make time. It's really unnecessary—to take me to lunch, I mean—but I look forward to it."

Molly beamed. "Having another girl in the office is nice." She giggled. "Now we're less outnumbered."

Janet laughed and raised her fist. "Girl power."

Molly did the same and giggled.

Janet turned, rolled her eyes, and walked to her office. The plaque next to her door read: *Janet Singleton, Commodities Analyst.* Janet rubbed her fingers over the letters and smiled just before she entered. It was the same office as two nights ago, but now it felt different somehow. The color of this desk was what had drawn her to this office in the first place. It was the only temporary office with a deep purple-colored desk. Now it was hers permanently.

As Janet approached her desk, Edgar entered.

"Congratulations, Janet. You seem to have created a stir all the way up the chain. I just got word this morning that the increase in teleporter crop shipment is 48 percent. That means you have single-handedly increased efficiency by 86 percent in total." Edgar was literally bouncing on his toes. "And . . . " He hesitated.

Janet opened her hands while gesturing his way. "And what, Edgar?"

"You get a vacation out of the deal. Where will you go?"

Janet sat down. This news was unexpected. "I . . . I don't know. I'll have to think about that."

"It's well deserved, Janet." He paused. "There is one catch, however."

Janet raised her eyebrows.

"While impressed, not everyone is sure the farmers will go along with changing what they grow on a routine basis. The company wants you to visit them and see if they agree."

"Visit? You mean you want me to travel and get their input personally?"

Edgar nodded. "Is that a problem?"

Janet shook her head and laughed. "Edgar, you just gave me a vacation and then said take several more!"

Edgar smiled. "Well, a business trip is not necessarily a vacation. Plus, the vacation is for two, your business trips are not."

"Good point."

Edgar turned to leave.

"Thanks, Edgar. I appreciate you listening to me."

Edgar turned. "From today . . . " He pointed his index finger downward, as if to emphasize the point. "Kick me if I don't listen to you." He paused and then shook his index finger at her. "But with respect."

Janet laughed. "Maybe I'll leave that for Administrator Billingsley."

Edgar chuckled as he left her office. She leaned back and gave a big sigh. It was amazing how things were coming together. She felt like she should pinch herself to be sure she wasn't really dreaming. After taking it all in for a few moments, she got to work.

She poured through her research and looked to see where the biggest changes to crop production would be expected based on her model. She categorized them and grouped them by location to see how few trips she could make and still accomplish her goal. She lost all track of time as she worked.

Molly knocked on her door. Janet looked up and motioned her in.

"Ready to go?"

Janet looked at her T-band. *Noon already?* "Sure. I can't believe how fast the morning went."

Molly smiled. "When I'm busy, it always does. The restaurant is only a few blocks away. OK to walk?"

"Sure."

The restaurant Molly picked was opposite another small park with a large sculpture. Both women ordered a salad. Janet's was spinach with fresh berries and walnuts; Molly opted for romaine with assorted citrus slices and almonds.

As they ate, Janet admired the sculpture. This one moved. A large hand would rise out of a marble base, a bird would seemingly fly into it, and at that point the hand would close and descend. When the hand rose again, it would open and a butterfly would emerge to fly away. This motion continued to repeat. It was beautiful to look at as the bird was pure white and seemed to glow while the butterfly was multi-hued and sparkled in the sunlight.

Janet pointed to the sculpture. "Molly, what does that sculpture mean to you?"

Molly swallowed a bite, looked over, and smiled. "I think it's why I come to this restaurant so often. I really like this piece. I get a sense of rebirth and transformation."

Janet nodded. "Transformation does seem to be the key element." She paused. "I wonder what the original artist was thinking." They continued to eat over small talk.

Molly looked at her T-band. "Oh, we have just enough time to stop by the new designer's shop on the way back. I have two dresses to choose from. Could you give me your opinion?"

"Well, uh, I'm probably not the best to give fashion advice. I don't want you to make a decision based on my poor taste."

Molly gave a quick wave with her wrist. "You always look fabulous. I trust your judgment. Just a couple of minutes?"

Against her better judgment, Janet agreed. As they left, she walked closer to the sculpture and noticed the inscription: '2 Corinthians 3:18'. She looked at the building. One half looked like stucco with patches deliberately left undone. The other side was smooth, a bluish purple in color. *Hmm, yes. Transformation did seem to be the key with this one.*

Molly turned down a side street and then left at the next block.

"Molly, aren't we heading away from the office?"

"Oh, it's right here. I promise. Fifteen minutes—max."

Janet looked at the name of the boutique as they entered: *Tell Your Story.* That seemed familiar, but she couldn't place her memory of the words.

The shop was cozy, to register a polite thought, Janet mused, as it had very little merchandise displayed. Yet the pieces showing were elegant. Some looked quite ethereal while others looked more plain yet elegant.

A woman came through a door in the back. "Can I help you?"

Molly gave a big smile. "Yes, I would like to try on my two dress choices and let my friend here help me decide."

The woman smiled. "Of course. Step over here onto the holographic design platform. Scan your thumbprint and the machine will know which designs you are considering."

Molly stepped on the platform. A 3-D hologram appeared around her with her dress selection. It looked as though she was actually wearing a dress. The platform had a motion sensor that made the dress move with Molly's motions.

Molly glanced at Janet and grinned. "What do you think?"

"It's lovely, Molly." The dress was white with bold splotches of color in random places. "It really suits your personality."

"And the other?" Molly pressed a different button on the wall. The hologram morphed her dress into the second one.

"It's also pretty," Janet offered. The dress was lavender with an uneven hem and had tiny white butterflies lining the bodice and hem. "What's the occasion?"

Molly shrugged. "Just everyday—or a date." She giggled. "Do you really want me to choose?"

Molly nodded. "Oh, please. I like them both and am having a hard time choosing."

"Well, I would say the first one. It's more you, I think."

Molly squealed. "Oh, thank you, Janet. I sort of felt that way too but couldn't decide for sure."

Molly went to the counter and talked with the clerk. "OK. Let me get Amanda so she can finalize the purchase," the clerk said.

A woman came from the back and talked with Molly. Janet knew her immediately. It was the woman she met at O'Brien's restaurant.

Amanda glanced at Janet. There was some recognition in her eyes, but she kept talking to Molly. Yet Amanda would also occasionally glance at Janet. After a few minutes, Amanda turned Molly back to her clerk and approached Janet.

"You look so familiar. Did I meet you the other night at O'Brien's?"

Janet smiled and nodded. "Yes. It's quite the coincidence. My colleague here asked me to come and help her decide which dress to select."

"You . . . were interested in my purse. Do you want to look at some purses?"

"No . . . I mean, yes . . . but I don't have the time right now," Janet said. "We have to get back to the office."

Amanda smiled. "I understand. Stop by anytime."

Janet looked over and saw Molly was still talking to the clerk. She cleared her throat and turned back to Amanda. "I, uh, overheard some of your conversation the other night."

Amanda's posture stiffened and her look went cold.

Janet reached out and touched Amanda's shoulder lightly. "Oh, don't worry. I was intrigued and would like to understand more."

Amanda's expression softened but her stance was still wary. Her eyes kept darting to see if anyone would enter the shop.

Janet whispered. "I never knew there were others who thought as I did." She smiled. "And to hear someone talk about them out loud. It was . . . just . . . wow." Janet made her hands go from her temples outward to show her surprise.

Amanda looked around and kept the same whisper Janet was using. "If you stop by after work today, I have some information you may be interested in. Say, eighteen hundred?"

Janet saw Molly approach and hurriedly whispered back, "Perfect."

"All set?" Janet raised her eyebrows.

Molly nodded. "Amanda, thank you so much. I just love your designs."

"You're welcome. I hope you enjoy your purchase. Come back soon."

As they walked back to the office, Molly was even more bubbly than usual. "Thank you, Janet. I think we really chose the right one."

"I'm glad you're happy about your decision."

"I saw you talking to Amanda. Do you know her?"

Janet laughed. "Not really. Believe it or not, I met her briefly at a restaurant the other night. I didn't know where her boutique was, though. I may go back and look at her purses."

Molly stopped and grabbed Janet's arm. "Oh, Janet, they are amazing. That's my next goal. I just love her stuff."

Janet chuckled. "Molly, you're a fashion junkie."

Molly laughed with her. "I guess I am."

Once back in the office, Janet went to her desk and worked—or tried. For being so focused that morning, she felt so distracted this afternoon. Her mind kept wandering. *What does Amanda know about 'total freedom'—and how is it attained?* What was Amanda going to show her this evening, Janet continued to wonder. Were there others with a similar mind-set and desire? The clock seemed to go ten times slower than it did in the morning.

As the clock reached seventeen hundred, most others began to leave. Many walked by her office and looked at her as they headed for the elevator. Some waved good night while others just looked at her, no doubt thinking the "overachiever" was trying to show them up. *Oh well, so be it.* Janet knew she wasn't given her recognition. She had earned it.

At 17:40, after a bit more work, she left the building and headed for Amanda's boutique. When she arrived, Amanda was finishing with a customer. Amanda looked up and smiled and went back to her customer. Janet looked around while she waited. Although there wasn't much to look at in the small shop, Janet discovered another holographic platform in the back corner that she hadn't seen before. As she stepped onto the platform, it activated. The screen in front presented a menu.

"Select style." The voice did not sound mechanical but feminine and pleasant. Janet raised an eyebrow and looked over the choices.

"Evening wear."

Several selections came onscreen. "Scroll, please." Several more selections appeared. "Number seven."

Next to the screen was a full-length mirror. The hologram made the dress Janet selected appear on her. As she twisted and turned, the dress did the same. Janet smiled. This particular dress was backless, and the hologram filled in skin where the outfit she was wearing had it covered. The effect let the buyer get a strong feel for what the dress would look like when worn.

"See something you like?"

Janet jumped as if she had been caught doing something she shouldn't. She laughed.

"Amanda, this can be addictive. I can see why Molly loves your boutique." She stepped down from the platform and the hologram dissipated as the menu screen went black. "I don't think I've seen anything like it."

Amanda smiled. "Thanks. It really helps with inventory. I don't have to have a lot of space or keep the same style with many different sizes to accommodate. You come in, select what you want, and I make it to your specifications."

Janet gave an approving nod, lips pressed together, and eyebrows raised. "Very impressive."

"Oh, and I can do the same for men as well. So pass the word."

Janet laughed. "I will."

Amanda turned more serious. "I know you came for another reason. Let me close shop. Mind eating a bite before the meeting I'd like to take you to? I'm starved as I had to work through lunch."

Janet froze. "Meeting? I . . . I'm not sure about a meeting."

Amanda gave her a dismissive wave. "Oh, don't worry about it. Let's talk first and then see what works for you."

Amanda took her to a bistro just around the corner from the shop. Amanda ordered some lentil soup and a small salad. Janet didn't feel very hungry, so she ordered only tomato basil soup.

Janet decided to break into a far heavier topic.

"So, what have you learned, Amanda?"

Amanda kept her voice low. "There's a prophecy of a coming one called the Overtaker."

Janet scrunched her brow. "That's an odd name. Why is he called that?"

"Well . . . " Amanda swallowed a bite of salad and took a drink of water. "Apparently, this coming one will overthrow the current King and set up a kingdom that will give total freedom to everyone."

Janet looked around to be sure no one was near. "Is that really true?"

Amanda shrugged. "I'm not sure how to be absolutely certain, but there is apparently a stone stele that has been found prophesying his coming."

"Who found this stele?"

"Some just call him The Leader."

Janet squinted. "He doesn't have a name?"

"I guess he does, but no one has ever seen him. I'm told he keeps his identity secret."

That made a lot of sense to Janet, and an idea began to form. "So, tell me about your meeting. You said it's tonight?"

Amanda nodded and took a glance at her T-band. "It's at twenty hundred."

"Where is it, and what do you do?"

"Actually, I have it in the back of my boutique. People enter from the alleyway behind the shop. There's only around eight of us right now, but it keeps growing slowly." Amanda ate the last spoonful of soup and pushed the bowl aside. "We talk about how people are unhappy with the King and what the coming Overtaker will bring us. We introduce new people and help them see they aren't alone."

Janet nodded and mindlessly moved her spoon through what was left in her bowl.

"Are you OK, Janet? Do you want to come to the meeting?"

Janet looked up and gave a weak smile. "I'm fine. I was just thinking about this Leader and your meeting."

"What do you mean?"

"Amanda, I'm supportive of your cause. But I travel a lot and I can't afford to have people know my true beliefs. I would like to attend your meeting but not be seen. Is that possible?"

"Well . . . " Amanda grabbed her upper lip between thumb and forefinger as she seemed deep in thought. "When you first go into the back room from the front there's a long counter with shelving almost to the ceiling. You could sit there and just listen. Or do you want to say anything like The Leader will do at his meetings? He leads the meetings but keeps his face from being seen."

Janet shook her head. "No, I just want to listen. Not let anyone know I'm there. Are you OK with that?"

Amanda shrugged. "Sure. I guess." She looked at her T-band. "We should go. Are you ready?"

Janet took a deep breath. "I guess."

They arrived a few minutes early so Janet could find a spot behind the shelves and wait. It wasn't long before she heard others gathering. After about fifteen minutes, Amanda had the attendees find a seat for their meeting.

"Hi, everyone," Amanda started. "Thanks for coming tonight. I'm delighted we have a newbie with us. Shannon, would you like to introduce your guest?"

"Thanks, Amanda. Everyone, this is Molly."

"Hi, Molly," everyone said, nearly in unison.

"Hi, everyone."

Janet's muscles stiffened. That sounded exactly like her Molly! She had no idea Molly had discontentment as she did.

"Welcome, Molly," Amanda said. "Can you tell us what prompted you to join us tonight?"

"Well, Shannon was telling me what happened to her brother. How the King took him because he had a different opinion from the Administrator at his office building. I was shocked. I had never heard of something like that happening. So I thought I'd come and see what this meeting was all about."

Janet listened as others told similar stories. She, like Molly, had never heard of this happening. All of this made her dislike of the King intensify. Yet she knew she had to keep a level head, and she realized it was important she keep her identity hidden.

Janet tensed when she heard footsteps coming closer . . . and closer.

"Where are you going, Molly?" Amanda's voice was higher than normal.

"Oh, Shannon said she needed a pen and that there are some on the counter over here."

"That's OK, Molly. I'll get them," Amanda said.

"It's no trouble. I'm already here."

Janet heard Amanda scurry to the counter and turn the corner just in front of Molly.

"Oh, here they are," Molly said.

Janet heard footsteps begin to walk in the other direction, and then she heard Molly's cheerful voice again. "Here you go, Shannon."

From behind the boutique door where Janet had hidden, she heard someone pace back and forth before returning to the others. After another half hour or so of general discussion, the guests could be heard leaving. Footsteps came closer.

"Janet? Janet, where are you?"

"I'm in here, Amanda."

Amanda opened the door to the boutique and peeked in. Janet was crouching at the corner of the shop counter.

"There you are. I was worried when Molly started to head behind the shelving."

"Yeah, me too. I dove in here to avoid her. I hope you don't mind."

Amanda laughed and shook her head. "I just didn't want to be the reason you were discovered. I had paced a few times looking for you but didn't want to call out to you and give you away."

"Something else good came of it," Janet said.

Amanda turned up her brow. "What's that?"

Janet pulled a purse from behind the counter and held it up. "I found the purse I want."

Amanda burst into laughter. "Glad I could be of assistance."

CHAPTER 7

G etting together with Bruce proved more difficult than anticipated. This was the third week since he left Chicago, and their schedules still hadn't allowed them to meet. Janet was getting discouraged even though seeing him on the holographic communicator was helpful.

"Janet, I'm so impressed with you. Look at all you've accomplished in such a short period of time," Bruce told her one day as they talked through the communicator.

"I couldn't have done it without you. I think you're my lucky charm."

Bruce laughed. "I'll take that credit."

Janet smiled. "I think it's truer than you know."

"Have you decided when you're going to visit the farmers? And what you are going to tell them?"

"I'm still working on it."

"Is Middle America on your list?"

"What are you thinking?"

"Well, if it is, why not 'come here' first? It will give you a chance to see how your presentation goes, learn what questions you're likely to get, and most important, give us some time together."

Janet's eyes widened. "Bruce, that's a great idea. I should have thought of that. We can target your territory and the four surrounding ones. Is your civic center large enough?"

"I think so. I'll work with Shepherd Morgan to get it scheduled. When do you think you want to do this?"

"Well . . . " Janet rubbed her chin with her thumb and forefinger. "Realistically, six weeks from now."

"Really? That's a long time."

Janet realized Bruce was right; her shoulders drooped. "I know. But I need to contact each territory and make my case to get them to come to the civic center in your territory. Some may be hard to convince."

"Oh. I think I have an idea."

"What is it?"

"If we get each Shepherd on board, they would likely be able to get the farmers to participate. Most really look up to their Shepherd. You could visit one every other day and have your meeting much earlier than six weeks from now. I could go with you to meet each Shepherd. That may be more convincing since I know each of them."

Janet's eyes lit up. "Bruce, that would be great." Then she frowned. "But if you can't get away to come here, how are you going to take two weeks away to come with me?"

Bruce scratched the side of his face as he tried to think. "Let me work on it. If you give me a week and a half before we start, then I can help, if we teleport back and forth from here rather than staying in each territory."

"OK. I'll see you a week from this coming Tuesday after work."

"I look forward to it."

They exchanged short blown kisses and ended the call.

Janet was getting excited. And, once again, Bruce was the catalyst for making her plans happen. And though she had a lot of office work to do tomorrow, that wasn't the only thing on her day's agenda.

She had to figure out where this "Leader" was and how to get in touch with him. Amanda was her only link.

Janet went to the kitchenette to get a snack. As she pulled some crackers from the shelf, a thought made her freeze. *Wait.* A communicator number may be on the card Amanda gave her. Leaving her snack on the counter, she went to find her purse and glanced at her T-band. It was late, but not too late.

Sure enough, Amanda's communicator number was on the card along with her office number. She dialed with the hologram activated. Amanda answered.

"Hello, this is Amanda Story." Amanda had her holographic display off.

"Hi, Amanda. This is Janet. Janet Singleton."

Amanda appeared on the holographic display. "Janet! What do I owe the pleasure?"

"I would like to talk to you more about some . . . things. Do you think you can stop by tomorrow night after dinner?"

Janet saw Amanda look down and then back at the communicator. "Sure, Janet. I can stop by. I'm just not sure how helpful I'll be."

"That's OK. I just want to ask a few questions. If nothing more, I can thank you for the purse. I really love it."

Amanda smiled. "OK, I'll see you tomorrow night. Around twenty hundred? Where do I go?"

"Lakeside Hotel. I'll tell the front desk to expect you."

"See you tomorrow." The communicator went silent.

Janet went back to her snack, finished preparing it, stepped out on the balcony, and made notes for what she needed to do over the next month.

＊ ＊ ＊ ＊ ＊

The next day, Janet put together an outline of what she wanted to present to the farmers as well as what she would request from the Shepherds. If this was successful, it meant Bruce had also identified the key to whom to reach out to in each area of the farming world—the Shepherds. She had to be sure she didn't let her bias get in the way of her progress. While the main job of the Shepherds was to teach Scripture to the masses, they had a lot of clout with individuals and could be extremely persuasive on other matters, not only those having to do with religion.

After getting home that evening, Janet made tea and set shortbread cookies on a small tray for Amanda's visit. Amanda arrived as scheduled and Janet suggested they sit on the balcony, her favorite place to relax.

"Janet, I appreciate you having me over, but I'm not sure I can be of much help," Amanda said as they took their seats.

"Well, let me ask this," Janet began. "How did you start having your meetings?"

"It only started a few months ago after I came back from my vacation. I met someone who got me to start thinking whether our King can really be trusted. I wanted to see if others had similar concerns and, as you saw, some do." Amanda took a few sips of tea and a bite of her cookie.

"Where did you meet this person?" Janet poured herself more tea.

"In Sydney, Australia. I attended a designer's conference. We met in the lobby one evening and got to talking. All the information I shared the other night was basically a repeat of what she told me."

"Were there any plans to talk after, or did you exchange any information with each other?"

Amanda shook her head. "No. The woman did encourage me to seek out others. She said that would prove others had doubts the same as I did." She took a bite of cookie and sat back, then jerked upright. "Wait. She did ask me for a business card, and I gave it to her."

"Did she say she would check in on you later?"

Amanda shook her head. Janet sat back and sighed.

"But . . ."

"Yes?"

"We had a drawing, and I told her she had to enter. She put in a card. I still have all the cards that were not pulled during the drawing. I haven't taken the time to throw them away."

Janet's pulse quickened. "Do you think you would recognize it if you saw it again?"

"I'm not sure, but I know most of those who entered, so I can likely find it by process of elimination. I'll look for it tomorrow."

"Thanks, Amanda. Please call me when you find it."

"Sure." Amanda set her teacup down. "I should be getting home. It's late. Thanks for the tea and cookies."

Janet thanked Amanda and showed her to the door. After putting things away, she got ready for bed. It had been a long day but a profitable one. With any luck, she would be able to find this Leader and understand what his plans were in preparing for a coming Overtaker.

Janet smiled. Things were coming together on multiple fronts.

CHAPTER 8

Janet spent the next week preparing for her presentation to both the farmers and the Shepherds. It was several days before she heard back from Amanda. For that she was actually glad; trying to focus on two different large areas of her life, at one time, seemed daunting.

One evening, as Janet entered her hotel lobby returning from work, Amanda was waiting for her in one of the plush chairs.

"Amanda. Is everything all right?"

"I'm sorry it's taken so long to get back to you, Janet," she said.

Janet sat next to her. "It's really all right. I've been so busy this week anyway."

"Well, I wanted to let you know what I found."

Janet raised her eyebrows. "You don't sound excited. Is it not good news?"

"Well, yes and no. I was able to reach the Leader's wife just before she left for Asia. She goes by the name of Isabelle. I'm not sure if that's her real name or not."

Janet leaned forward. "So, what did she say?"

"Well . . . " Amanda took a deep breath and exhaled. "She's willing to meet with you. I reached her right before she left for southern China."

"That's good—isn't it?"

Amanda gave a grimace. "I had to go ahead and commit to when you would see her. Otherwise, she'd be unreachable until she returns. Something about staying under the radar."

Janet straightened and her muscles stiffened. "What did you tell her, Amanda?"

"She's only going to be there for three weeks."

Janet's eyes widened.

Amanda raised her hand. "Oh, that's only the half of it. She has to see you before she lets you meet the Leader. And he isn't even with her. She has to tell you where to meet him."

Janet gave a small laugh. "And I thought I was being cautious."

"Janet, you have to get to Guilin, China, no later than three weeks from today."

Janet rubbed her forehead. "That's . . . that's extremely challenging." Her mind rushed through everything she had to get done. Panic set in, and she felt herself getting warm all over.

"I'm sorry, Janet. I had no idea when the window would be open again."

Janet patted Amanda's knee. "No, no. I don't blame you. It's just overwhelming right now. There's a lot of planning I have to get done in the next few days."

"Well, I hope it works out for you. This woman, Isabelle, stated she will leave you a note at the hotel in Guilin as to where and when to meet. I told her to leave a note for Ms. Story. I'll call the hotel later and let them know to give the note to you." Amanda stood. "I have to get home. I hope it all works out."

Janet stood and gave Amanda a hug. "Thanks, Amanda. Thanks for all the help."

As Janet headed to the elevators, she clutched her fist and shook her head. How was she going to get everything done and still make this appointment? She had to talk to Bruce.

As soon as she reached her suite, she called Bruce on her communicator and hoped against hope he was there. Apparently he wasn't, because he didn't answer; he was likely out in one of his fields. She left a message trying not to sound panicky but realized she had pretty much failed miserably.

She warmed some leftovers and sat down to eat and figure out how to make all the upcoming activities work. It would be a week before she left, and she would be at least a week in mid-America. How was she going to set up a meeting with farmers in China in less than a week? She really needed to have a meeting with farmers in Guilin to cover her need to visit Isabelle.

A thought hit her: What if she turned the China trip into her vacation? Would Bruce be able to go on short notice? Her hope plummeted as she realized she was already waiting a week because of his schedule. What made her think he could get away so quickly? She took her last bite, dropped her fork on her plate, and sighed. Pushing the plate to one side, she propped her chin on her hand.

The communicator beeped, and she had it on nearly before the first beep had ended.

"Janet? Wow, you must have been sitting right next to it. Is everything OK? Your voice message sounded frantic."

"Sorry. I'm feeling a little stressed. I found out this afternoon I have to be in China within three weeks. It freaked me out knowing all I have to do before I get there—and I now have to get things set up there."

"You have to give the same talk in China you're going to give here, and you have to set that up before you even come here? Why?"

"The why isn't important. I just need to get it done. Do you think that's possible?" She felt guilty not being totally honest with Bruce, but the less he knew the better.

"I might be able to help."

"Are you my knight in shining armor again?"

Bruce laughed. "I'll try. After talking to Shepherd Morgan, he came back and said he had mentioned this to Shepherd Randall, who talked to Professor Tiberius. Because Professor Tiberius was so impressed with the idea, Shepherd Randall suggested he and Shepherd Morgan go ahead and get all the Shepherds involved. They're going to get several farmers from their respective territories to come here so you only have to give one presentation."

Janet's mouth fell open as she leaned forward slightly. "Bruce, you really *are* a hero."

Bruce chuckled. "I wouldn't go that far." He shrugged. "But if you want to, then who am I to deny, well . . . you adoring me?"

Janet laughed and shook her head. "I can always count on you to lighten the mood."

"Does that mean you're not going to adore me?"

"How could I not?"

Bruce laughed. "Well, since you're going to do that, maybe I can take it a step further. Send me the names of the Shepherds in the area you're going to, and I'll see if Shepherd Morgan can get them as enthused as he is."

Janet put her hand to her chest. "Bruce, I can't thank you enough." She shook her head. "I so wish you could be able to come to China with me."

Bruce looked down and then back into the communicator. "I wish I could too. But I can't. Not right now, anyway. Sorry."

Janet held up her palm. "No need to apologize. I understand. I was just wishing."

"Me too."

"You have saved me so much time. I'll see you next week."

"Have a good night." He gave her a wink and terminated the connection.

She breathed a deep sigh. Her task no longer seemed as daunting as it did an hour ago. Some restful sleep now seemed possible.

* * * * *

The week seemed to fly by, and Janet spent each day putting her presentation together and reviewing all her data to answer the questions she anticipated and, more importantly, to be ready for the ones she couldn't anticipate. During this time, Molly helped her get all the needed China reservations scheduled so she could arrive immediately after her mid-America trip.

The day finally came. She checked in for a final time with Edgar, left her office, and headed for the elevator. As she did, she heard Molly's familiar voice.

"Good luck, Janet. Call me if you need anything."

"Thanks, Molly. I guess I'll see you in a couple of weeks."

"Take care." Molly gave a wave as the elevator descended.

Janet felt excited and nervous as she headed for the short-range teleporter. She locked in the desired destination and pressed "Engage." Her skin prickled and vision blurred; the latter was something like looking across a hot pavement. In a matter of moments her vision cleared, and she was now in a rural town rather than a city. Taking a deep breath, the smell of earth, hay, and mowed grass filled her nostrils. These were smells she had not remembered since childhood.

She turned, and there was Bruce with his arms open, inviting her to walk into them. She hurriedly did so. He hugged her tightly, and this caused her to be overcome with emotion and gasp instinctively, her eyes watering. Bruce released his grasp and looked into her eyes while giving her a smile. He gave her a kiss, then held her even tighter as he leaned in. She reciprocated.

Bruce released her and whispered, "I've missed you, Janet." "And I, you."

Janet looked around. They were in the town square, and she saw a vegetable stand across the square in front of the civic center. The stand was closed but still had fruit and vegetables displayed.

"Why don't we get something to eat, catch up, and get you prepared for tomorrow?" Bruce said.

Janet nodded. Thinking about tomorrow made her heart palpitate. She needed to feel more comfortable with what she would say and do.

Bruce took her to Mable's Restaurant. As soon as they entered, the smell of vegetable soup and fresh baked bread made Janet's stomach growl. She suddenly felt very hungry and knew her stomach would not be able to resist either of these foods tonight.

After eating some soup and a few bites of bread, Janet was ready to hear what Bruce had found out. "So, what should I know about tomorrow?"

Bruce smiled and took her hand. "Don't worry, Janet. I think you're overthinking it. The Shepherds are already on board. Just tell them what you know and what you want to accomplish. Then, the next day, they'll help you convince the farmers."

"Do you really think all the farmers are willing to change the way they've been growing crops, or which crops they grow?"

"As I said, most farmers are." He suddenly turned more serious. "I don't know if I am, though."

Janet had a bite of food halfway to her mouth but froze in midair.

Bruce laughed. "You know I'm your biggest supporter."

Janet chuckled. "Well, I think I'm so nervous everything is throwing me off."

Bruce took her hand again. "Janet, as a farmer, my bigger concerns are being able to do what I know, understanding what I'm doing, and seeing the value of it. I think most farmers are that way."

"Thanks, Bruce. That helps me understand better."

Bruce patted her hand. "You've got this. Now, let me give you a quick tour before it gets dark."

Janet stood. "Oh, is there enough time?"

Bruce stood and laughed. "I think five minutes may be just enough time."

Janet took the hand he held out to her. "Come on. You're exaggerating."

Bruce nodded. "Yes. It'll take at least six."

Janet bumped her shoulder into his. "You're impossible."

Bruce laughed even more. As they stepped outside, Bruce took her just north of the town square to a gazebo in a small park.

"This is the highest point in the town," he said. He pointed forward. "You saw the town square. Where we are now is where some concerts and events are held." He pointed west. "The majority of the town is that way, including Mable's on Elm where you ate. Other businesses are on Main. Most of the other streets have houses." He pointed east. "The main things that way are the ruins of an old pre-Refreshing building and some more houses."

"Can I see them?"

Bruce gave her a second take. "See what?"

"The ruins."

Bruce cocked his head; he didn't seem to understand. "The ruins? Why?"

Janet shrugged. "I've never seen ruins."

Bruce chuckled and shrugged in return. "OK." He put his arm around her shoulders and they walked in that direction.

"What's the purpose of the ruins anyway?" she asked as they walked.

"Well, that's a good question. I think early on it was a way for those here to remember how life is now better. Over time, maintaining the ruins became a town project for people to work together."

The sun was close to setting by the time they reached the area. Janet walked around the entire building while stepping over stones here and there. It was rectangular in shape with some of the stone walls almost waist high, while other parts were only as high as her ankles. One of the wall ends was a little higher than she could reach. This larger wall had an indentation, and it had stones that seemed to come together into a column that went as high as the wall.

Janet reached out and touched the stones. "What is this?"

Bruce came over and patted the rough edifice. "This indentation and this column are what was known as a fireplace."

70

Janet's eyes widened. "They had a fire *inside* the building? Wasn't that dangerous?"

Bruce chuckled. "It seems that this indentation helped contain the fire, and its smoke would go up through the column, through what they called a chimney."

Janet shook her head. "Well, that doesn't make any sense to me."

Bruce chuckled. "It evidently made sense to them."

He stepped closer and leaned in for a kiss. "I'm glad you're here. I've missed you."

Janet smiled. "I feel calm when I'm with you." She looked around a bit more while holding Bruce's hand. "It's getting dark. Where should I stay?"

"There are a few rooms behind Mable's restaurant." He grimaced. "This is a small town, and if I have you stay at my farm, people will talk."

Janet nodded. "I understand. Don't forget. I come from a farming town as well."

"I'll take you to see the farm after your meeting with the Shepherds tomorrow."

She tiptoed and gave him a quick kiss. "Thanks for everything."

They held hands on the way back to Mable's. There, Bruce helped her secure a room. He gave her a final kiss.

"I'll come by and get you a little before 10:30, and we'll meet them in the civic center." He paused. "Oh. Mable's has an awesome breakfast special if you're interested before I get here."

Janet stood watching Bruce head down the street. She sighed. While still nervous, she was less so now compared with when she first arrived. Could she see herself living in this type of town again? *Don't jump the gun, Janet. Focus on what you came to do.*

Sleep came quickly, but a restful sleep it was not. She dreamed of her talk to the farmers here—but they all seemed to be Chinese.

CHAPTER 9

Bruce came by just as Janet finished her breakfast. He sat across from her. "I see you didn't get the breakfast special."

Janet shook her head. "There's no way I could eat that much. Yogurt and granola were enough for me." She turned up her brow. "I got some strange looks, though."

"Around here, breakfast isn't breakfast without eggs."

Janet gave a slight smile. "Well, hopefully that's my only faux pas for the day."

"Are you ready to go?"

Janet sat up with a determined look. "As ready as I'll ever be."

As he stood, Bruce chuckled. "I'm sure you'll be great."

Once they entered the civic center, Bruce directed her to one of the adjacent rooms alongside the two-story atrium, which had a stained-glass ceiling. The sun cast a kaleidoscope of color on the walls. The room they entered contained an elongated oval conference table. Around it sat six men. Janet had expected five.

All the Shepherds stood as she and Bruce entered. Shepherd Randall stepped forward and held out his hand.

"Hi, Janet. It's been a while."

Janet shook his hand. "Hello, Shepherd Randall. Yes, it has. I trust you are doing well."

He smiled. "Let me introduce you to some of my colleagues." He pointed to each one. "These are Shepherd Morgan from this territory, Shepherd Alexander from the territory west of here, Shepherd Andrew from the territory south of here, and Shepherd Barry from the territory to the east."

Each nodded at Janet as they were introduced. The sixth man stepped forward. "Hi, Ms. Singleton. I'm Administrator Mattathias, from the Jerusalem Science Center."

Janet shook his hand. "Just call me Janet." She shook her head slightly. "I'm sorry. But why are you here?"

Mattathias smiled. "I report to Professor Tiberius. I'm now Administrator over the teleporters. He did that for a long time, but now, being in charge of the entire Science Center, he has much less time to devote to them than he once did."

"I see. Well, it's an honor to have you here."

Randall continued. "Morgan and I felt having Mattathias here would help the farmers understand the importance of what you're asking them to do."

Janet nodded. "Thank you. I appreciate it."

Bruce interjected. "Shall we get started?" Everyone settled around the table.

Janet linked with the monitor and flicked her files onto the large screen at the end of the table.

"Before we go further," she began, "I want to show you what we've discovered about crops grown and used around the world."

"By 'we,' you mean 'you,' is that right?" Bruce asked.

Janet smiled at Bruce but didn't say anything.

Mattathias chuckled. "Don't worry, Mr. O'Brien, the Science Center is well aware that Ms. Singleton—I mean, Janet . . . "

He gave her a smile. " . . . came up with this concept on her own."

Janet cleared her throat as she felt heat rush to her cheeks. "Anyway . . . " She had the map onscreen animate. "What you see on the map on the left are the crops grown today, and the one on the right shows where they are consumed. The geographic placement of the colors doesn't always match."

"And you've gotten them to match, is that right?" Shepherd Morgan asked.

Janet looked his way and smiled. "Almost. If farmers change up some of the crops they grow, then more crops can be utilized locally and the need for teleporter shipment will go down."

Shepherd Andrew leaned in and pointed at the monitor. "I, for one, am glad you were able to keep Africa out of the equation. There's a delicate balance between the grazing land and herd migrations."

Shepherd Barry laughed. "Andrew, you've always wished to be stationed in Africa."

"You know that's not true." Andrew sounded irritated. "There's nothing wrong with wanting to help out on the Sabbath Year safaris. Teaching Scripture is my first love, but animals are my second. I'm thankful the Master allows me to enjoy both."

"I'm just kidding, Andrew. I know everyone in your territory loves you."

Shepherd Alexander put his hand on Barry's shoulder. "Let's get back to the task at hand," Alexander gently said.

Mattathias jumped in. "This comes at an important time. With many crop shipments coinciding around the time of Sukkot, when teleporter traffic into Jerusalem is at its highest, and with the increased size of earth's current population, we were reaching a point where we had to decide how to handle the teleporter traffic."

"So, how does this change that?" Shepherd Randall asked.

"Our King likes order and efficiency," Mattathias said, then pointed to Janet. "Thanks to Janet's first finding of better predicting the timing of crop shipments, the long-range teleporter efficiency jumped to 73 percent. Now, thanks once again to Janet, the teleporter efficiency is up to 86 percent. Now we don't need to build new teleporters."

"Divine serendipity?"

Mattathias looked at Shepherd Randall and gave a small laugh. "Randall, you know serendipity never fits into the King's equation."

Randall laughed and nodded.

Janet glanced between the two of them. That seemed a strange statement for a man of science. The King planned her finding? She couldn't accept that thought process. It didn't seem logical.

"Any questions?" Janet looked at each of them.

Mattathias gave a slight wave. "I have a question, but it's one for Mr. O'Brien."

"Bruce. Call me Bruce."

"So, Bruce, you're a working farmer. What are your thoughts about changing the way you farm?"

Bruce shrugged. "I don't see it as changing the way I farm. I'll use the same equipment, plant and harvest in a similar manner. I don't think the crop itself is the issue. I think knowing what I'm doing will impact the world positively is what will drive me to do something a little differently."

"But you'll change your secondary crop every few years to ensure the soil is fit for the next crop, and you'll use ground cover you haven't used before," Mattathias said. "You don't see that as a concern?"

Bruce shook his head. "The ground cover just gets plowed under. No big deal there. Since I'll be using the same farming equipment for the other crops, it isn't a big learning curve." He looked at each of them and shrugged. "I don't think it's a big deal."

"And you don't think others will see it as a big deal?"

"No, I don't."

Mattathias sat back in his seat. "Well, I'm satisfied. I guess the true test is tomorrow."

Janet jumped back in. "So, what information or tips do you have for me for tomorrow?" She looked around the room at each of them. "What do you think the farmers want to see and hear?"

Everyone turned to Bruce, who replied, "I think plain and simple is best." He gestured toward Mattathias. "Hearing that the Jerusalem Science Center is behind this, and why . . . " He gestured to the Shepherds next. "And hearing that you Shepherds are supportive, I think, will go a long way." He pointed to Janet. "Then Janet can answer questions they may have and give more details at that time."

Everyone nodded.

"OK, that makes sense to me," Mattathias said. "Janet, are you OK with this plan?"

Janet nodded. "Sure. That sounds great to me."

All stood to end the meeting. It was planned that they would meet back at the civic center the next morning. Handshakes were given, papers gathered, and all headed out.

Janet walked with Bruce across the town square and stopped at a parked AGA.

"Ready to see the farm?" Bruce asked.

"Sure. Is this your AGA?"

Bruce nodded. "They're pretty necessary here since farms are several kilometers from each other."

Bruce opened the door for her and then entered the driver's side.

Janet leaned back in her seat and let out a long breath. "I'm glad that's over." She looked at Bruce. "I think it went well."

Bruce glanced from the road to Janet. "Are you kidding? It went great." He patted her hand. "You were great."

She smiled. "So were you. I feel a lot of the pressure is off now with just having to answer questions."

Janet sat back and enjoyed the ride. They passed field after field of corn. In between were fields of vegetables.

"How many farms are here?"

Bruce glanced her way. "That's a good question." He rubbed his chin. "I would say about one hundred large farms and at least another hundred smaller farms for fruits and vegetables."

"And that's just in your territory?"

Bruce nodded. "There's no doubt what you're asking the farmers changes a lot of things. But I don't think that in and of itself is the issue. Most love and adore our King. If he is for it, so will they."

"So you're saying most people aren't as skeptical as I am about the King?"

"There are all kinds of people in the world, Janet. You're just a smaller minority, I think." Bruce gave a big grin. "But, I like different."

Janet gave a half laugh and leaned back in her seat. If Bruce was right, then it really did make her job easier. Yet, at the same time, it put her personal beliefs in greater jeopardy. It was important that she and her thoughts be kept private. She had to be sure no one but Bruce knew those thoughts, and even he couldn't know everything she was planning. He couldn't know about her trying to meet the Leader of The Order.

Bruce turned off the main road. "Well, this is it. These fields are mine." It seemed like a long drive before they reached the house. It was typical of what Janet had grown up with: house, barn, animals, even a small pond.

"Bruce, this is lovely. Your house is larger than I expected."

Bruce laughed. "It was built with further contingencies in mind." He looked at her and raised his eyebrows a few times.

Janet rolled her eyes and laughed.

Bruce quickly stepped out and came around to open her door and help her out. As she looked around, a beagle came bounding over and licked her fingers. She bent over and petted him.

"Hi, there. What's your name? You're a sweetie. Yes you are."

The beagle wagged his tail excitedly and followed Janet as she and Bruce started walking.

"His name is Oliver."

"That's . . . an interesting name for a dog."

Bruce laughed. "Well, the story behind it is a little embarrassing."

Janet leaned into his shoulder. "Well, you have to tell me now."

Bruce looked down for a while and then back at Janet. "Well, I got Oliver when I was young. I thought the initials 'B' and 'O,' together, were funny. You know, 'B' for me, for Bruce. Then I needed something for an 'O.'"

Janet looked confused. "Why is that funny?"

"What do you immediately think of when you hear 'B-O'?"

A smiled spread across Janet's face. "No!" She laughed. "That's why you named him Oliver?"

Bruce nodded. "As a young boy, body odor was just a funny phrase to me. I nicknamed us B-O. Of course, once I got older, I just stuck to Oliver for him."

Janet shook her head.

"See, I told you it was a little embarrassing."

"No." Janet grabbed his arm and leaned into his shoulder. "It's kind of sweet. It makes you seem more real."

Bruce showed her around the farm and then the house. She was impressed with how he had managed to keep everything so immaculate.

As the sun set, they sat next to the pond and fed the ducks scraps of bread Bruce had brought from the kitchen. One of the ducks kept going from one crumb to another as fast as it could, but it never seemed to get there fast enough. Feeling sorry for the poor duck, Janet threw a crumb near him. He gobbled it up.

Janet giggled. "Look at that expression. 'I did it!' it seems to be saying."

Bruce smiled at her. "I could see you here."

Janet didn't know how to respond, so she just smiled back. "It's getting late, Bruce. I should get back. I want to spend some more time preparing for the questions I may get asked tomorrow." Bruce nodded and helped her to her feet.

Not much was said on the way back to Mable's. When Bruce dropped Janet off, he kissed her good night, and she leaned in to return his affection. She wanted him to know she was definitely interested.

"I'll stop by in the morning at the same time," Bruce said.

"OK. I'll see you then."

She stepped from the AGA and waved as Bruce left.

As she walked to her room, Janet thought about Bruce's comment at the pond. Could she see herself living here? Maybe her father's prediction was coming true—it just would not be back with him.

She shook her head. She loved the city. She loved Bruce. Which did she love more?

CHAPTER 10

*D*éjà *vu*, thought Janet as Bruce arrived at the same time as the previous day and once again sat across from her.

"Something's different. I see yellow on your plate."

Janet smiled. "I had some eggs with my yogurt and granola."

"Acting like a native already," Bruce said with a chuckle.

Janet laughed and shook her head. "Just avoiding stares from the natives."

Bruce stood and held out his elbow for her to take. "Ready to go?"

"I am," Janet said as she took his arm.

When they reached the civic center, only Mattathias was there waiting for them.

"Where is everyone?" Janet asked, turning around. She was wondering if this meeting was a bust before it even got started.

Mattathias put his hand on Janet's shoulder. "Don't look so worried, Janet. The farmers wanted to be outside, so the meeting was moved to a spot near the ruins."

Bruce laughed. "That makes sense. We farmers like to be outside."

Mattathias escorted them to the large crowd of farmers that had gathered. Janet walked with Mattathias to the front of the crowd where the Shepherds were standing. Bruce stayed near the front with the farmers.

Janet didn't count them, but as she looked over the crowd there seemed to be at least two hundred or so farmers who had gathered. Her jittery feelings returned. Maybe she shouldn't have eaten those eggs after all.

Shepherd Morgan stepped forward. "Thank you all for coming. As you know, all your hard work in growing crops feeds not only your families but families around the world. As you also know, every town has to deal with an ever-increasing population. We have changed over time. Now we have the opportunity to help the entire world deal with its growing pains. Here to give more information on this is Administrator Mattathias from the Jerusalem Science Center."

Mattathias stepped forward. "Hello, everyone. It is my pleasure and honor to be here and represent all those who help maintain our teleporter system. As you know, the long-range teleporters are used to carry your crops around the world for everyone to enjoy. People like Ms. Janet Singleton, here with us today, work tirelessly to help understand how our citizens utilize your crops. Our King is a King of order and efficiency. Ms. Singleton, and others like her, help the King maintain that order and efficiency."

He motioned for Janet to step forward and join him.

"As Shepherd Morgan stated, to accommodate the teleporter traffic and crop shipments, changes have to be made," Mattathias said. "We either make their use more efficient or we have to build more. Just building more is not always the best solution, and it sometimes creates additional problems we must work through. Ms. Singleton has single-handedly been able to devise a plan which will increase the efficiency of our current long-range teleporter system by 86 percent. Just changing a few things on your end will yield huge benefits to our entire world population."

Janet stepped to the microphone. "I am willing to answer any of your questions. Feel free to address me as Janet. What questions may I address?"

A muscular farmer near the front raised his hand. "Exactly what kind of changes are we talking about?"

"Not to simplify things too much," Janet said, giving a warm smile. "But you will change your secondary crops every few years and add cover crops in between plantings to help enrich your soil for the next crop. You'll use the same farming equipment for each of the crops you would be growing."

"That's it?" the man asked.

Janet nodded.

The man shrugged. "Seems simple enough to me."

Others nodded in agreement.

"Do we all grow the same crops at the same time?" This came from someone near the back.

"Our thoughts are that would be best. Everyone can then help and assist others if needed. Less experienced farmers can take advantage of the experience of their neighbors." Janet looked over the crowd. "Any objections to that approach?"

From the back, Janet heard, "No objections."

Janet nodded. "Other questions?"

Someone else called out, "We live to serve our King. It's a small change for a great purpose."

Janet smiled and gestured back to Mattathias. Bruce was right again. Most of these farmers seemed extremely supportive of the King. All her worries were unfounded.

"Thank you all for coming," Mattathias said. "We will all be here for a time, so if you have further questions you can stop by and we can address them for you." He gave a warm smile. "Instructions will come shortly. Stay tuned."

The crowd began to disperse. A handful of farmers came forward to ask a few more questions. Some seemed a little skeptical, but none seemed against the proposal. Most felt that once they received the instructions they would understand things even better.

All of this was also starting to make Janet believe her time in China would go well.

Once everyone dispersed, Mattathias approached her. "I heard you are traveling from here to China for a similar talk."

"Yes. I was worried, but the success here makes me feel better."

"I agree," Mattathias said. "I plan to stop and see Shepherd Keung before I return to Jerusalem. I'll be there for support when you speak. However, if things go well there, I don't see a need to continue these meetings. We can just let the local Shepherds handle the expected changes."

Janet nodded. "I agree, Administrator."

Mattathias smiled. "I'll see you in a few days."

With that, he took a few steps back and . . . disappeared.

Janet flinched, feeling a slight pull toward Mattathias as he teleported, and her arm closest to him felt a slight tingle.

Bruce put his hand on her shoulder. "You didn't expect that?"

Janet smiled. "Yes, but I've never been that close to someone when they disappeared. It seems so . . . so . . . "

"Miraculous?"

"Abnormal."

Bruce laughed as he put his arm around her and hugged her lightly. "You're such a skeptic."

Janet looked into his eyes. "If you feel like that, why do you want to be with me?"

Bruce released his grip and faced her. "Janet, you are one of the most unique people I have met. It is you I am learning to love. If you don't hold what I believe against me, I certainly will never hold what you believe against you."

Janet's gaze softened. "You're the most unique individual I have ever met as well."

"That has to mean something, right?"

Janet hugged his arm. "Give me time. I left a farming community thinking I'd never return. It's not that easy for me."

Bruce kissed her on the head. "I understand."

They went back to Mable's, had a late lunch, and continued their conversation.

"So you're heading to China this afternoon?" Bruce asked as their time drew near a close.

Janet nodded. "Yes, although I'm hoping things go as smoothly there as here. But I do have more prepping to do." Bruce nodded. "I'll try and get a few hours rest here and then take the teleporter. It will be early morning there."

Bruce took her hand. "I'll miss you."

Janet put her other hand on his. "Same here. Molly will have my schedule if anything important comes up. I should be reachable by communicator, though."

Bruce sighed. "I'll leave and let you get some rest." He stood, leaned over, and gave her a kiss. "See you soon."

She smiled and held onto his hand until his stepping away separated their touch. She blew him a kiss as he turned and left.

Janet sat back and thought about the two of them. She was really falling for him, but to move back to farming territory seemed like a step backward. After finally reaching her goal to live in the city and work in the building she loved, what was she going to do?

She shook her head. She told herself she couldn't think about all that right now. Rest was paramount so she could be alert for her visit to China. Coming to grips with personal decisions would have to be dealt with later.

CHAPTER 11

nce Janet's view cleared as she arrived in Guilin, she gasped. She had not expected the city to be so beautiful. The long-range teleporter was on a platform high in the middle of the city. A view of the Li River lay to one side; the river looked clear and blue running through a green landscape. The city itself was immaculately designed. Many of the buildings had the traditional curved eaves, but they were arranged in a way to form an appealing design to the eye. In addition, a fruity aroma filled her senses.

When Janet arrived at street level, she saw the hotel just across the street from the teleporter location. In front of the hotel a small tea garden with various flowering shrubbery, a koi pond, and a paifang were visible. As she walked near the hotel, a light, peachy aroma grew stronger. Several shrubs along the garden path displayed small golden flowers. Bending down, she breathed in their aroma. Yes, these flowers were the source. The sign at the bottom of the plant read: *Osmanthus fragrans.*

Janet pulled from her memory what this Greek designation meant and smiled: sweet fragrant flower. *Aptly named,* she thought as she continued into the hotel.

The front desk allowed her to check in early, and the clerk handed her a message waiting for her. She took the envelope and went to her room, which wasn't large but was decorated tastefully. It had scenes from the area with a picture grouping on the wall over a small bonsai garden placed on the table opposite the bed. She sat on the bed to read the note.

Her eyes widened as she read.

Unfortunately, our plans have changed. Hopefully, you get this note in time. I will have to leave the area early. I will await you in the Reed Flute Cave at 14:00 two days after the date on this note. Take the tour and when you get toward the halfway point of the tour, a cave-in will be pointed out. Go around the large stalagmite and enter the cave produced by the cave-in. As you enter, a torch will be awaiting you. I hope to meet you then.

She looked at the date. Her pulse quickened. The final date they could meet was *today*. She glanced at the clock: 11:25. Was there enough time to get to this cave? She quickly changed into jeans and a pullover and raced downstairs to the front desk.

Janet smiled and tried not to look frantic. "I need to get to the Reed Flute Cave. How can I do that?"

The clerk smiled. "There are several tours a day. It's only five kilometers north of here. We have an AGA leaving at noon. Would you like to reserve a seat?"

Janet smiled. "Yes, please."

"Meet right outside the front doors and the driver will get you there in plenty of time for a tour."

"Thank you." Janet turned and headed to the restaurant, her T-band revealing there was just enough time for a quick bite. After ordering some steamed dumplings, she sat back and let out a long breath. She was anxious to meet this Isabelle. Would she let Janet meet the Leader? She hoped.

Three other women were waiting outside to go to the cave. The driver pulled up with an open AGA design with three passenger seats. It seemed the three knew each other, and all three climbed into the same seat. Janet got into the next seat and sat by herself. The three women did not totally ignore her but spent most of their time talking and laughing with each other.

The trip was less than twenty minutes. It went more slowly than normal, she heard the women say, but the traffic did allow them to enjoy the scenery more than a fast trip would have. Janet was impressed with the tiered gardening practices still employed here. The farms were beautiful as they undulated with the hills to which they clung. The water from the terraced rice fields reflected their surroundings and made them look almost glassy.

Once at the cave, a number of people were awaiting the next tour. Janet joined them, and as they first entered the cave, everyone gasped. While the cave itself was impressive with its huge stalactites and stalagmites, multicolored lights throughout added another awe-inspiring effect as they highlighted different and various geologic structures. *Mesmerizing* was the word that came to Janet's mind.

About a half hour into the tour, the tour guide explained what they were seeing in the distance. "The Great Earthquake, which occurred when our King returned to us, caused this particular cave-in that you see here. While it destroyed some of the present cave, it has opened another, even larger, cave. Work is under way to allow tours. I hope you come back next year when the first tour will be open to the public."

In front of the cave-in was a huge stalagmite twice the height of Janet and a couple of meters wide at the base. Janet assumed this must be the place to which the note referred, so she purposely lagged behind the tour group and then quickly ducked behind the large stalagmite. She heard the tour guide talking about the next section of cave that would lead them back to the surface.

As Janet scanned the area, she almost laughed out loud when she noticed the tip of an overlarge stalactite pointing directly over a small cave entrance. It would have been hard to not notice. Because she had to almost double over to enter the opening, she was starting to have second thoughts as to whether this was the correct cave. Once inside, it was pitch-black, and this elicited a slight sense of panic until her eyes adjusted. At that point, she saw a small glow to her left. As she approached, she realized it was coming from a battery-powered torch; the note had mentioned the torch that would be waiting for her.

She took the torch and looked around but didn't see anything yet, just more of what the other cave looked like. As she turned a corner, she saw what looked like glow sticks on top of a flat rock. Walking closer, she saw several of them had been put together to spell the word *sit*. Her eyebrows shot up. Still, she complied, taking a seat on the front portion of the rock.

"Good afternoon," a female voice said.

"Isabelle?"

"Yes. Is this secretive enough for you?"

Janet nodded but then realized no one could see her. "Yes, thank you."

"Why do you want to see the Leader?"

"I understand the reason for his anonymity and why he needs others to help lead a resistance."

"Not everyone can have anonymity, though, as you have been requesting."

"I understand that," Janet replied, "but I think several key people will need that in order to be successful overall. There needs to be at least, say, one per continent, to help ensure all goes according to plan."

"And you want to be one of those people?"

"I feel I already am. I'm the one seeking him out and not the other way around."

"How do you plan to be effective being anonymous?"

"The person with anonymity needs to be mobile and able to meet a lot of people. I feel I fit that model as I travel all the time. I would need anonymity in order to stay effective by meeting who I think is loyal to our cause and then have others reel them in, so to speak. The Order needs both, but in order to ensure the entire Order is never shut down completely, the key people need to not know everything or everyone."

"There is some sense to this," Isabelle said.

"Thank you. Now, what is the proof of this Overtaker I hear about?"

"The Leader found a stone stele that prophesies his coming."

"What does it say?"

Janet heard something being pushed her way over the flat stone surface. She reached out, pulled it to her, and raised it to her lap. It was a wooden case. Once opened, her light revealed symbols that looked Hebrew in origin. She couldn't tell for sure, however.

"What type of writing is this, and what does it say?" Janet asked.

"It's Hebrew, and it says, 'The Overtaker consumes with device of doom.'"

Janet looked more closely at the stele. "And you think there are more of these because of the Roman numeral VII on it?"

"I'm impressed. Yes, that is what we believe."

"But you haven't found any of the others?"

"Not yet. Where they are is unknown. We're making certain calculated assumptions and investigating to see if they pan out. That's what the Leader is doing now. I think you should meet him."

Janet jerked up straighter where she sat. *Wow, that was a quick turnaround.* "I would love to—in anonymity of course."

Isabelle laughed lightly. "That can be arranged."

"Where and when?"

"He'll be in his current location for only another week. If you miss him, I can't guarantee when you would see him."

"You don't make it easy for me."

"Sorry. But we have to always stay under the radar. Moving around quickly is one of the means to do that."

"I understand. Where?"

"Iceland."

"Iceland?" Janet knew her surprise was louder than she wanted. She finished her response in a more normal tone. "I thought he would be here somewhere."

"He's following up on a lead." The voice paused. "So, can you make it?"

"I'll try. I have a meeting here in a couple of days, and then I'll meet him in Iceland. I'll be there in four days. Will he still be there?"

"Yes. I doubt he will be there past five, though."

Janet nodded her head and sighed. "I understand. Where should I meet him?"

"There's a small inn close to the teleporter in Reykjavik," Isabelle said. "I'll leave a message for Ms. Story there. Goodbye for now. You have just enough time to catch up with your tour group before they exit the cave. You must hurry."

Janet had forgotten about the tour; she had become so caught up with the stele. She quickly headed back to the cave entrance and literally ran to catch up with the group. The beautiful colors of the cave continued to mesmerize her, but her pounding heart rate didn't allow her to slow down. When she reached the tour, she carefully eased herself into the back of the group while trying to not let anyone notice how heavily she was breathing.

She enjoyed the rest of the tour, spent some time in the gift shop, and then took the AGA back to the hotel, where she tried to get some rest before dinner. A lot was going through her mind, however, keeping her from getting serious rest. She was proud her plans were coming together and felt fortunate she had arrived in time for the meeting.

Again, Bruce seemed to be the key to everything coming together. At some point, she had to consider how to have this man more permanently in her life.

For now, she had to focus on the immediate. Rest was what she needed. She closed her eyes.

CHAPTER 12

Janet woke to the sound of her room communicator beeping. Turning over, she pressed the button.

"Yes?"

"Ms. Singleton, Administrator Mattathias is here to see you. He was wondering if you could come to the lobby."

She replied instinctively. "Yes. I'll be right there."

She sat up, confused and disoriented. Looking at the window, she saw the sun. That confused her even more. The clock in the room read 08:47. The logic came into focus: she never woke for dinner. That would explain why she was still in her clothes—and very hungry.

Janet quickly freshened up and changed. No time for a shower. She headed downstairs to the hotel lobby. Administrator Mattathias was sitting in a chair next to a large wall water structure, with water cascading down a mosaic.

As she approached, he stood.

"Good morning, Janet." They shook hands. "Sorry. I'm early. Did you want to get some breakfast before we leave to see Shepherd Keung?"

"Yes, thanks. I seemed to have slept through dinner last night." She chuckled. "I guess the time change had a bigger effect on me than I thought."

"No problem. We don't need to meet him until 10:15."

They found a spot in the hotel restaurant. Janet ordered a couple of steamed baozi and an egg pancake. They were served in a matter of minutes.

Between bites, Janet asked, "Do you expect anything different here than in America?"

Mattathias shook his head. "The crops are different, but the scenario is the same. We'll talk to eight Shepherds this morning and then address the farmers after that."

Janet stopped chewing. She swallowed hard. "Both meetings are today?"

"Is that a problem? You don't foresee any problems, do you?"

"I guess not. It's just . . . " Janet shrugged. "I expected the same timing as before."

"The Shepherds seemed supportive, so I thought we could cover more ground more quickly."

Janet finished her pancake and pushed her plate aside. "OK. So, where do we meet them?"

"By the river. There's a place large enough to hold the farmers. The Shepherds and I had a small area set up to address them. We'll talk to the Shepherds there as well." Mattathias raised his eyebrows. "Ready to go?" Janet nodded.

They headed down the street and turned toward the river. The beauty of the city continued to amaze Janet. It was hard for her to understand what amazed her so. It seemed planning went into every detail: buildings, plants, walkways, gardens, sculptures. Maybe there was something to feng shui after all. If so, these people had it mastered.

When they reached the area, Mattathias introduced Janet to Shepherd Keung.

Keung bowed and Janet bowed in return.

"Ms. Singleton, I appreciate you being here." Keung smiled. "I have been thinking something like this was necessary for some time. I am glad you are now implementing it."

"Thank you, Shepherd Keung. Seeing patterns in data is not always easy, but I'm glad to be able to help put it into practice."

He nodded and gestured toward other glorified individuals. "Let me introduce you to the other Shepherds."

Janet smiled and bowed in greeting to seven other men. She tried to remember their names, but the names were so unusual to her that she couldn't remember them. Hopefully, that would not come back to haunt her during the meeting with the farmers.

"And behind me here is my great-granddaughter, Huizhong," Keung said.

Huizhong bowed in greeting. Janet did the same, but she felt a little underdressed as her dark business suit was in stark contrast to Huizhong's dark red cheongsam, decorated with lotus flowers.

"She has a position similar to yours, Ms. Singleton."

Janet's eyebrows went up. "Oh, how so?"

Huizhong gave a half smile. "I oversee the crops produced in most of Asia."

"Oh, very impressive."

"Thank you. I have looked over your proposal. I only have data from the territories I oversee, but I anticipate very little modifications needed to fulfill your requests."

"That's very good to hear, Huizhong. Not all territories have such detailed oversight." Janet smiled. "I look forward to working with you more closely."

Huizhong gave what seemed, to Janet, a half-hearted bow.

Hmm. I wonder what's going on with her, Janet asked herself. Huizhong's answers were positive, but her tone seemed too deadpan to be sincere.

"Your city is amazingly beautiful," Janet said, hoping that supplying some compliments would help Huizhong open up.

Huizhong smiled. "Thank you. We take great pride in it." She gave a small laugh and her eyes twinkled. "There is a saying that when the Refreshing occurred, no one in Guilin knew because nothing changed."

"Now, Huizhong."

"Sorry, Grandfather. It's just a saying."

Janet thought there was something deeper there not spoken. She replied, "Well, your city is exceptionally beautiful. I could see why some may have said that."

Huizhong gave a small smile in return.

Mattathias began the meeting with the Shepherds by giving the same presentation he had previously. Janet also had the same role, except she did not give any presentation this time. She did, however, try to engage Huizhong in her presentation, thinking the Chinese analyst may be concerned not knowing what her role would be in this new model for growing and shipping crops.

The Shepherds nodded and expressed no concerns with what either Mattathias or Janet said. Huizhong seemed too quiet for Janet's taste, but she was unsure how to address any of Huizhong's possible concerns if she did not express them.

Janet looked up and saw farmers congregating. Many had on regular trousers and shirts. Some wore the traditional conical-shaped straw hats. Most were holding them, but some were still wearing them. Once again, there seemed nearly two hundred farmers present.

Shepherd Keung said almost the identical words to the farmers that Shepherd Morgan had a few days earlier. To Janet, it was interesting how this meeting was almost a mirror image of the previous one. After Shepherd Keung talked, Huizhong stepped forward and basically reiterated what Keung had said. She did not, however, step back once finished, as Janet had expected.

Janet waited a few extra moments, but Huizhong remained motionless. Assuming she wanted equal credit for what Janet had put together, Janet stepped forward.

"Thank you, Huizhong, Shepherd Keung, and Administrator Mattathias. Does anyone have any questions?"

The same questions as in America were asked: would everyone grow the same crops? Would they be expected to use different equipment from what they were used to? What were the major differences going forward from how they were farming today? What Janet found interesting, and a little annoying, was Huizhong answered all questions. Janet added a sentence here and there to appear knowledgeable on the subject. It was, after all, her meeting. Janet was unsure why Huizhong felt she had to take charge.

Before all questions were answered, Janet noticed one farmer kept moving closer to the front. He did not come forward quickly, but steadily squeezed his way between other farmers. Once at the front, he continued coming forward. He uttered one word—loudly.

"Why?"

Huizhong stopped talking and turned to Janet.

Janet looked at Huizhong and then at the farmer. *Well, that's just great.* When she really needed local input, Huizhong refused to provide it. Janet tried to smile. "Excuse me? Why what?"

"Why did you come?"

Janet shook her head slightly. "You mean us, or me specifically?"

The farmer pointed his finger at Janet, brushing his hat so that it hung down on his back, and his eyes locked onto Janet's with an icy stare. "*You*. You take another decision away from us."

Janet stiffened. Her heart rate increased even though she tried to remain calm—at least on the outside. She glanced at Huizhong, who remained still as a statue. It seemed obvious Janet would get no help from her.

Janet swallowed hard and tried to keep her smile even though her muscles were telling her to bolt. "As Huizhong and Shepherd Keung have mentioned, we are not asking you to change much of what you are doing. It's not really changing your decision, but seeking your help to help everyone."

"You hide behind their words? You have no opinion of your own?"

"What?" Janet shook her head. "No. No, I think you're misunderstanding. Yes, I did the calculations and take full responsibility for that work. Your leaders here—" She gestured to those onstage with her. "They just want you to understand they also support the work I have done. It not only benefits you—you most of all—but also benefits the people of the world."

The farmer kept approaching. His stare did not waver. *Is someone going to do anything?* Janet looked at Huizhong, whose stare rivaled that of the farmer. She glanced at the other Shepherds. Surely, they were on her side. Still, no one stepped forward.

"I don't trust anything you say." The man was now coming up the steps to the stage where she was standing . . .

Janet took a step back. "Do you want to address the crowd and have a more thorough discussion?" she asked the man.

The farmer shook his head. "I want to send you back to the King."

"I . . . I didn't come from the King. I came from the Commodities Department in Chicago. We just want to have crops that are efficient for everyone."

The man stepped onto the stage and continued coming closer. Janet took a few more steps back. Beads of sweat were forming on her forehead. *Is no one going to do anything?*

At the last moment, before this man came within arm's length of Janet, Shepherd Keung stepped between them.

"Yunxu, what is the meaning of this?" Keung interjected.

The two of them were now face to face.

"You are in favor of this?" Yunxu's face now was turning red. "Letting outsiders tell us what to do?"

"There is no such thing as an outsider, Yunxu. We are all children of the King. Our ethnicity is something to be proud of, but we cannot let it define us. We live to serve our King, and we work to serve each other."

"I serve no one. The King is an imposter. He will be overcome."

Gasps could be heard throughout the crowd. Janet glanced at Huizhong and saw her eyes water; she was trying to hold back tears. *Does she know this man?* Janet had to give the man credit for his boldness, but she felt this was not the time to take this approach. Or was she just upset he had lumped her into all of this?

Keung grabbed Yunxu's shoulders with his hands and shook him slightly. "Yunxu, you do not mean such words. Be careful. You verge on the border of blasphemy."

Yunxu laughed. The laugh turned almost maniacal but then ended abruptly. His eyes now bore hatred, and his words dripped loathing. "Blasphemy? I despise the King, and I look forward to his demise."

Suddenly, Yunxu disappeared. Janet jumped back with a small shriek. Shepherd Keung's hands, which had been holding Yunxu, fell to his side. His shoulders drooped; he dropped his head and shook it slowly.

Janet looked at Huizhong. She remained motionless, but tears were now trickling down her face.

Shepherd Keung stepped forward to address the crowd. "My fellow citizens. We have just witnessed what we, our Administrators, and our loving King wish to never happen. Yunxu lost his vision for himself and his family. We are all here to help each other and serve our King." He gestured toward Janet. "What Ms. Singleton has presented is pure logic. Although supported by the King, it is not an edict from him. He only wishes it because it is the best for everyone."

There was silence across the crowd for several seconds.

"We serve the King!" someone in the crowd shouted. Others followed suit. Soon the whole crowd was announcing their support of the King.

Shepherd Keung smiled and lifted his hands. "Go, my children. Go forth and prosper. May our Lord and King bless you all."

The crowd applauded and began to disperse. A few came forward to ask a few more questions. Others came to pay their regrets regarding what happened. Soon, all the farmers had left.

Janet walked over to Huizhong and placed a hand on her shoulder. "Are you all right? I couldn't help but see this was very emotional for you."

Janet saw so much sadness in Huizhong's eyes. "I was afraid Yunxu was going to do something like that."

"You knew him?"

Huizhong nodded. "He is a great farmer and comes from a loving family. Yet his purpose for living never seemed to match that of most others." Her eyes darted over Janet's face as if looking to see whether she could be totally honest with her. "Not everyone serves the King with abandon."

Janet nodded, but didn't say more; she sensed she had met someone of common spirit. Huizhong likely believed similar to Yunxu, but perhaps not as strongly, and would never put her life at risk so willingly.

"I'm sorry for your loss, Huizhong."

Huizhong nodded as her eyes watered again.

"Please, let me know if there is anything I can do for you."

Huizhong looked at Janet again, perhaps trying to determine if any common bond might now exist between them. Still, all she said was, "Thank you."

Janet saw Administrator Mattathias talking to Shepherd Keung and walked over to where they were standing. Keung nodded slightly. Janet returned the nod with a weak smile.

"Shepherd Keung, what will happen to Yunxu? Will he be allowed to return?" Janet asked.

"That, I'm afraid, is up to Yunxu."

Janet cocked her head. "But isn't it really up to the King?" Janet saw the raised eyebrows on the Administrator's face and wondered if she had gone too far. Shepherd Keung, however, seemed to take the question to heart.

Keung smiled. "I guess that is true. But the King has allowed us to determine our ultimate fate. If Yunxu remains as resolute in the King's presence as he did in ours, I don't have the hope he will return to us." He shook his head. "I'm afraid of the message I'll soon receive from Ruach HaKadosh and the difficult talk I'll then have to have with Yunxu's family."

Keung excused himself and joined the other Shepherds. Janet was left alone with Administrator Mattathias.

"Janet, I appreciate you coming," Mattathias said. "It seems most of the farmers are on board with our approach. I think it is safe to say we can have Shepherds in other parts of the world relay the message and gather their subjects' support. You don't have to schedule another meeting like this one."

Janet gave a weak smile. "Well, that's good to hear."

"I'm just sorry you had to have such an experience. It's never easy to see someone disappear knowing the likelihood of the outcome. It is really sad." He reached out and put his hand on her shoulder. "Are you OK? Do you need to talk or anything?"

Janet shook her head. "No. I'll be fine. It was a jolt. I'll have to come to grips with it, I guess."

Mattathias nodded. "I'm always available if you need me. I've enjoyed getting to know you these last couple of weeks."

"Thank you. Same here."

"Well, I'll be off and get things rolling with the other Shepherds. Take care, Janet."

He walked to the other Shepherds, shook their hands, and then he too disappeared. Within a few minutes, the other Shepherds did the same.

For some reason, Janet found it odd how disappearances of those with glorified bodies seemed natural and right, but a disappearance of one who was nonglorified always brought panic to those who saw it. The *why* of the disappearance made all the difference.

Would she ever come to accept the decisions of the King? Were differences, even extreme, enough to justify individuals being taken? She was unsure if she could ever come to accept that.

CHAPTER 13

Janet got back to the hotel late and collapsed on the bed. Huizhong had asked her to dinner, and she felt she couldn't say no. With that behind her, all she wanted now was to rest, but she knew she couldn't. Next on the agenda was Iceland. She needed to get a message to Amanda if she was to keep her anonymity. Working through Molly was probably best. Hopefully, Molly wouldn't be upset with her calling so early.

Molly answered, but by audio only. "Hello."

"Hi, Molly. This is Janet. I'm sorry for calling so early."

"Oh. Hi, Janet. No problem. Sorry for no video. I'm getting dressed."

Janet grimaced. "I'm sorry, Molly. Something unexpected has come up and I need you to make reservations for me to stay at Reykjavik."

"Iceland?" She sounded puzzled.

Janet laughed. "Yes, can you do that this morning? I need to get there today. I hear there's an inn not far from the teleporter."

"Sure. I'll do it even before I head to work."

"Molly, I really appreciate this. Can you also let Amanda know where I'll be?"

"Amanda? Amanda Story?"

"Yes, she needs to get a, uh . . . a package to me."

"OK, Janet. I'll call her right after I make your arrangement."

"Molly, you're the best. Thanks. I'll see you soon."

"Have a safe trip."

Janet disconnected and then decided to rest for a couple of hours to give Molly time to make arrangements. She set her alarm and collapsed.

Her exhaustion overcame her adrenaline.

* * * * *

When she arrived in Reykjavik, Janet found the inn just around the corner from the teleporter as Isabelle had said. It provided a breathtaking view overlooking the ocean. On checking in, the clerk, seeing her name, handed Janet an envelope.

"A Ms. Story asked that you receive this."

Janet smiled. "Thank you."

She opened the envelope and took out the note, read it, looked at her T-band, and sighed. It almost felt as if she was in some type of sorority hazing ceremony.

"Excuse me. Can you tell me where the Seljalandsfoss cave is?"

"You mean the waterfall?" the clerk asked.

Janet looked at the note again. "No, the cave."

The clerk frowned and shook his head. "Ms. Singleton, I don't think you want to go to the cave. It's very unstable and dangerous. The waterfall . . . " He smiled and his eyes twinkled. "Now that is something you don't want to miss."

"I'll be sure and not miss it. But I do need to see the cave as well."

The clerk pursed his lips and sighed. "Well, the cave is about a half kilometer north of the waterfall. The Great Earthquake that occurred several centuries ago caused the fault line running through the island to shift and form a large scarp face. It created an opening into a large cave."

"Do you have automated AGAs here?"

The clerk nodded. "Yes. But are you sure you don't want a guide? It's very dangerous to go to the cave alone. Getting a guide is no trouble."

Janet shook her head. "No, that won't be necessary." She smiled. "I'll be fine."

The clerk shrugged and shook his head. He handed her the key card to her room. "Use the green AGA out front. You will have to walk to the cave from the waterfall."

Janet nodded. "Thank you." She went to her room and freshened up quickly. The note stated she had to meet the Leader in the cave that very afternoon. Perhaps she would at least get this over more quickly. Maybe then she could actually rest.

Janet went back downstairs, got in the green AGA waiting outside the inn, and had it scan her thumb. A polite mechanical voice responded.

"Good evening, Ms. Singleton. Where to today? Address or point of interest?"

"Point of interest. Seljalandsfoss cave."

"That landmark is not recognized. Can you state again?"

Janet thought for a second and then changed her entry. "Seljalandsfoss *waterfall*."

"Very good, Ms. Singleton. Travel time will be ninety-three minutes."

Janet's eyes widened. She had no idea it was that far away. Looking at her T-band as the AGA pulled onto the highway, she calculated the trip would put her there around fifteen hundred. Then she would have to walk to the cave, and that would take . . . she had no idea. Hopefully, the Leader was in no hurry to leave.

Janet leaned back in her seat and looked out the window. Although not in her plans, she found herself nodding off. At first, she resisted, but after a few minutes, she allowed herself to succumb to the inevitable slumber . . .

She didn't awake until she heard the AGA announce their near arrival.

"Destination will be achieved in five minutes."

Janet slowly woke and sat up. Looking out the AGA window, her mouth fell agape. The waterfall came from a cliff overhang several stories high and plunged into a pool below. Where the water fell was in front of a hole that went all the way through the cliff. Grass and moss surrounding the cliff added a stark contrast. It looked as if the stone broke through the green and towered into the sky.

Janet wanted to take a closer look, but she knew she had to make it to the cave. Finding a small trail at the base of the cliff that headed north, she followed it while hoping the cave entrance would be obvious. There were no stalactites here to point the way.

After walking no more than fifteen minutes, Janet saw several boulders blocking her path. As she walked around them, a large opening became visible in the cliff face. This had to be the place . . .

She entered the opening with trepidation. It was pitch-black inside. This time, there was no torch set aside to help her find her way. She mustered determination and held her hands out to feel her way farther in. Darkness enveloped her as she forced herself to remain calm. *Is the Leader even still here?*

She talked herself into going a little farther rather than bagging the whole thing. Her hands touched something solid. *The cave wall.* She followed with her fingers. It soon had her turn left. Only then did she see a glow farther ahead and toward her left. This gave her a focus, somewhere to head. Once there, glow sticks again were laying out, and again they made the single word: *sit.* She took a seat on a nearby rock.

"Good afternoon," a masculine voice to her left stated.

"You didn't make this easy."

"I needed to test your determination."

"And?"

"I can tell you're determined. So, explain your plans."

This guy got down to business from the get-go. Janet liked that. "I sought you out because I feel your tactics made sense."

"And how so?"

"Your anonymity made sense to me. You need well-traveled leaders to have the same type of anonymity, and then local individuals to be the face to others in their locale. This gives both strategy as well as a personal touch."

"And you want to be one of the leaders?"

How condescending. As if I'm a groupie or something. Janet didn't hesitate. "Well, no disrespect, but I didn't come here to apply. I'm going to do what I feel I should do. I like what you have started and would like to be part of it, but I don't have to. I think we can accomplish more together, but if you don't want that, that's fine with me. Should I go?"

"Whoa, whoa. Don't get defensive. Tell me what you envision."

"I think you need one anonymous individual on each continent to help lead The Order. That way, no one person can lead to the downfall of the organization as no one person can point to the discovery of everyone. It's a safeguard to ensure continuity. These individuals need to be well connected to discover potential recruits, notify others to follow up, and provide the necessary personal touch. I feel I can provide that for North America."

"I'm impressed with your insight and deduction."

"And I have just the person to lead Asia."

"Are you trying to take over my organization?"

Janet knew it was her personality to be bold, so she decided to hold nothing back. "Now who's getting defensive? I told you I agree with your tactics and feel I can contribute. I could start my own organization if I wanted to. But no, it makes more sense for us to band together with a common goal. Pardon my bluntness, but I thought you'd be more focused."

"I have to say, you have a strong personality. I certainly feel you can command and lead a continent. Who do you feel could lead Asia?"

"Shepherd Keung has a great-granddaughter named Huizhong who is well connected throughout Asia. Although she is not necessarily against the King as much as maybe you and I, from what I gather she has doubts and has been upset about certain people whom the King has taken. With a little guidance, I think she can be a great leader for our cause."

"I will certainly be in touch with you." She heard something scooted across the cave floor in her direction.

She reached out and picked up a small box. "What's this?"

"Use that with your computer or tablet and it will put us in touch with each other. All communication will be encrypted."

"Looks like you have a plan after all. May I ask why you are here in Iceland?"

"My wife showed you the stone stele I found centuries ago?"

"Yes, she did. And you are looking for others. Any idea where they are?"

"I am investigating places where volcanic activity occurred centuries ago. I feel that will eventually lead to finding others. Once we find a couple more, I think we can discover a pattern and find the others."

"Until that time, we need to spread the promise of the coming Overtaker," Janet said.

"Absolutely. I look forward to working with you."

"Same here."

Janet stood and groped to find the cave wall. Once she reached the curve in the wall, the light from the cave opening easily guided her to the entrance. The bright sunlight made her squint hard once she exited, so she stood with eyes closed for some time until opening them was no longer painful. She then worked her way back toward the waterfall.

Janet had mixed feelings about this Leader. He seemed more interested in leading than in the cause he was leading. That didn't sit well with her, but he had the resources and network she needed. Playing along was important—for now—but she made the decision that she would try and guide the outcome to how she felt things should be done.

When she got back to the waterfall, she stood and looked at it for several mesmerizing minutes. Once she walked around the pool formed by the falling water, she noticed another AGA parked next to hers. Turning several times, she scanned her surroundings but didn't see anyone else. She cautiously went to the AGAs to investigate. A note stuck to her windshield caught her eye. Opening the note, she read the words: *Come to the back of the falls.* Janet looked around again. Who even knew she was here?

Janet reluctantly, and cautiously, headed back to the water-fall and edged her way around the pool to the backside of it while trying to stay as dry as possible. The spray didn't allow her to be totally successful in that regard. Once at the backside of the falls, there was an opening leading through the cliff to the other side. She grabbed her shirt between thumb and fore-finger and jerked it back and forth to get the water droplets off before they had time to sink into the fabric. She looked around but saw no one. Was this all a prank? Was this yet another test from The Order? That's the only possibility she could think of.

She decided to go back. She turned, took a step, and froze. There standing in front of her was Bruce.

"Bruce! How . . . what . . . why are you here?"

Bruce laughed. He came forward and gave her a big hug and kiss. "Teleporter. To see you. To ask you something."

Janet cocked her head.

"That's the answer to your three questions."

She slapped his arm. "Don't patronize me. How did you even know I was here?"

"Molly." He laughed. "But she wasn't easy to convince."

She smiled. "Well, I'm glad to hear that, but equally glad she caved in for this particular instance."

He pulled her in and gave her another hug and whispered in her ear. "I do have something to ask you."

She raised her eyebrows. "And what would that be?"

He held her shoulders and pushed her backward gently, guiding her to sit on a boulder.

"I have something to say. Let me finish before you say anything."

Janet gave a half shrug. "OK."

Bruce cleared his throat. "Janet, I miss you when I'm away from you, I think about you all the time, and I'm constantly wondering what you're doing when I'm not with you." He pulled at his collar. "What I'm trying to say is, I have fallen in love with you and want you in my life."

Janet opened her mouth to say something, but Bruce held up his palm.

"I don't want to change you, change what you do, or even how you do it. I just want us to be together as much as possible and be there for each other."

He got down on one knee.

Janet's eyes widened.

"Janet Singleton, I am madly in love with you." He pulled out a small box and opened it, displaying a ring. The diamond wasn't large, but all Janet saw was its bright twinkle.

"Will you marry me?"

Janet's voice caught in her throat. She opened her mouth but nothing came out. Tears welled in her eyes.

Bruce reached out and took her hand. "Janet, are you OK?"

Janet nodded, wiping a few tears away. "Bruce, I can't tell you how happy that makes me. Before I answer, I have to tell you some things."

Bruce nodded. "OK."

"I really love you, too. But I need to continue to work, and I'm not sure if I want to have children. I know that is very different from other women in your territory."

As she talked, Bruce patted her hand and shook his head. "Janet, as I said, I don't want to change anything about you. I think you being so different from anyone I have known is a big appeal to me. I just want to spend more time with you. I'm willing to do whatever it takes to make it work."

He stood and pulled her to her feet, then drew her back into a tight hug. "So, what is your answer?"

She pulled back and looked into his eyes. "Yes. My answer is yes."

Bruce smiled brightly. He leaned in and gave a lingering kiss. "Janet, you have made me the happiest man alive."

She gave him another hug. The sun was setting. Its red and gold colors were glistening through the waterfall. It was mesmerizing. She reached up with her hands and turned Bruce's head to see the view.

"Wow. It's beautiful. Almost as beautiful as you."

Janet grabbed his arm and leaned into it. "You always know what to say at the right time."

Bruce smiled. "Let's head back."

Bruce put his arm around her shoulders and she around his waist as they walked to the AGAs. Janet sent her vehicle back to the hotel empty so she could ride back with Bruce.

Once in Bruce's AGA, Janet leaned back in her seat. Should she pinch herself to be sure this wasn't a dream? She kept smiling at Bruce. He was smiling back.

CHAPTER 14

" **B**ruce, I want to get married today."

Bruce glanced over at her and back to the road. "What? Don't you want a regular wedding with family and friends?"

Janet shook her head. "I've never been traditional. I think it's about you and me and not about them. I have a vacation coming. I can take it now. We can stay here and just enjoy each other."

"You're serious?"

Janet nodded. "Very."

With eyes slightly wide, Bruce said, "OK." He then laughed and responded more forcefully, "OK. So, who's the Shepherd here?"

"Let's ask back at the inn."

"You think he'll do it on such short notice?"

"Well, we're not asking for thrills. It would only be a few minutes of his time."

Bruce shrugged. "Hopefully that's how he'll see it."

Janet set back in her seat and drummed her fingers on her thigh. It seemed the time to get back was taking way too long.

Once back, both jumped out and ran to the front desk hand in hand.

The clerk looked up with raised eyebrows. "Ms. Singleton. I guess your adventure went well?"

"Better than expected." She held up her hand with the ring displayed on her finger.

"Oh, congratulations." He glanced between them. "When's the date? Have you settled on one?"

They looked at each other and laughed.

"We want to get married today."

The clerk looked at Bruce with eyes wide. "I don't want to be a downer, but it's already late. That may not be possible."

"Who's the Shepherd here? Can we talk to him?"

"Shepherd Fridrik will be here in a couple of hours. He's already performing a wedding tonight." His eyes perked up. "Oh, here comes the bride now."

Janet turned. A brown-skinned, toned woman wearing a long white dress with purple lilac prints throughout the pattern came forward and stopped at the counter. "Excuse me, Stefán. Did you ever hear from our friends?"

"I'm sorry, Ms. Okoro. No one has called."

Her shoulders drooped.

Janet leaned closer to the woman. "Is everything all right?"

She seemed to come out of deep thought. "Oh, I'm sorry for interrupting. It's just . . . our friends were supposed to come and be our bridesmaid and best man as well as the witnesses to our wedding." She threw up her hands. "They haven't shown up."

"When are you getting married?"

She looked at her T-band. "In just a couple of hours. Supposedly at twenty hundred." Her eyes watered. "But I'm not sure that's now going to happen."

"Well, this couple here was asking about getting married," Stefán said. "Maybe the two of you can work out an arrangement?"

Janet looked from Stefán to the woman and back. "What do you mean?"

"You can have a double wedding, and you each can serve as each other's witnesses."

Janet looked at the woman. "Are you willing?"

The woman smiled and nodded, holding out her hand. "Hi, I'm Afia."

Janet smiled. "I'm Janet, and this is Bruce."

Bruce gave her a nod with a smile.

A man rushed in carrying a tuxedo and practically ran to the desk. His skin tone was slightly darker than Afia's. "Afia, I have the tux. Did they call?"

Afia shook her head. "Chika, this is Janet and Bruce."

He looked at them and nodded.

"They also want to get married."

"That's nice." The look on his face made it clear he wasn't connecting the dots.

Afia grabbed Chika's arm. "Sweetie, our friends didn't make it. These two will be our witnesses. And we will be theirs."

His eyes widened as his mind made the connection. He glanced back at Afia. "But shouldn't we wait for our friends?" He looked at Bruce and Janet. "No offense, but we've planned all this with them."

Afia shook her head. "Chika, I want that too, but time's running out. I don't think they're going to make it in time." She glanced at Janet. "If they come, they can be our witnesses, but we'll still be yours. OK?"

"Sure," Janet said as she looked at Bruce, who also agreed.

"All right," Chika said to Afia. "If you're sure."

Afia nodded.

Chika looked at the tux he was carrying and then at Bruce. "Uh, we have a problem. There is no way this tux, for my best man, is going to fit you."

Afia looked at her T-band. "We don't have much time." She pointed her finger from Bruce to Chika. "Bruce, you go with Chika to get the tux replaced."

Chika kissed his fiancée. He tapped Bruce on his shoulder. Bruce raised an eyebrow at Janet and followed Chika out the door.

Afia stepped back and looked at Janet. "I think the dress I brought for my bridesmaid will fit you." She paused. "Or did you have something already prepared?"

Janet shook her head.

Afia turned to Stefán and put her hand on his. "Stefán, could you influence Shepherd Fridrik to prepare two marriage licenses?"

Stefán cocked his head and sighed. "That's really overstepping my bounds."

Afia gave a pouty face. "Please. You'd be making four people very happy."

Stefán looked at Janet. She just smiled and nodded.

Stefán's cheeks reddened as he rubbed the back of his neck. "Well, I, uh, guess I could call him and see if he would be willing."

Afia pulled her arms into her chest, smiled, and bounced slightly on her feet. "Thank you, thank you. Call me in my room as soon as you hear back."

Stefán nodded.

"You're amazing, Stefán," Afia said one more time as she turned.

He smiled as he headed to the other end of the counter and picked up his headset.

"Janet, come to my room," Afia said. "Let's see how well the dress fits."

Janet followed her up the stairs. "Thanks for being willing to do this," she said.

Afia glanced back with eyes wide. "Are you kidding me? Thank you. Without you, I wouldn't be getting married."

Janet chuckled. "I guess neither of us would be getting married without each other."

Afia opened her room door. "That's very true."

When Afia retrieved the dress for Janet from her closet, Janet's eyes widened. "Afia, this is beautiful." It had the same white background as Afia's, but the flowers were various colored roses. "What made you choose these?"

Afia smiled. "I've always loved lilacs." She chuckled. "The more purple the better."

"And your friend loves roses?"

Afia put her fist to her mouth, shook her head, and started to laugh. "She actually hates roses."

Janet's mouth dropped open.

"This was supposed to be a prank for her." Afia shook her head. "I guess the prank's on me."

"Well, I love it."

"Oh, good." She gestured toward the bathroom. "Go try it on." She smiled. "Then we'll accessorize."

Janet found the dress not a perfect fit, but not terribly bad under the circumstances. She reentered the bedroom portion of the suite.

Afia turned and froze. "Janet, you look stunning."

"Thanks. It fits pretty well. Just a little loose in the bodice."

Afia gave a dismissive wave. "No one can tell. Come sit down. I think I have just the thing for your hair."

There was a knock at the door. Afia opened it and Chika and Bruce entered.

"We got it." Chika was all grins.

Janet entered the main room with her room key card and handed it to Bruce. "You guys can change in my room."

Bruce stood there staring at Janet.

"What's wrong?"

"Nothing. You look gorgeous, Janet."

Chika grabbed the key card. "Come on, Bruce. We have to hurry." He looked at Afia and Janet. "Be downstairs in fifteen minutes. We have to sign the marriage contracts and get to the waterfall."

The men left.

"Waterfall?" Janet asked Afia.

Afia nodded. "Didn't I tell you? We're getting married at the Seljalandsfoss waterfall." She pulled Janet back into the bedroom and had her take a seat in front of the mirror.

"It's already night. Why at the waterfall?"

Afia brushed Janet's hair and worked some baby's breath into it.

"It's beautiful at night. They have colored lighting in strategic places. You'll love it."

Janet did the same work on Afia's hair using tiny blossoms of lilacs.

After a few more minutes of this, Afia looked at her T-band. "We'd better go."

They hurried downstairs. Bruce and Chika were already at the desk in their tuxedos talking to Shepherd Fridrik. Janet was surprised to see Fridrik was almost the same size as Bruce and just as muscular. *Maybe that's a good sign, one that the two*

IRON IN THE SCEPTER

of them will get along, she thought. She certainly hoped so as she wanted no complicating issues for this night.

Introductions were made all around. Everyone complimented each other on how well they looked. Shepherd Fridrik had them all sign their marriage certificates on an electronic tablet and place their thumb in the tablet corner, where a small pinprick took a blood sample.

Janet sucked her thumb. "What's the purpose of the blood sample?"

Shepherd Fridrik certified the signatures. "Oh, it's just part of the process. It helps every Shepherd to know and care for their subjects better."

Janet nodded, but it all seemed a little controlling to her. So Shepherds Morgan and Randall would know of their marriage before they even got home? That was unsettling. She pushed those thoughts aside, however. Being with Bruce was all that mattered right now.

"Shepherd Fridrik," Janet said, "we're so thankful you're willing to do a double ceremony for us."

Fridrik chuckled. "Well, it's not every day one gets to conduct a double ceremony. Bruce was just telling me about your crop schedule. Before you go back home, I'd like to discuss that with you and be sure Iceland is part of that plan."

"Oh, absolutely." She mouthed a "thank you" to Bruce when Fridrik wasn't looking. Bruce was turning out to be a good luck charm once more. It amazed her how fast Bruce was able to not only get Shepherd Fridrik on their good side but also make him want to be there.

Chika put his arm around Afia and pointed everyone to the door. "It's time to go."

Afia inhaled quickly and grabbed Chika's arm. "The photographer."

Chika rubbed her arm. "Relax, Afia. He'll meet us at the falls."

Once they were outside, Afia sighed. "We don't have an AGA for Janet and Bruce."

"No problem. They can ride with me," Shepherd Fridrik said while turning to Janet and Bruce.

"Let's do it," Bruce said, taking Janet's hand and following Shepherd Fridrik to his AGA.

Fridrik's AGA had a back seat that allowed Janet to cuddle with Bruce along the way. After a few minutes, Janet had a thought and got a confused look on her face. "Shepherd Fridrik. Why are you driving the AGA when you could teleport to the falls?"

Fridrik chuckled. "Well, it's a little selfish on my part. It gives me a chance to talk to you about your crop rotation plan."

Janet laughed and went through all the details she had presented to the other Shepherds. "It's pretty simple, really," she concluded. "I'll send you an instruction packet when we send out the others. You change a few crops you grow, but there's no need to change any farming equipment."

"OK, I look forward to it. We never had much farming here until after the Refreshing. I guess that's why it interests me so much."

Bruce leaned forward. "Does that have anything to do with why you call this country Iceland?"

Fridrik laughed. "Actually, it does. I can see that would be confusing to you today as it's considered part of the Northern Scandinavian Territory. Before the Refreshing, there were many extreme climate differences, far more than we have today. The farther north, the colder it was, and this land was covered with snow and ice for many months of the year."

"I've heard Shepherd Morgan state something like that." Bruce cocked his head. "But if all of that ice melted, didn't the water table go up?"

Fridrik nodded. "It did, but the Great Earthquake also caused a lot of changes. This entire island also rose. I know most islands disappeared because of those two factors. I'm glad my island didn't. I grew up here and feel blessed to be able to still serve here."

Fridrik pointed. "Here we are."

Janet looked out the window and whispered. "Wow." She patted Bruce's arm. "Bruce, look."

As they got out of the AGA and approached the falls, the beauty was breathtaking. There were up-lights and colored lights that slowly made the falls change color. Other up-lights and spotlights highlighted the surrounding rocks. Janet could see why Afia wanted her wedding here. While she would have settled for a very simple wedding, she was glad things had worked out for her and Bruce to be married here as well.

The photographer took over from that point, telling everyone where to stand and what to do. During the ceremony he was like a gazelle hopping here and there—on this rock, over to that rock, then leaning over another.

Fridrik performed a traditional wedding with traditional vows. When it came time for the ring, Janet stiffened and gave Bruce a quick, wide-eyed look. That detail had totally slipped her mind. Bruce just smiled. He reached into his pocket and pulled out a wedding ring and placed it on her finger. It was a simple but elegant gold band with minute filigree around both edges.

After repeating the ring vow, Bruce whispered, "I did more than get the tuxedo."

She smiled, adoring him even more. Yes, he was the calm in her chaotic world.

After Shepherd Fridrik announced them husband and wife, they gave a passionate kiss, and the photographer immediately took over again. Janet was sure she had posed and smiled more than she had in a lifetime. At the end, the photographer gave both Afia and Janet the information needed to access their pictures via the nebula drive.

Fridrik approached Bruce. "You and Janet take the AGA back to the inn. I'll teleport back and take care of the AGA later." He gave a wink, took a few steps back, and disappeared.

Janet walked up to Afia. "Thank you again for allowing us to do this with you." She gave her a hug.

"The inn is giving us a small reception," Afia said. "You and Bruce will surely come?"

Janet nodded. "For a little while."

This time, the trip back to the inn seemed short to Janet. It did, however, give her time to contemplate things. Her decision to marry Bruce was so quick she really hadn't thought about how her life would change. She had no regrets about her decision, but now she had to consider how to make her life in Chicago and her life in a farming town mesh.

If she wanted to stay under the radar, as the Leader had put it, where better than in the middle of a rural farming community?

It seemed her life with Bruce would be excellent on many fronts.

CHAPTER 15

All four of them were in a great mood as they entered the inn. Stefán greeted them and pointed to a small side room. Janet and Afia were talking and giggling as they entered. Afia immediately stopped.

Janet looked at Afia, who had frozen in place. "Afia, are you all right?"

"Candis?"

Janet turned. There was a couple, wearing more traditional African clothing, next to a table bearing a wedding cake and other refreshments. Janet found the woman's multicolored fabric headdress with teal background and matching dress stunning. The man's dashiki-style shirt was simpler in design but complemented the woman's dress.

Candis came forward and gave Afia a hug. "I'm so sorry for being late and missing this. Will you ever forgive me?"

Afia smiled. "Of course. It all worked out in the end. But I'm glad you're here now. Let's get something to eat and have a seat. I'm starved."

Afia introduced Candis to Janet and Bruce. Candis, in turn, introduced them to her husband.

He shook both Bruce and Janet's hands. "My name is Zuri. Zuri Turay. It's a pleasure to meet you. Please come and sit down."

They each got some food and sat together at the table.

After taking a couple of bites, Afia glanced between her two African friends. "OK, spill the beans. What happened? Why were you so late?"

Candis's dark cheeks reddened. "It's my fault, I think. When we teleported, I chose the geographic display. I guess I hit Greenland rather than Iceland."

"You couldn't tell after you got there it was the wrong place?"

"We were already running late," Zuri said, twisting the glass he was holding on the table. "That, I think, was my fault."

"That part I know was your fault," Candis said. Everyone laughed.

"OK, so that part is fact," Zuri said. "Anyway, we were rushing and didn't pay attention."

Candis nodded. "There was an inn not far from the teleporter, similar as it is here, which we had read about, so we thought that made it the right place. We rushed to the front desk and asked the clerk if he knew anything about a wedding at a nearby waterfall. He said the wedding party had just left. We asked how to get there, and we took off in one of the hotel's AGAs."

Janet thought that strange. "Why didn't you first ask if Afia and Chika were staying there?"

Candis stopped, cocked her head in thought, and looked at Zuri. "Yeah. Why didn't we do that?" She shook her head. "I guess we were so rushed we weren't thinking straight."

"So what happened after you got there?" Bruce asked.

Chika nodded. "Yeah, you must have discovered it wasn't us."

Zuri grinned. "It was pretty obvious once we got there the couple wasn't the two of you. But for whatever reason, it still didn't dawn on us that we were in the wrong place."

"We just assumed you were nearby waiting for this couple to complete their ceremony." Candis looked at each of them. "I know that sounds pretty dumb now, but we just weren't thinking straight. Zuri went looking for you."

Zuri nodded. "I followed a path upstream thinking maybe you went sightseeing for a little bit."

"Yeah. You only found a dumb cave, right, Zuri?"

He nodded. "I went in just to see if perhaps you had gone inside. I got turned around, and it took a while for me to find my way out." He looked down and shook his head. "It was kind of spooky."

Janet didn't say anything, but found it too coincidental that Zuri had a similar experience to hers. Was that the reason Isabelle left China early? Did Isabelle have an appointment with Zuri and Zuri was now concocting this story to cover his tracks? She would have to find a way to understand Zuri's feelings about the King.

"Once he got back and the other wedding was over, I asked the Shepherd when the next wedding was." Candis laughed. "He looked at me like I had three heads or something."

Zuri laughed with her. "He introduced himself as Shepherd Oluf." He looked at Candis. "We looked at each other. I think that's when the light started to dawn for us."

Candis nodded. "I knew you stated the Shepherd who would marry you was Frederick, or something like that." Candis put her hand to her mouth and giggled. "He told us to try Iceland for Shepherd Fridrik."

Zuri nodded. "We said, 'Isn't this Iceland?'" Zuri laughed. "He jerked his head back and said, indignantly, 'This is Greenland.'"

"I gasped, took Zuri's hand, and we got back to the teleporter as quickly as possible." Candis's eyes began to water. "Unfortunately, by the time we got here, it was too late." She took Afia's hand. "I'm really sorry."

Afia patted her hand. "It's OK, Candis. You're here now."

Candis smiled. "I love your dress, though. I know you've always adored lilacs." She sat up. "So, what was the dress surprise you had for me? What did I miss out on wearing?"

"Janet's wearing your dress."

Candis looked at Janet and back to Afia, incredulous. "Roses? You were going to have me wear roses?"

Afia laughed. "I thought it would be funny. It is a beautiful dress, though."

Candis put her hands on her hips. "Afia, I can't believe you."

"Well, look at the bright side. You didn't have to wear it after all."

"I love the dress," Janet said as she looked between the two of them. "Candis, what do you have against roses?"

"I'm allergic to them!"

Janet jerked her head back. "But it's a dress."

"Yes, but it's the principle of the thing." Candis looked back at Afia. "You have some serious making up to do."

Afia gave a smirk. "And so do you."

"Touché." Candis smiled. "Let's call it even."

Afia laughed. "Deal."

Zuri interrupted their giggling. "Well, now that we're all friends again, let's cut the cake."

"Great idea," Chika said as he got up and motioned for everyone to stay. "Don't get up. I'll serve."

Afia grabbed his hand as he walked behind her. "Thanks, sweetie." He bent over and gave her a kiss.

While Chika was getting the plates of cake, Janet took the opportunity to engage Zuri. "How do you two know Afia and Chika?"

"We're best friends. I've known Chika since we were little. Candis and Afia went to school together. When they started dating, I met Candis. We were the first to take the plunge."

"And you still live close to each other?"

Zuri nodded. "Chika and I work together. We help manage African tourism."

Bruce filled their glasses with water as he asked, "Oh, like the King's Sabbath Year safaris?"

Zuri's smile vanished. "Chika likes to do that. I help with individual family tourism and coordinate those activities."

Janet found that statement and his change of expression interesting. It was just a hint, but if Zuri had met with Isabelle in Greenland, perhaps she now had an ally in Africa. Could Zuri play a key role for The Order on that continent? Janet sought to probe deeper into Zuri's feelings.

"It sounds like you want more for Africa than it currently has."

"Many in my country are happy with Africa's position in today's world. They are grateful for the King's personal visits."

Bruce nodded. "Not every country gets to have that."

Zuri nodded. "True." He shrugged. "But I would like to see Africa have a bigger stake in the world's economy than just being a gigantic zoo for the world."

Seeing Afia give him a strange look, Janet diverted the conversation. She felt she had the answer she sought. "Zuri, forgive my prying, but I see you're stretching your earlobes."

"And you want to know why?"

"Well, yes, kind of." She held up her palms. "I think they look great. I was just curious." She shook her head. "But you don't have to answer if you don't want to."

Zuri smiled. "It's no big secret. Centuries ago, people in my area of Africa did this. I thought it interesting. I'm using a small gauge right now. I don't think I'll go any bigger." He laughed. "It's a good conversation starter with the tourists."

Chika came back with cake slices and passed them around. The conversation turned more lighthearted and festive. Before all six knew it, midnight had come and gone.

Bruce stood. "I hate to be a party pooper, but Janet and I are heading upstairs."

Everyone said their goodnights. Afia grabbed Janet's hand as she walked by. "Dinner tomorrow night?"

Janet nodded. "Sure. We'll see you then."

Janet and Bruce left the reception arm in arm and took the elevator upstairs. When they got to Janet's room, he opened it, but before Janet could enter, Bruce scooped her up in his arms.

"It's traditional for the groom to carry his bride across the threshold."

She smiled. It was an awesome feeling having such strong arms holding her. Being independent and doing everything on her own had always been so important to her. Yet she found Bruce was now filling a need in her she never knew she had. She kissed him. "And why is that?"

He laughed. "I have no idea. But better safe than sorry."

She laughed with him. "So, you do what's expected?"

He carried her in, closed the door with his foot, turned the lock with a free hand, and entered the bedroom. He looked into her eyes. A smirk came across his face. "Not always as expected."

He threw her up, tossing her onto the bed. She gave a short shriek as she bounced. "Be careful of the dress. It isn't mine."

"I can remedy that." He took her hand and pulled her to her feet and into himself. He looked into her eyes again and slowly leaned in, giving her a lingering kiss. As he did so, he unzipped her dress and let it fall to the floor. Their lips parted; still, he didn't budge. Janet felt his warm breath on her cheeks. Without warning, he scooped her up in his arms and threw her back on the bed, eliciting another shriek from her followed by laughter.

"Well, that definitely changed the mood in a hurry."

He smiled as he picked up her dress and hung it up along with his tuxedo jacket. He faced her and began unbuttoning his shirt. She stood to help, but he pushed her back onto the bed. She watched as he removed his clothes. He then climbed on the bed and gave her another kiss, which turned into one of the most passionate Janet had ever received. It was a good thing she was already on the bed. She went totally weak.

Bruce looked into her eyes. "I'm going to take a shower. Do you want to take one with me?" He smiled. "I'll wash your back."

She smiled back as he held her. Their lips were only millimeters apart. "Oh, I'm going to need much more help than that."

"I think that can be arranged."

He went into the bathroom and turned on the water while she finished undressing. He was already in the shower when she entered. Stepping in behind him, she wrapped her arms around his torso.

"You feel nice and warm," Janet said.

He turned around and placed her body under the warm water.

"Oh, that feels nice," she said.

"It sure does."

She smiled, leaned in, and give him a kiss. He wrapped his arms around her and pulled her even closer.

Yes, she had certainly made the right decision, even if a rash one. She didn't care how the logistics would work out. All she knew was that they would. But none of that mattered tonight. She took a step backward, pulling the two of them under the flowing warm water, never separating their kiss. There was no rushing tonight. They had a week alone—and she was going to take every advantage of that fact.

132

CHAPTER 16

Janet awoke. Looking over at Bruce next to her, still sound asleep, she gave a contented sigh. Last night had been wonderful. She glanced at the clock: 11:53. *Oh well, who cares? There were no agendas today.* Time was on their side. She pulled back the sheet, sat up, and watched Bruce sleep, his abdomen rising and falling in an easy, smooth rhythm. She thought his reddish disheveled hair looked so adorable. As she glided her hand over his torso and arms, he sighed but didn't wake. These were the muscular arms that made her feel so safe when wrapped around her.

Pulling the sheet back farther, she laid on top of him and placed her head on his chest. She could hear his heart beating—steady and slow. She looked up and kissed his chin and then stretched farther, kissing him lightly on his lips. He stirred, not waking completely, but wrapped his arms around her body. That made her feel as though she had melted over him like butter on hot toast. She began kissing his torso and moved up to his face, kissing his forehead, cheeks, chin, and then lips. Softly at first, but then more forcefully.

Bruce awoke and smiled. "Good morning. Looks like you already have plans for this morning."

"Indeed, I do. Breakfast may be a little sweet this morning."

"Everyone needs a little decadence once in a while."

Bruce held her tightly as he rolled over, putting her under himself and kissing her at the same time.

"I'll start the entrée and you can serve dessert."

She smiled. "Sounds like a balanced meal to me."

Janet lost track of time. The next time she looked at the clock it was 13:45. She turned to look at Bruce. "Are you getting hungry?"

"I thought we just had breakfast." He had an ornery smile.

Janet laughed. "Well, my stomach felt left out."

Bruce sat up. "There's some fruit on the table." He brought the basket over. "You eat while I get cleaned up."

Janet ate a peach as she watched Bruce through the open bathroom door as he shaved.

"What did you think of Candis and Zuri last night?"

Bruce turned and glanced at Janet for a second. "What do you mean? They seem like great people."

"I agree. But didn't you find it odd they confused Greenland with Iceland?"

Bruce stopped shaving for a second. "In a way, their story made sense. But I would have asked different questions—and earlier, I think."

"Yeah. I felt it was a little odd."

Bruce rinsed his face after shaving. He turned to Janet with towel in hand. "So, speaking of odd, why are we in Iceland?"

Janet froze with peach in midair. "What do you mean?"

Bruce shrugged. "Well, it's no big deal, but I knew you were going to China, and when I confronted Molly on your whereabouts, she told me you're in Iceland. You didn't come to meet farmers, because Shepherd Fridrik was asking you questions."

Janet wondered what to tell Bruce. She didn't want to get him further involved. "Let's just say I had some ancillary business here I had to take care of before I went back to Chicago."

A worried look came across Bruce's face. "Did I mess anything up?"

Janet hopped off the bed and hugged him. "There is no way you can mess up anything."

Bruce pulled her back, looked into her eyes, and smiled. "That's not true." He then stepped aside and showed her the sink.

She slapped his arm playfully. "Gross. That's a mess. You have to clean that up before I brush my teeth."

It took a couple of hours for them to get dressed. Every time Janet put on an article of clothing, Bruce came along and took it off her. By the time she finally got dressed, Janet's sides were sore from so much laughing. She had to dress faster and faster to keep ahead of Bruce's disrobing. Of course, she tried to do the same to him, but he was able to hold her at bay more easily. Although she knew he let her win a couple of times.

By the time they made it downstairs, it was already midafternoon. They got some yogurt to hold them over until dinner, took a walk through the city, and then along the shore, where terns and seagulls were active on the beach. Bruce threw some of his granola and watched a pack of gulls try to get the few chunks on the sand.

After a couple of hours of sightseeing, meandering through shops, and just being with each other, they headed back to the inn. Afia and Chika were in the lobby.

Afia waved. "Hi, Janet. Hi, Bruce. About ready to go out and eat?"

They walked over. Bruce shook Chika's hand and gave Afia a hug, and Janet hugged them both.

"Where's Candis and Zuri?" Janet looked around trying to spot them.

Afia smiled. "Oh, they'll be down in a minute."

"There's a fish restaurant nearby," Chika said. "I thought we'd all go there for dinner. Game?"

Bruce nodded.

"Oh, I haven't eaten fish in a long time," Janet said. "I guess fish with scales being the only animal protein allowed to us . . . " Janet gave a half shrug, laughing. "And not living near the ocean makes me forget to even order it."

Afia's eyes focused behind Janet. "There you are."

Janet turned to see Candis walking over with Zuri.

"What's the game plan?" Candis asked.

Chika pointed toward the front doors. "Fish. Let's go. I'm starving."

The restaurant was only a few blocks from the inn. The maître d' sat them immediately upon arriving. A three-course meal, suggested by the waiter, was ordered. The first course delivered was brauðterta, a salmon and egg sandwich loaf. The waiter explained the dish as he served it to each person.

Janet found it a little heavy, but tasty and filling.

Bruce took a bite and nodded his approval. "Chika, being from Africa, what made you choose Iceland for a wedding?"

"It's all Zuri's fault, really."

Bruce looked at Zuri, who held up his palms. "Hold on there. Don't make me the bad guy just because I had the guts to propose first."

"Uh-oh, I see a family feud developing here," Bruce said, laughing.

Chika shook his head. "No, it's just that when Zuri and Candis got married, it turned into a lot of fanfare and . . . " He glanced at Afia. "We felt it was too overwhelming."

Afia nodded. "Since we all know pretty much the same people, we didn't want a large wedding, and we were looking for a way to go simple." She laughed. "We felt the farther away we went, the less chance of people coming even if they found out."

Candis's eyes widened, and she shook her head. "You would not believe the pressure put on Zuri and me from family members wanting to know when and where their wedding was going to happen." She took her fork and pointed it at Afia. "That's one of the reasons we were so late. We tried to leave at the last minute so no one had time to find out where we went."

Afia grinned. "So, going to Greenland was a diversion tactic?"

Candis laughed. "Well, I wish I could say that was planned, but now that you already know it wasn't, I won't try and claim it now."

Janet noticed Zuri smiled but didn't laugh like the others. *Is he hiding something?*

"But that doesn't exactly explain why Iceland," Janet said, looking at Afia. "Had you been here before?"

Afia shook her head. "It was Zuri's plan."

Janet's eyebrows went up and she turned to Zuri. "Oh, how's that?"

Zuri shrugged. "We get a lot of brochures. I remembered seeing this colored waterfall in one of the brochures and gave it to Chika."

"Yes, it seemed like a perfect spot," Chika said, smiling. "And now that we've done it, I have to say it was."

Bruce chimed in. "Lucky for us, too."

Everyone laughed. But Janet found herself wondering. *If Zuri knew about the waterfall, how would he have confused the two countries?* It seemed planned to her. But she wasn't going to spoil Afia's dream wedding to get a confession.

The waiter brought the next dish: curried haddock with pineapple. It had a slight citrusy aroma that made Janet's mouth water before the first bite. Everyone raved at how wonderful it tasted.

"Chika, this was a great choice for a place to eat," Bruce said. "Thanks for the invite." He filled his mouth with another bite.

Chika smiled. "I'm happy with my decision also."

Janet set her fork down for a minute. "So, what happens once you all get back?"

"You mean besides getting scolded by family and friends?" Afia asked.

Janet chuckled and nodded.

Afia shrugged. "Pretty much back to life as usual." She looked at Chika and patted his arm. "But a little different." He smiled back.

"What about you, Chika?"

Chika finished chewing and laid his fork down. "We're already preparing for the next Sabbath Year safari. You'd be surprised at how much work it takes to get them set up. It's for the King, so it has to be perfect."

Janet noticed Zuri rolling his eyes. Others seemed not to notice.

Suddenly, Candis uttered words which stunned them all: "At least until the Overtaker comes."

All eyes turned her way.

"Candis!" Zuri looked mortified—as if she had given away a secret.

Candis laughed. "Oh, come on, Zuri. I'm just joking. It's just a saying anyway. There can't be any truth to it."

"What saying?" Janet leaned in.

Candis twirled the fork in her hand. "In the territory north of ours, there's a rumor of a stone tablet that tells of a coming Overtaker."

Janet's eyes widened.

Chika gave a dismissive wave. "Yeah, and some say the King comes to Africa on his safaris just so he can find and destroy that stone piece. Pfft. Like he wouldn't know where it is if it existed. A total fabrication, I can tell you."

"Sorry, I didn't mean to get everyone so riled," Candis said. "Chika, I was joking, OK? I'm sorry I mentioned it."

Janet felt like she had just hit a gold mine. She would have to get this information to the Leader. Or was that what Zuri had been doing in Greenland: meeting with the Leader's wife to give such information?

Janet focused on Zuri. "Zuri, if we ever wanted to come to Africa to view the animals, would we get in touch with you, or who?"

Zuri came out of the thought fog he seemed to be in. "Oh, yes, please contact me. I can set you up with a customized tour."

Janet smiled. "Do you have a business card? I'm not sure when we'd make it, but I can keep the card to remind me."

"Oh, sure." He reached into his pocket and pulled out a small case that contained his cards. "If for some reason you can't reach me, ask for Chika."

"Absolutely." Chika grinned. "I'll give you a better deal than Zuri."

Zuri gave Chika an irritated look. Chika laughed. "I'm only kidding. I'd be happy to help, though."

Janet nodded. "Well, I thank both of you. I've learned something new from all of you. I hope we stay good friends."

Afia held up her water glass. "I'll toast to that." They all held up their glasses and clinked them together.

The waiter brought their dessert: djöflaterta. He explained it had rhubarb jelly for the filling but assured them the taste would contrast well with the chocolate icing on the cake.

Every time someone took a bite, a soft *mmm* was heard.

"Whoever picked this dessert gets extra points," Bruce said.

Everyone nodded. The waiter came back shortly with coffee and tea.

Janet stirred her tea. "When does everyone have to go back home?"

"We have to go back tonight," Zuri said, patting Candis's hand. "I only took a couple of days." He looked at Chika. "And I have to make up work for the slacker over there."

Chika's eyebrows went up. "Now see here. Everything was caught up when I left. Besides, we'll be back in a couple of days."

Afia smiled at their banter and looked at Janet. "What about you two?"

Janet lightly rubbed the back of Bruce's hand. "We're here until the end of the week."

"Then we also go back, and we also face upset family and friends," Bruce said.

There were laughs and looks of understanding around the table.

Afia nodded. "Seems like a common theme."

After the last few bites were finished, Zuri stood. "Well, we do have to get going."

Everyone gave goodbye hugs and Candis and Zuri headed for the teleporter. Janet, Bruce, Afia, and Chika walked back to the inn.

Once in bed, Janet cuddled next to Bruce, who put his arm around her, making her feel so secure in his arms. Bruce was asleep in a matter of minutes. She sighed with contentment as she pondered their enlightening evening.

Maybe The Order now had a leader on three continents. Also, there now seemed to be a lead for another stone stele. Janet smiled to herself. She felt sure she had accomplished, in just a couple of weeks, what the Leader had not accomplished in centuries. She eventually dozed off with a smile on her face.

CHAPTER 17

The rest of the week went by uneventfully. Afia and Chika said their goodbyes in the middle of the week; Janet and Afia exchanged contact information. Janet and Bruce spent their last couple of days exploring the island. They spent their last night having dinner on their balcony looking out over the ocean.

"Bruce, thank you for this week. It was much needed downtime."

He reached over, took her hand, and gave it a kiss. "Same for me." He smiled. "But what's the game plan for when we get back home?"

Janet looked at him and sighed. "I guess we do have to face that now, don't we?"

Bruce raised his eyebrows and nodded. "Afraid so."

Janet sat up, took a drink of water, and pushed her plate aside. "I guess we should have a get-together of family and friends so they don't feel totally left out."

Bruce nodded. "And we could display several pictures of the wedding."

Janet's eyes lit up. "Oh, that's a great idea, Bruce." She sat back and tapped her lip with her forefinger. "And I suppose we should have a cake and some other refreshments." She turned to him. "Any idea where we should have it?"

Bruce rubbed his chin. "I prefer to not have it at home. That just turns into too much preparation." He inhaled quickly with eyes wide. "I know. Why not have it at the park just off the town square? We can have a quartet play in the gazebo, and it's not too far from the teleporter so it would be easily accessible for visitors."

Janet sat up straighter shaking her forefinger. "Then we wouldn't have to worry about space since it will be outside." She paused. "OK if we just cater the whole thing?"

Bruce nodded. "Oh, definitely. Why put more stress on ourselves? Plus, you and I will be working."

"Good point. OK, we'll send out invitations as soon as we get home. You think next weekend is an OK time to have it? Or is that too early?"

Bruce laughed. "I don't think it can be too early. With all the questions we're going to get, the earlier the better. I would like to answer questions once rather than a million times."

Janet gave a grimace. "Maybe I'll stay in Chicago until the get-together." She laughed but then noticed Bruce was fixing her with a blank stare. She rubbed his hand. "I was kidding."

Bruce continued to stare but was looking through her, not at her.

"Bruce? Are you OK?"

Bruce leaned forward, talking slowly. "No. No, that's good. I've been gone a week. One more won't matter that much." He looked at Janet. "I could stay with you in Chicago this next week." He scrunched his brow. "Are you OK with that?"

"Sure." She squinted. "What are you thinking?"

"We'll set everything up remotely. Once everyone is there, we'll arrive and face everyone together—united."

Janet smiled. "I like it."

Bruce nodded. "Now that we have that settled, what about us?"

"Us? What do you mean?"

He took her hand. "Janet, I said I didn't want to change you, and I meant that. Yet we have to decide how we're going to live and work. Have you thought about that?"

Janet nodded. "What keeps coming back to me is what you stated that night in my office. You said a teleporter makes a lot of things possible. If you're going to continue to farm, and I'm going to continue to be a commodities analyst, both of us will have to use the teleporter more often so we can be together. Are you willing to do that?"

Bruce smiled and kissed her hand. "I meant what I said. I'll do whatever it takes. Sometimes, you'll come home. Sometimes, I'll go to Chicago. Other times we'll be apart for a short time. None of that will ever change how I feel about you."

"Bruce, I love you."

Bruce stood and held out his hand. "Now come to bed. We have a big day tomorrow."

The next day, Stefán congratulated them again as they checked out. They headed for the long-range teleporter, entered Chicago as their destination, and Bruce pressed "Engage."

Their vision went blurry, and in only a few moments they were standing in the middle of downtown Chicago. They walked to the Lakeside Hotel, which was only a few blocks away.

"You realize, this is the first time I'll be seeing your place," Bruce said.

Janet thought about that. Did she leave it a mess? She couldn't even remember. "Well, just remember I wasn't expecting anyone coming back with me." She laughed. "I can't even remember if I left it presentable."

"Ah, I get to see the real Janet. What secrets can I find?"

"Oh, if that's what you're looking for, you married the wrong girl."

"Oh, OK." Bruce turned and started walking the other way.

Janet stopped and turned. "What? Bruce, what are you doing?"

"Looking for someone more mysterious."

She grabbed his arm and turned him around. "Oh no you don't." She laughed. "You already said, 'For better or worse.'"

"Oh, so I had the better, now I'm getting the worse?"

Janet slapped his arm with a laugh. "Hey now."

He stopped and made her face him. "I can't wait to spend the rest of my life with you." He gave her a lingering kiss. "I'll face any danger—including a dirty hotel room."

She smiled. "Well, there you go. You've discovered my secret—dirty laundry."

He chuckled and put his arm around her shoulders. "Let's go face the giant together."

Once inside, Bruce looked around: living area, kitchenette, bedroom. "This is nice, Janet." As she rearranged the bedroom, he stepped out onto the balcony. "Oh, this is nice too. I like the view." He smiled. "Not like looking over wheat fields, but I still like it."

She came out and put her arms around him. "This is one of my favorite spots."

He nodded. "I can see why."

145

She tugged on him. "Come to the bedroom. I'll show you the space I made for you."

Janet showed him the closet and drawer space she cleaned out.

He smiled. "I guess it's official."

"Yep. Too late to back out now."

Bruce laughed and gave her a kiss. "I'm willing to take my consequences."

"Let's order in and go over our get-together this weekend."

"Good idea."

While eating spinach salads with fruit and walnuts, they made their invitation list. To their surprise it was longer than they expected.

"Should we trim it down?" Janet picked up the list and scanned it. "But who to take off if so?"

"I doubt everyone will be able to come," Bruce said. "Anyway, let's just do it and get it over with."

Janet handed him the list. "OK. You'll take care of this tomorrow?"

Bruce nodded. "I'll also order the caterer and the musicians."

"So, we're done?"

Bruce smiled. "I think so."

"Good." Janet let out a sigh. "My brain's mush anyway. Let's head to bed."

Once in bed, Janet cuddled up to Bruce . . .

The next thing she knew, she woke but found herself alone in bed. Sitting up, she looked around, but Bruce wasn't there. She heard some noise in the other room. Entering, she saw Bruce scrambling eggs.

"What are you doing?"

Bruce looked at her and smiled. "Good morning, sleepy-head. I thought I'd send you to work with a good breakfast."

She went over and gave him a kiss.

"Why don't you get your shower, and I'll have it ready for you."

I could get used to this, Janet told herself—unless this was a one-time deal. At any rate, Bruce's actions were sweet. She showered, dressed, ate, and headed out the door as Bruce gave her a final kiss as she left.

On the way to the office, Janet looked at her ring and pondered how she was going to tell Molly. Maybe talk to her and casually place her hand in view, or perhaps put her hand on her cheek to put the diamond in view. Janet smiled. She could almost see Molly jumping up and down with excitement.

As the elevator climbed, her heart beat faster. The elevator doors opened—and Janet froze with eyes wide and mouth open. Molly's cobalt-colored desk lay in pieces on the floor, her desk items strewn everywhere. Some people were running here and there while others were standing in groups crying. She saw Edgar in Administrator Billingsley's office, so she headed there. Others looked at her as she passed, but no one said anything.

At the Administrator's doorway, Janet gasped and put her hand to her mouth. The Administrator's clear desk also was demolished with objects scattered everywhere around the floor. Some type of long metal bar was on the floor in the corner of the office.

"Janet." Administrator Billingsley motioned for her to enter.

"Administrator—I mean, Beth—what . . . what happened?"

Beth put her hand on Janet's shoulder. "Janet, I'm sorry. I know you were good friends with Molly."

A knot formed in Janet's stomach, and a feeling of nausea swept over her. No one had said anything yet, but she knew something bad had happened.

"Did . . . did something happen to Molly?" Janet looked from Beth to Edgar. Her eyes watered. "What happened?"

Beth shook her head. "I don't know why, but Molly came in this morning extremely angry and holding that bar in her hands." She pointed to the piece of metal on the floor behind Edgar. "I heard something breaking and came out to see her desk in pieces. I yelled, 'Molly, what are you doing?'" Beth put her hand to her chest. "She had such hatred in her eyes."

Janet shook her head. "Why?"

Beth looked crestfallen. "I couldn't understand it. She was always so cheerful." Her eyes watered. "She approached my office. I stepped back in, but she kept coming." Beth shook her head. "She said something like, 'You people just never let up, do you?'"

Janet tried to understand why Molly would do this, or what she meant by that statement. *Maybe Amanda will have some insight,* she thought to herself.

"I backed into the corner. Then she demolished my desk." Beth's voice caught in her throat. "She . . . she turned to me with that bar raised. I . . . I tried to calm her down, but . . . she kept coming." Tears came down Beth's cheeks. "When she got near me, she disappeared."

Janet gasped. "You mean . . . "

Beth nodded. "I'm afraid so." She put her hand on Janet's shoulder but then withdrew it. "Janet, I'm . . . I'm so sorry."

Janet turned, feeling disoriented, unsure what to do next.

Edgar touched her arm. Janet jerked to face him.

"Janet, come to my office," he said softly. "We can talk there."

Janet nodded but still felt disoriented. It all seemed surreal.

As they stepped from Beth's office, the Administrator softly called to her. "Janet."

Janet turned.

"Congratulations."

Janet turned up her brow, confused.

Beth pointed to Janet's hand, and her rings. "I'm sorry it wasn't a more festive homecoming for you."

Janet nodded and followed Edgar to his office. People were already starting the cleanup work on the mess Molly had left.

Edgar motioned for Janet to sit on the sofa in front of the window overlooking the park across the street. He sat on the other end of the sofa.

"What did Beth mean? Why did she congratulate you?" Edgar asked.

Janet held up her hand and gave a slight smile.

Edgar's eyes widened. "Was that expected?"

Janet shook her head and gave a half laugh. "Pretty impromptu."

"Congratulations." He shook his head. "This has been quite the morning."

"Edgar, what happened when I was gone?"

He gave a half shrug and shook his head. "What do you mean? What, specifically?"

Janet gestured wide. "Like anything. Anything that may have made Molly upset."

Edgar's eyes darted back and forth in thought. "No. Everything seemed to go as normal." He sat up. "There was ... one thing." He shook his head. "But it couldn't be anything."

Janet took his arm. "Edgar, what was it?"

"Molly took a call for Administrator Billingsley, and right after that she left the building."

"Do you know why?"

Edgar shook his head. "I never found out why Molly left, but Administrator Billingsley said the phone message was about the Chinese farmer who disappeared."

Janet cocked her head. "You think that's what pushed her over the edge?"

Edgar shrugged. "I don't know. I'm not sure why it would, but I don't know."

"Did Beth do anything to provoke Molly?"

Edgar's head jerked back. "What? Why would you even suggest such a thing? You know those with glorified bodies can never do anything like that. They represent and promote the King. Beth, as all Administrators, only wants the best for us." He shook his head. "Janet, sometimes I don't think I know you at all."

Janet realized she had probably gone too far, especially with Edgar. Shaking her head slightly, she put her hand to her forehead. "Yes. Yes, of course, you're right. I'm just grasping for straws trying to understand this."

Edgar sighed. "I understand. It's hard on all of us."

What would have made Molly go ballistic? Janet knew she was upset about her friend's brother disappearing, but would that provoke her to such an extreme? She needed to talk to Amanda.

"Janet, I wanted to get an update from you today, but let's cancel and do it tomorrow. I'm going to send everyone home early today so we can get everything cleaned up." He glanced at the work being done on the other side of his office wall. He held up his palm. "This being your first day back, you stay here as long as you need. I need to take care of some things out there. We'll catch up tomorrow. OK?"

Janet nodded as Edgar left his office to supervise cleanup work being done in both Molly's and Beth's areas.

Janet sat back on the sofa and sighed. *Poor Molly. Why would she do such a thing?* She shook her head. But why would the King take someone who was obviously confused? Janet couldn't imagine Molly doing harm to anyone. Maybe she was upset, and perhaps even threatened Beth, but she couldn't believe Molly would actually hurt someone intentionally. This made Janet even more upset with the King.

She stood to leave. Her best move now was to find Amanda and see what she knew. Maybe something significant happened at one of her meetings in the back of her boutique that would have turned Molly violent. Janet had to find out.

CHAPTER 18

Janet walked into Amanda's boutique and saw her in the front waiting on a male customer. The man was wearing a dark purple suit. It was so dark it almost appeared black if Janet stared at it too long. The coat had white lines over the top two-thirds and down the arms as if a white string was randomly intertwined throughout. It looked stunning. Of course, the guy being somewhat muscular, having short black hair, and a thin mustache and beard outlining his jaw only added to the overall effect.

Amanda motioned for Janet to approach them.

"Well, ask this lady that just entered."

Janet raised her eyebrows.

"Jeff, here, is unsure if this style is really for him," Amanda said to Janet.

"Yes, ma'am. What do you think?" he asked.

Janet smiled. "Let me ask two questions."

The man straightened. "Uh, OK."

"How old are you? And are you married?"

"Twenty-five, and no."

"Then you have to buy this suit. You'll have to fight off every single woman in this city. If I wasn't married, you'd probably have to fight me off too."

Jeff laughed. "Well, I guess I *have* to buy it now."

Janet smiled.

Amanda went from smiling at Jeff to giving a wide-eyed stare at Janet and mouthing, "What?"

Jeff stepped off the holographic pad and the suit dissipated.

"Come by tomorrow afternoon and I'll have all the alterations completed," Amanda said.

"Wonderful. Thank you, Amanda." He turned to Janet. "And thank you . . . "

"Janet."

"Thank you, Janet." He waved and stepped from the boutique.

Amanda came over and grabbed Janet's hand. "That's quite an unfair way to tell me! How and when did this happen?"

"It was an impromptu thing that happened just a week ago."

Amanda hugged her. "Congratulations, Janet. I'm happy for you."

Janet smiled, but her tone suddenly went solemn. "Uh, Amanda, I need to talk to you about something."

Amanda's jaw went slack. "Janet, what's wrong?"

"It's Molly."

"What's wrong with Molly?"

"She . . . " Janet cleared her throat to keep her voice from cracking. "She was taken."

"Taken?" Amanda shook her head slightly.

"Taken by the King."

Amanda's mouth fell open. "What?" She took Janet's arm. "What happened?"

"She confronted Administrator Billingsley—and the King took her."

Amanda leaned against the counter as if to support herself. "I . . . I can't believe it."

"Amanda, what happened when I was gone?"

Amanda scrunched her brow. "What do you mean?"

"Well, something must have gotten Molly so riled up she did something out of character for her." Janet put her hand on Amanda's arm. "Did something happen at your last meeting?"

Amanda looked down in thought and shook her head. "No. No, I don't think so. It seemed to be fairly routine. There was a new guy there. Jeff. You just met him." Amanda looked up and smiled. "He's very cute, isn't he?"

Janet gave her a hard stare.

Amanda's smile vanished. "Sorry." She shook her head. "He told of an experience of a coworker disappearing, and we all expressed our condolences." She shrugged. "I don't remember Molly being any different than normal. She took it hard, but she always does."

"You don't think that pushed her over the edge?"

"It didn't seem to. She cried, and so did others." Amanda shrugged. "Like I said, it appeared to be her normal reaction."

Janet nodded. "Did she come to see you the other day?"

Amanda shook her head. "I haven't seen her since the meeting. Why?"

Janet gave a quick shrug. "I heard she left work unexpectedly, so I just assumed she went to talk to someone."

"I don't know, Janet. She didn't contact me."

Janet patted Amanda's arm and gave her a sad smile. "OK. Well, I should go and let you get back to work." She headed toward the door, then turned. "Bruce and I are having a reception this weekend. You're coming, right?"

"Where is it?"

"Check your e-mail. Bruce is sending the instructions."

Janet waved as she stepped from the shop. As she headed for home, her mind drifted to a number of other things. Molly was certainly an excitable person, but not really a self-starter. Something had to have set her off. But what? Or who?

She was in such deep thought that she walked right by her hotel entrance—or would have if the doorman hadn't been outside.

"Good afternoon, Ms. Singleton—I mean, Mrs. O'Brien."

Janet came out of deep thought and looked around with recognition of her surroundings slowly coming back. "Oh, hi, Charlie. Sorry. I guess I was too wrapped up in thought." She turned and headed into the hotel. "How are you doing today?"

"Very good, Mrs. O'Brien. Thanks for asking."

As Janet entered, she stopped and turned. "Charlie, how did you know I was married?"

"Your husband, Mrs. O'Brien. He asked me to help him with some of your reception arrangements. I was very happy to do so." He smiled. "You have a very nice husband, Mrs. O'Brien. I really like Bruce."

"Thank you, Charlie. I think he's a keeper."

Charlie chuckled. "Indeed, Mrs. O'Brien." Then, almost as an afterthought, he replied, "Bruce asked me to the reception, but I wanted to be sure that was OK with you before I did something so bold."

Janet shrugged and smiled. "I don't see why not. I'm probably closer to you than some of my actual relatives. I would love to have you come. And, oh—bring someone with you."

"Thank you, Mrs. O'Brien. That's very sweet of you."

"No. Thank you, Charlie. It will be an honor to have you there."

Janet walked to the elevator and headed up to her floor. As she did, she was thinking about the reception. Bruce was quite the charmer, she thought. Maybe the event would go well. She would just stay close to him and let him do the talking.

As Janet entered her hotel room—*their* room, she reminded herself—Bruce looked up from the dining table.

His eyes widened. "Oh, hi. I wasn't expecting you back so soon." He stood. "It's all done. Everyone's invited." He walked over and gave her a kiss.

She smiled weakly.

Bruce's face turned solemn. "Is everything all right? Did something happen?"

Before she could answer, he led her to the balcony. "You sit here and relax. I'll get you some tea and you can tell me all about it."

She nodded and sat in her favorite spot. As Bruce went inside to prepare the tea, she leaned back and sighed. All this was leaving her more determined than ever to find as much information as possible about a coming Overtaker. It sounded like he might be the answer to what she had been looking for. She deeply wanted to investigate further.

Bruce came back with the tea and set it on the small table next to her. He sat in the other chair.

"OK, tell me what happened."

Janet picked up the teacup and took a sip, feeling the comforting warmness go all the way down. This used to be her most comforting thing. Now it was her second favorite; Bruce's big arms around her was her new number one.

"For some reason, Molly went ballistic at work and destroyed a couple of desks and allegedly attacked Administrator Billingsley," Janet said.

She could hear genuine concern in Bruce's voice. "And where is she now?"

Janet couldn't help but reply—in agitation. "As you would expect, she was taken by the King."

Bruce pursed his lips and nodded. After a couple of seconds, he cocked his head and looked at Janet. "You said 'allegedly' attacked Administrator Billingsley."

Janet gave a shrug. "Well, that's what she said."

"And you don't believe her?"

Janet set her teacup down and sat up. "It's not that I necessarily think she's lying. It's just that this is so out of character for Molly." She sighed. "I know she's emotional, but she's usually pretty timid at work and doesn't speak out to anyone." Janet shook her head. "It just doesn't make any sense."

Bruce went over and sat on the lounge chair with Janet. He kissed her and gave her a hug. "I'm really sorry, Janet." He had her lean back. "You just relax here for a while. I'm going for a walk. Charlie told me about a great little eatery down the street. I'll bring you something back. How does that sound?"

She reached up and gave him a quick kiss. "You're wonderful."

As he stood to go, she added, "Charlie thinks you're wonderful, too."

Bruce laughed as he reentered the apartment. "He's a neat guy," he called back. He then stuck his head back outside for a moment. "Oh, I asked him to the reception. I hope that was OK."

"Sure. He told me. It's fine. What's two more anyway?"

"Two?"

"I told him to bring somebody."

Bruce laughed. "I'll see you in a few."

Janet heard the door open and close. She leaned back and closed her eyes. She knew she was lucky in so many ways. Never in her wildest dreams did she think she would find someone like Bruce. He didn't always side with her, but he let her be herself. That was rare.

As her mind began to calm, she remembered the little box the Leader had given her. After retrieving it and her tablet, she inserted the small device. It seemed to copy something onto her tablet and then formed an icon. When she clicked on the icon, a welcome screen displayed.

As it came online, she saw a place for electronic mail, so she sent a message about Zuri Turay and where he was located. Janet could see him becoming a leader for the cause in Africa, and she hoped he and the others she met in Iceland could become good friends.

But her new African friends could never know she worked for the Leader. Anonymity had to be a priority.

CHAPTER 19

The day of the get-together arrived. Bruce took Janet's hands and looked her way. "Ready for this?"

Janet laughed. "No. But we can't get it over with without it starting."

Bruce smiled. "Very true." He selected the teleporter near his home and pressed "Engage."

In a matter of seconds they were standing in the town square. They heard music behind them. It was soft and melodic. They turned and saw the string quartet in the gazebo on the far end of the square. Janet would have enjoyed the music if she didn't have such an adrenaline rush going at the same time.

Bruce held out his hand. "Shall we?"

Janet took his hand and a deep breath. Then, into "the land of a thousand questions," as she presumed it would be, they went.

As soon as they walked by the gazebo, the musicians changed their tempo. Everyone turned and clapped. The crowd converged around the gazebo. The lead musician motioned for the two of them to step toward where he was standing.

Janet followed Bruce onto the gazebo. Bruce raised his hands and the clapping died down.

"Thank you all for coming. I know what Janet and I did was unconventional."

"You can say that again."

Janet saw a woman, looking angry, step forward.

"Now, Mom. Don't start," Bruce said. "We'll talk later."

"You bet we will."

Everyone laughed.

"She's always been unconventional," a man next to Janet's mother said while his eyes gestured toward Janet.

"That's my dad," Janet whispered to Bruce.

Bruce smiled and put his arm around Janet. "Yes, sir, Mr. Singleton. That she is. And I love her for it."

The expression on Mr. Singleton's face turned to one of satisfaction. Janet could barely hold back a gasp. It had been a long time since she had seen that look on her father's face.

Bruce cleared his throat. "Like I said, although unconventional, we still want you a part of our lives and to share our happiness. That's why we've invited you here today. Please enjoy the music, food, and each other."

The musicians started playing again and the crowd began mingling. Bruce took Janet's hand and they stepped from the gazebo. To the right was a table with their wedding pictures. Each of their parents approached the table.

"The pictures are beautiful," a woman said, and Janet put her hand on the woman's shoulder.

"Thank you, Mrs. O'Brien. It was a lovely place."

"And you think it isn't lovely here?" Bruce's mother said, turning, her tone suddenly colder.

"Mom, don't start," Bruce said.

"I don't understand why you shut us out."

"Mom." Bruce breathed hard through his nose. He swept his arm wide. "Look around you. You're shut out of nothing.

We're here. Everyone's here." He put his hands on his hips and sighed. "Can't you just embrace it?"

"It was . . . spur of the moment," Janet said, looking at Bruce's mother. "Haven't you ever done anything like that?"

Mrs. O'Brien shot a hard look at Janet. "No. And Bruce never did before either."

"What are you implying about my daughter?" Janet's dad said, walking up.

Janet waved her hands. "It's . . . it's OK, Dad."

"No. No, it isn't." Bruce turned to his father. "Dad, take mom home. Now."

"What?" His mom's expression was now wide-eyed and as if in shock. "I thought you said you weren't shutting us out?"

"I'm not. *You* are." Bruce stepped in front of his mom. "Mom, what you want is in the past. Take what is offered now. Be happy for us. If not, and if you're going to insult my wife, then you're not welcome here."

"You . . . you don't mean that."

"John." She took her husband's arm and shook it. "John, reason with your son."

Bruce looked at his father. "Dad. Talk to your wife."

"Give me a minute with her," John said, taking his wife's arm and leading her away. They appeared to be in a heated discussion.

Bruce was breathing hard. Janet went over and touched his arm. Bruce lifted it and wrapped it around her shoulders.

Janet's father walked over and kissed Janet on the forehead. "I'm happy for you, Janet." He then shook Bruce's free hand. "I'm happy for both of you."

"Thank you, sir."

Janet's mom approached and gave Janet a hug. "We've never seen eye to eye." She smiled. "But I'm happy for you. I always hoped you'd find the right man." She shook her head. "But you kept chasing them away."

Janet chuckled and nodded.

She put her hand on Janet's cheek and looked at Bruce. "But you've found a good one. And one that adores you." She gave Bruce a hug. "Thank you."

Janet's mother and father walked away together.

Bruce leaned in and whispered in Janet's ear. "Having fun yet?"

She put her forehead to his chest and laughed. "So much fun. I may even throw up."

Bruce smiled. "Hang on just a little longer."

She looked up. "Oh no. More fun."

"What?" Bruce turned as Shepherd Randall approached. "Shepherd Randall. I hope you are enjoying yourself."

"You two surprised us all."

Bruce laughed. "Yeah, well, we even surprised ourselves."

"I hear your parents took it hard."

Bruce nodded.

Shepherd Randall patted his shoulder. "Let me and Morgan talk to her." He smiled. "We'll get her to turn around."

Bruce gave a half laugh and shook his head. "I hope so." He grabbed Shepherd Randall's arm. "But she has to understand she does not get things her way this time. She either accepts Janet or loses both of us."

Shepherd Randall nodded and walked to where Shepherd Morgan was standing.

Bruce took a deep breath and let it out quickly. "Let's go to the food table. Maybe we'll find someone who actually likes being here."

Once they neared the table, Janet grabbed Bruce's arm. "Look, isn't that Charlie with Amanda?"

As they approached, Amanda turned with her full plate. "Janet. Wow, you look beautiful. You really did choose the right dress. Taupe really looks good on you. And the swath of cherry blossoms across the bodice looks elegant."

"Thanks, Amanda. You also look great, as usual. I see you met Charlie."

Charlie shook Bruce's hand. "Hi, Bruce." He nodded. "Hello, Mrs. O'Brien."

Janet squinted. "Charlie, why are you and Bruce on a first-name basis and you call me by my last name?"

Charlie shrugged. "I don't know. It just feels right."

Bruce laughed.

Janet gave Bruce a curious look. She really didn't understand. "Why is that funny?"

Amanda grabbed Janet's arm. "Janet, you never told me Charlie works at your hotel."

Janet shook her head slightly. "I didn't know you two knew each other." She turned her head sideways. "Wait a minute. How *do* you two know each other?"

"Jeff took me to a meeting the other night, and Amanda was there," Charlie said.

Janet felt like she was reading a book two pages behind everyone else. "I'm sorry. Who's Jeff?"

"Jeff is my grandson." Charlie looked around. "He's around here somewhere."

"He's getting our drinks," Amanda said, her eyes then lighting up. "Here he comes now."

"Here you go, Granddad." Jeff gave Charlie a cup of punch, then handed one to Amanda.

Janet swore she knew this man, but from where? Once he turned and faced her, their recognition was simultaneous.

His eyebrows went up. "Janet!" He smiled. "Well, it certainly is a small world."

Bruce looked from one to the other. "You know each other?"

Jeff stuck out his hand to Bruce. "Hi, I'm Jeff. Jeff Starling. Your wife helped me make a suit selection the other day."

"Oh, really?" He looked at Janet with a turned-up brow.

"He was in Amanda's shop the other day when I went by."

Just then, Charlie dropped his cup of punch and some of it splashed on Bruce's left shoe.

"Oh, Bruce, I'm so sorry."

Bruce chuckled. "No worries, Charlie." He put his hand on Charlie's shoulder. "Come with me. I'll get you another cup."

Bruce gave Janet a quick kiss on her cheek. "I'll be back in a sec."

Janet nodded, then noticed Amanda and Jeff looking at each other and nodding.

Janet put her hand on Amanda's arm. "What is it?" Janet asked her.

"Janet, I found out who Molly visited the other day before her . . . disappearance."

"Who?"

"It was me." Jeff briefly looked down at the ground.

Amanda took his arm. "Go ahead and tell her, Jeff."

He looked up and then glanced around. "I'm really sorry, Janet. It was the next day after our meeting when she came to me in the middle of the day and said she had heard about another person being taken by the King."

"And?"

He put his hands in his pockets and shrugged. "I was still upset about my friend as well."

"And who was your friend?"

"I'm a geologist and I work at the Chicago museum," Jeff said. "My coworker thought our Administrator was hiding something and went berserk one day. He was taken before I knew what it was all about. That's what made me so upset."

He glanced at Janet periodically but didn't look her in the eye. "Molly asked what she should do. I . . . I didn't think she would actually do it." He glanced back at Janet, eyes watering.

"What did you say, Jeff?"

"Well, I said something like, 'If I could, I'd take something precious away from the Administrators and make them think twice about what they did.'" He shook his head. "I wasn't meaning for her to do anything. I was just spouting off. Really, I had no idea she was going to do anything like that."

Janet looked around. "OK. OK, Jeff. Calm down. Don't let anyone see you making a scene here. In the future, please keep your thoughts in check. We can't afford to have more incidents like that."

Jeff nodded.

Bruce returned with Charlie. "Here we go." He handed Janet a cup of punch. "All's now right with the world." There was a bit of laughter; it was needed in this tense afternoon.

"Well, Jeff, Amanda, Charlie, I hope you all have a good time." Bruce took Janet's hand. "Janet, let me introduce you to some of the people in this area." He smiled. "Excuse us."

Bruce gave Janet a wry smile as they turned and headed to another area. "So, trying to ditch me already, are you?"

Janet looked at Bruce and replied with a matter-of-fact tone, "Yes, I tire easily."

He put his arm around her. "Well, it's a good thing I don't."

Janet leaned into him even more. *How did I get so lucky meeting this man?* Janet laughed. "I think he's into Amanda anyway."

Bruce smiled. "That's what I wanted to hear."

Janet smiled back and patted his chest.

Bruce had Janet meet a large number of the townsfolk. Most seemed happy for them, except for some of the younger women. Some acted as if their chances for marriage had totally evaporated. Janet tried to remember their names. She was going to have some interesting conversations with Bruce later, she told herself. However, after a while, she met so many different people she was unsure whether she was going to remember any names. They all began to run together after a while.

Some of the men converged on them and engaged Bruce in conversation about crops and farming. Janet was able to contribute to some of the conversation, which the other men found a bit odd but also interesting. However, some of the women came over and pulled her from the conversation the men were having.

"Thank you for the invitation," one of the women said. "We haven't had a get-together like this since the last ruin renovation."

The other women nodded. One said, "Living so far apart doesn't give us as much chance to get together as we would like."

"What's the importance of the ruins?" Janet looked from one woman to the other. "Everyone seems to adore them, but I'm not sure why."

Some of the women looked at each other as though unsure how to explain. "Well . . . " one of the women started. "I guess you could say it's a way for us to honor the King."

Janet cocked her head. "Really? How so?"

"The ruins date to before the Refreshing. Shepherd Morgan speaks at each renovation day to remind us how blessed we are to live post-Refreshing. We renovate the ruins to remember that fact."

"I see. It's like a memorial, then," Janet said.

The women smiled. "Exactly," one said.

Shepherd Morgan approached. "Good afternoon, ladies. May I steal Janet from you for a few minutes?"

The women nodded and walked off together.

Janet smiled. "It's good to see you again, Shepherd Morgan."

The Shepherd smiled back. "Likewise. I just wanted to let you know I had John take Mildred, Bruce's mom, back home."

"Is she OK?"

Morgan nodded. "She will be. I'll stop by their place later and talk to her again." He chuckled. "You know, this may have been the first time Bruce ever did something without her knowledge."

Janet's eyes widened. "Really?" She glanced at Bruce, who was still talking to the other farmers. "He doesn't strike me as a momma's boy."

"Oh, he isn't. But it's never stopped her from prying."

Janet grimaced. "Oh, my. What have I gotten myself into?"

Morgan patted her arm. "Don't worry. From what I hear from Shepherd Randall, you can hold your own."

Janet sighed. "Shepherd Morgan, please don't let the stories of my past define my present. I'm not that person anymore." She smiled. "I think Bruce has had a positive effect on me."

"Knowing something about both of you helps me see why you are good for each other."

Janet shook her head just a bit. "What do you mean?"

"Well, from what I've heard, your independent nature needed someone who could accept it, and Bruce has needed someone not clingy." He smiled. "I think you're perfect for each other."

Janet chuckled. "Well, I'm not sure of your analysis, but I'm definitely sure about your conclusion."

Morgan laughed. "OK. I'll accept that." He touched her arm. "I'll let you get back to your guests."

"Um, Shepherd Morgan?"

He turned her way. "Yes?"

"I was talking to some of the women about the ruins."

His eyebrows went up.

"I understand it has become a type of memorial."

Morgan nodded. "That's a good description."

"And I heard it's difficult for these farming families to get together due to their living so far apart."

Morgan again nodded.

She touched his arm. "What if we turned the ruins into a living memorial?"

"A *living* memorial?"

"What if we rebuild the entire building and turn it into a type of lodge for families to get together more often? We can even put a plaque of some type on it to remind everyone of its original purpose." Janet took a sip of her punch. "I know you have the civic center, but having something more rustic, I think, would be appealing to the people here."

Morgan put his hand to his chin and nodded.

"Would you be supportive of that?" Janet asked. "I could help organize it."

"Janet, you've been here less than a day, and you've come up with a great idea that could benefit this entire town. I'm not sure why no one ever thought of that, but I really like it. Let's talk more about it later. OK?"

Janet nodded. "Anytime."

Bruce approached. "Everything going OK?"

Shepherd Morgan nodded. "Bruce, your wife is one of a kind."

Bruce smiled. "That's why I married her."

Morgan shook Bruce's hand and patted his upper arm. "I'll talk to you both later."

Morgan walked off and Bruce turned to Janet. "Well, it seems you've made a good impression on everyone."

Janet turned up a corner of her mouth. "Well, almost everyone. It looks like I have some work to do with my mother-in-law."

Bruce chuckled. "Don't think you're in that boat all by yourself."

They went back to the gathering and mingled some more. People began trickling back home little by little. It was almost sundown before the last guests had left. The caterers packed everything away and the musicians did the same with their instruments.

Bruce took Janet in his arms, gave her a hug, and kissed her. "Well, it's finally over."

Janet breathed in and let it out slowly. "Hallelujah. Now we can focus on us."

"Speaking of us. Now I get to make some space for you at my home." He put his arm around her. "OK walking home?"

"Is it far?"

"Oh, it will take a while. But I know just how to cool down once we get there."

Janet's eyebrows went up. "Oh?"

"We can go skinny-dipping in the pond and then do some other fun things after."

Janet turned and looked at him as they continued walking. "You're serious?"

Bruce held up his palm. "Oh, don't worry. I've sworn Oliver to secrecy. The ducks . . . now they are a little fickle. They tell you one thing but then do another."

Janet laughed and hugged his arm. "Bruce, I simply adore you."

"All part of my elaborate plan, my dear. All part of my plan."

They walked arm in arm toward Bruce's home.

CHAPTER 20

J anet woke to a strange sensation on her hand. She flicked her wrist and felt something furry. When she looked over the side of the bed, there stood Oliver with an expectant look in his eyes. She smiled and rubbed the dog's head.

"Good morning, Oliver. How are you today?"

The dog wagged its tail excitedly.

Janet turned over, but the other side of the bed was empty. She stepped out of bed, put on her robe, and went to the kitchen where Bruce was at work behind the stove.

"You're going to spoil me. I may expect this every morning."

Bruce turned and smiled. "Maybe that's part of my plan."

"Well, I think it's working." She walked up and gave him a kiss.

"Now the ultimate test," Bruce said.

She looked over his shoulder. "French toast?" She nodded. "Yes, that puts you in a precarious position." She looked in his eyes. "What if I don't like it?"

"I may have to do something to take your mind off your disappointment," he said with a grin.

"What if I do enjoy it?"

"Then you'll need to show your appreciation."

She put her face millimeters from his. "Well, it seems the odds are in my favor."

"Hmm. Depends upon your perspective. It's not looking bad from my side either."

"Shall we sit down and see who the winner is?"

Bruce pulled out a chair for Janet. He set a plate of French toast in front of her.

"You start, and I'll scramble some eggs with cheese."

She took a few bites and put her fork down.

Bruce turned. "Uh-oh. Not as good as I thought, huh?"

Janet shook her head. "No, it's perfect." Her eyes watered and tears welled up and spilled over her eyelids.

Bruce put the plate of eggs on the counter. He knelt next to her. "What's wrong?"

"You're too perfect."

He took her hand. "What? What do you mean?"

"No one has ever treated me this way."

He smiled and kissed her hand. "That's because no one else is me."

Janet chuckled between sniffles.

"Janet, I'm not perfect. You're just the person I've been looking for, and I'm appreciative of it." He moved in closer. "We have something unique. I accept you as you, and you accept me as me." He smiled. "If you think I'm perfect, then that just spoils the magic."

Janet smiled. "Well, now that you mention it, the cinnamon was a little heavy."

Bruce leaned back, gasped, and put his hand to his chest. "You stab me." He held up his forefinger. "But the secret is you need to eat the toast with the eggs."

To play along, Janet offered a deadpan expression. "That's your explanation?"

Bruce waved his forefinger back and forth. "Don't judge without evidence."

He reached for the eggs and put some on her plate. She reached for the fork, but he grabbed it first. "Uh, wait. You don't know the portion control."

"Portion control?"

"Oh, absolutely." He smiled. "You can't ignore the food balance."

Janet chuckled. "Now you're just making things up."

"I can see I have to educate you." He pointed to the eggs. "You see, the cheese in the eggs counterbalances the extra cinnamon and makes the bite perfect."

"But I don't like to eat my food together."

"Trust me."

She gave a smirk but took the bite he offered her. Her eyes lit up. "Mmm." She smiled. "May I have another?"

They fed each other bites. Once the last of it was eaten, Bruce looked at her with raised eyebrows. "So, who won?"

She put her arms around his neck. "Well, let me see. You put too much cinnamon, so I won." She touched the tip of his nose with her finger and smiled. "But then you made the wonderful eggs, so you won." She shrugged. "I guess it's a draw."

Bruce chuckled. "So, I need to take your mind off your disappointment, and you need to show your appreciation. You think we can do that simultaneously?"

Janet smiled. "I can start." She leaned in, wrapped her arms around his neck, and pulled him closer as she gave him a lingering kiss.

When their lips parted, Bruce stood and pulled Janet to her feet. "Let me see if I can match that." He scooped her up in his arms and she wrapped her arms around his neck again. He carried her to the bedroom.

He placed her on the bed and returned her passionate kiss. Oliver then bounded in, jumped on the bed, and began licking Bruce's face.

"Oliver!" Bruce's voice was scolding. "That was bad timing."

Janet laughed.

Bruce took Oliver to the door, put him out, and closed it.

Janet heard Oliver whine. "Aw."

Bruce headed back to the bed. "My next move is for our eyes only."

A couple of hours later, they took a shower and dressed. Bruce helped Janet get the house the way she wanted it. Several pieces of furniture were moved to places Janet felt was more suitable or provided a better flow to the room. What Bruce called the den had a large picture window that looked out into the backyard and to the field in the distance. Janet decided to make this room her office; from here she could work when at home.

Bruce brought in an old mahogany desk that had been in his family for generations. A flowered swivel chair was also brought in and placed behind the desk. He carried in a table with four chairs so Janet could use it as a conference table when needed. A decorative table for the tea and coffee maker was placed near the door, and a sofa was placed on the opposite wall. Janet added some finishing touches with pictures for the wall, desk, and table. Once completed, it looked both homey and businesslike rolled into one.

Bruce stood in the doorway, composed of French doors, and looked at the achievement. "Does it meet your specifications?"

Janet turned to him and smiled. "And then some. It's perfect." She went over and gave him a hug. "Thanks for being willing to donate this room just for my work."

Bruce shrugged. "It wasn't getting that much use anyway. At least now it will."

They heard a knock at the front door.

Bruce kissed her on the forehead and went to answer the door. Janet stayed in the room to admire her office. It wasn't as modern-looking as hers in the Chicago office, but it would give her a feeling of being *home* when home.

This could also be her covert office for working with The Order, she told herself, and she could use her Chicago office for her commodities work.

She heard Bruce talking with someone in the living area. The voice sounded familiar, but she couldn't place it. She walked into the room to find out.

"Shepherd Morgan, what brings you by?" Janet tried to sound pleasant but felt it a little unsettling the Shepherd deemed it OK to come by unannounced. That pointed to one of the reasons she liked the city. People didn't feel like every domicile provided an open invitation for visitation rights.

Morgan smiled. "Hi, Janet. I can see you've already had a positive influence here."

Bruce laughed. "So, my bad tastes were always so obvious?"

Morgan shook his head and laughed. "No, Bruce. Your house was always well kept. Yet . . . " He glanced around the room. "I have to say, I really like the new arrangement."

"So, what brings you by, Shepherd Morgan?" Janet said while taking a seat; Bruce and Morgan followed suit. "Can I get you anything?"

Morgan smiled. "I'm fine, thanks." He shifted slightly in his seat. "I just came by to remind everyone, and to tell you, Janet, that it's our town's turn to support Sukkot in Jerusalem this year." His smile went to a large grin. "We are doubly blessed this year."

Janet's eyebrows when up. "How's that?"

"It's not only Sukkot, but Sukkot in a Sabbath Year."

"Oh, that's right." Bruce looked in thought for a few seconds. "That would make it the last Sabbath Year before the next Jubilee."

Shepherd Morgan nodded. "I'm already gathering things for the honoring ceremony. Various things people have achieved or created in honor of our King are being placed in the civic center. Priest Ya'akov from Jerusalem will be here in three weeks to check on them." He beamed. "Isn't it exciting?"

Janet smiled, but that pointed to another reason she had originally wanted to move to the city. It was easier to get lost than required to attend religious festivals, in Jerusalem or otherwise. It looked like she would not be able to do that this time.

"Janet, you should present something about your crop rotation schedule. It is revolutionary," Morgan said.

Janet felt a knot in her stomach. That was the last thing she wanted to do. "Well, I don't want to take full credit. There were a lot of contributing factors by others."

"Now you're just being modest." Morgan beamed. "I tell you what. I'll reach out to Administrator Billingsley and see what she would like to do. OK?"

Janet nodded and smiled—but didn't like the idea at all.

"Oh, and we have two people who will be having their sacrificing ceremonies this year."

Bruce raised an eyebrow and smiled. "Oh, and who are they?"

"The Cumberland twins. They placed their faith in the King as their future hope just the other night after my teaching session." Morgan rubbed his hands together. "I just love being able to present people to the King who yield themselves to him, and their burnt offering will represent that."

Janet wanted to change the subject; this type of discussion made her uncomfortable. People who came back from their sacrificing ceremonies always acted differently somehow—almost as if they had been brainwashed. They even *talked* differently. She never seemed able to relate to them in the same way as before the event.

Janet decided to change the subject.

"Shepherd Morgan, did you have a chance to think more about my proposal?"

"Proposal?" Bruce looked from Janet to Morgan.

Morgan nodded. "Bruce, your wife made the most insightful observation yesterday."

"Well, I don't find that hard to believe."

Janet looked over at him and smiled.

"She wants to have the ruins rebuilt to pre-Refreshing standards so the community can have more get-togethers and feel more tight-knit—more like a family rather than distant neighbors."

Bruce nodded. "I think that's a great idea."

Morgan slapped his knee. "And I do too. I think we should make the reconstruction of the building a community event and have everyone part of it."

"I agree," Janet said. "That way everyone will feel connected to it and coming to it will become more endearing to them."

Janet didn't mention, of course, that her biggest motivation was to interact with more people in the community to determine who wasn't so loyal and devoted to the King. The faster the building got built, the faster she could work within the community. "So, Shepherd Morgan, when do you propose we get this project started?"

"The Sabbath Year celebration is only six weeks away, so I think we can start construction right after we get back. Everyone will still be on a high from that trip, and this will just add to the experience."

Janet nodded. "OK, you work on getting the people together. I'll work on the agenda. I do hope you'll be willing to say a blessing for the building at that time."

Morgan beamed. "Oh, that would be my honor, Janet. My honor indeed. I'll also talk to each farmer and see what each can donate or contribute for the construction project. I think everyone will be excited to contribute."

"Wonderful. Perhaps you can give me a list of the families here and I'll coordinate getting the food together."

Morgan stood. "I can and will. Well, I should be going and not overstay my welcome."

He shook their hands and left. As Janet and Bruce watched Morgan leave, he disappeared as he passed the pond. Janet chuckled; his vanishing startled some of the ducks standing nearby.

Bruce went about catching up on chores as Janet prepared dinner. Hopefully, Janet thought to herself, Bruce knew what he had married into. Cooking had never been her thing, but she was willing to give it a try.

Janet laughed to herself as she went about her preparations. Bruce had said he didn't want to change her. Dinner would be a true test of whether he would hold fast to that statement—after he'd tasted one of her meals.

CHAPTER 21

The following weeks developed into a pattern for Janet and Bruce. She spent the week in Chicago and came home every other weekend while Bruce went to Chicago on alternate weekends. Janet knew this wasn't sustainable for the long haul and began working with Edgar on a way she could eventually work more often from home.

Although her ultimate plan had been to have her office at the house be her main place for interacting with The Order, she found being alone at the hotel during the week allowed interactions with the Leader and meetings of The Order to be better accommodated. It was there that she received word of The Order's first meeting of its core team.

Janet was unsure how this meeting would go. She clicked the link-to-meeting icon in the invitation. Her screen divided into six squares, her camera activated, and the sound initiated. Instead of her picture, her silhouette displayed. The software seemed to not only encrypt communications but also video. Other silhouettes, as well as the name of their continent, displayed as each came online.

The Leader initiated the call. Janet noticed the words "The Leader" highlighted when he talked. "Hello, everyone. Welcome to our first meeting of The Order. As you can see, anonymity is important for us. While we can't know each other, we are bound to each other with a common cause. We look forward to the coming Overtaker, and we need to spread the word of his coming."

Janet had to admit it surprised her that the Leader had all five continents covered already. She was pretty sure Huizhong was the anonymous leader in Asia and Zuri in Africa. While Huizhong was a hunch, Zuri's silhouette showed the enlarged holes in his ear lobes. Not necessarily proof, but if not, extremely coincidental.

Janet saw "The Leader" come off highlight status and saw "Asia" highlight. "What are our plans for moving forward?" the Asian leader asked.

"Similar to what you were doing before. Meet people, find those who are unhappy with the King. Work through someone you can trust and have them teach about the Overtaker."

Other questions were asked, but the answer was essentially the same: meet, reach, teach.

* * * * *

On the home front, Janet spent the weekends leading up to the Sabbath Year with various farm ladies to ensure food and activities were coordinated for the "lodge raising," as people started calling it. Although small talk was not Janet's forte, she didn't find it difficult as she merely had to smile and nod while the other women did most of the talking. The best thing was the project allowed most of the women to begin trusting her.

The evening before the town was to leave for Jerusalem, Shepherd Morgan had everyone gather in the civic center auditorium and bring their luggage.

"I'm having a schedule passed out to you now," he said, addressing everyone. "Please note your time of departure. It's very important we stick to this schedule in order to get everyone to Jerusalem on time."

Someone from the crowd asked, "What if we miss our scheduled departure time?"

"The teleporters are very busy right now. If you miss your turn, I'm not sure when you'll be able to arrive."

Another raised his hand. "What about the things for the honoring ceremony? How do we get them there?"

"Everything is already in Jerusalem. Priest Ya'akov came the other day, inspected everything you'll be presenting, and had it all teleported to Jerusalem." Morgan smiled. "He was very impressed with everything you will be presenting and showing to honor our King."

Clapping and a few whistles came from people around the room.

"You all will be staying in the Guest House that is not far from the King's palace."

Janet heard someone behind her get very excited. "Oh, that is the best place to stay in Jerusalem," the woman said. "You can see the whole city from there. This is too good to be true."

"After arriving, go to street level and follow the signs to the Upper Guest House," Morgan said. "There will be a lot of people there, but everyone is friendly and courteous, so if you get lost, just ask someone." He gestured with arms open. "Any further questions?"

"What about our luggage?" someone asked.

"When you exit, leave it near the long-range teleporter. It will be waiting for you in your hotel room. Just be sure your names are on each piece." He looked over the crowd. "Any other questions?"

No one said anything.

"OK, then. Stick to your schedules, and we'll see you all in Jerusalem!"

More clapping erupted as people stood and dispersed. As Janet and Bruce were heading to leave, Shepherd Morgan approached them.

"Excuse me, Janet. Do you have a minute?"

Janet turned to see an extremely excited Morgan looking at her. She smiled at him to look interested but knew she likely would not be happy about what he wanted from her.

"I heard back from Administrator Billingsley. She had your boss, Edgar, pull something together that will be presented at the Jerusalem Civic Center with many of the other objects that will be on display. She would like you to be present the first night to help answer questions."

Janet smiled. "Of course, Shepherd Morgan. I'd be happy to do so." Although she wasn't nearly as supportive as she made herself out to be, if this would help her career, she was more than willing to participate.

"Wonderful." He took her hand and patted it. "I'm sure many will be impressed."

Someone else approached Morgan with questions. "Excuse me, Janet," Morgan said. "I'll see you tomorrow, then."

As they headed home in Bruce's AGA, both Bruce and Janet were quiet for some time.

"Janet, have you ever been to Jerusalem?"

"Only once. I think I was maybe six or seven at the time." She shook her head. "I really can't remember much about it. I remember a lot of people." She paused in thought. "Beautiful singing." She smiled. "And eating a falafel."

Bruce laughed. "That sounds like what a six-year-old would remember."

"What about you?"

"Hmm. Well, I was probably a little older. Eleven or twelve, I guess. I remember seeing the King." He glanced at Janet. "I thought he had kind eyes."

Janet turned and looked at Bruce. "Where did you see the King?"

"On the palace balcony. I was pretty far away. But his eyes . . . I still remember those eyes."

Janet sat back in her seat. *Kind eyes don't exactly make a person legitimate,* she thought to herself.

Finally, Bruce pulled up beside the house. "You go ahead. I'm going to take care of a few chores in the barn first."

Janet nodded, they kissed briefly, and she headed into the house.

The next morning came early. Their departure time was 08:30. They made it to the town square with fifteen minutes to spare. Everyone was abuzz with excitement. Janet and Bruce got in line for the teleporter. When their turn came, they stepped on the pad. The destination was already set, so Bruce hit "Engage."

Janet felt her skin prickle, her vision turn blurry, and her stomach go a little queasy. In a matter of seconds, her vision returned and the prickliness and queasiness subsided. Someone motioned for them to quickly step off the teleporter pad. People seemed to be everywhere going here and there. Yet, in spite of it all, it didn't seem chaotic. Busy, but not chaotic.

Various aromas surrounded Janet. She took a deep breath and detected hints of coriander and cumin. *A restaurant must be nearby,* she thought. When they left street level they saw several street vendors with various breads, gyros, and falafels. Well, that answered the question of those enticing aromas.

It was midafternoon here. The first day of Sukkot would start at sundown—only a few hours away. They turned right and headed toward the Upper Guest House. Once they got away from the main foot traffic, Bruce had Janet stop and look around. The city cascaded down before them toward the east. The temple could be seen to their left with water gushing from beneath it and down the escarpment to the valley below. They saw a river flow between two small mountains in the near distance and then merge into a larger river in the distance. The valley was lush and green.

The city was beautiful. The buildings were a combination of old and new, but still they seemed to harmonize quite well. There were numerous small parklike areas throughout the city with trees and flowering shrubs. The city appeared to be in three parts, and various ornate bridges connected the three areas together. In the distance, two trams led down the escarpment to the valley below.

Janet took a deep breath. "I remember it being pretty, but I'd forgotten just how beautiful this place is." She looked at Bruce. "But I still like Chicago."

Bruce laughed and put his arm around her. "Just the comment I expected."

She poked him in the ribs.

"Umf." He laughed all the more.

There was a long check-in line at the Guest House. After about thirty minutes they were finally in their room.

Janet looked at her T-band and laughed.

Bruce looked her way. "What is it?"

"We finally get to our room, and it's nearly time to leave for the ceremony."

"Well, before we do, come to the balcony. The city's even more beautiful from here."

Bruce was right. More of the intra-city parks were visible, and she could see farther into the valley beyond the escarpment. Closer by, she could see people leaving various shops and restaurants as they closed up for the day in anticipation of the beginning of Sukkot.

Janet stiffened and gasped at the same time.

Bruce put his hand on her shoulder. "What's wrong, Janet?"

Janet pointed. "Look . . . look at that woman leaving that shop over to the right." She glanced at Bruce with mouth open. "It's . . . it looks just like Molly."

"What?" Bruce tried to glance where she was pointing, but the area only looked like a sea of people to him. "Janet, what are you talking about?" He looked back at her. "You know that's impossible, right?"

"But that dress. No one else has a white dress with those bold splotches of color. Who else could it be?"

Bruce gave an exaggerated shrug. "It could be anybody. Why couldn't someone else have a dress like that?"

Janet shook her head. "No. No, it's impossible. Amanda created that dress for Molly. She doesn't create another until about a year after the original is sold." Janet looked back over the edge of the balcony trying to see where the woman was heading.

Bruce put his arms around her shoulders. "Or, she did because Molly was taken. That could be almost anyone."

"I have to go find out." She quickly headed back into the hotel room from the balcony.

Bruce grabbed her arm. "Janet, be reasonable. How are you going to find her in all those people?"

"I have to try." She pulled out of Bruce's grasp. "If I don't get back in time before the ceremony, meet me in the civic center later. OK?"

"Janet, please." He walked back into the room as Janet was leaving.

She turned back. "I'm sorry, Bruce. I . . . I have to."

"Wait—"

She heard some muffled sounds as she closed the door. Not wanting a confrontation, she hurried down the hallway, down the stairs, and out of the Guest House. Rushing as near to the area where the woman had exited the shop as she could find, Janet ran as fast as she could. There were so many people. Would she be able to find her?

Frantically looking right and left, she pushed her way against a flood of foot traffic. She came to an intersection. Should she continue straight, go right, or head left? Standing there, she turned, craning her neck to see as far into the distance of each direction as possible. Seeing a splash of color on white disappear behind a building to her left, Janet walked in that direction as quickly as possible without bowling someone over in the process.

She turned the corner at the building she had seen. There, up ahead, climbing the small incline of the street, was the woman. Janet pressed on, determined to get to her before she was out of sight again. She was now breathing quite heavily and sweating intensely. Still, the woman turned another corner before Janet had a chance to get close enough to shout Molly's name.

Janet kept trying to increase her pace, but the crowd made it difficult. She turned the same corner as the woman did but then found herself at a small open area that looked over the escarpment to the valley below. Janet looked right but didn't see her. She looked left—nothing. She turned and turned and turned. *Which way to go?* Putting her hands on her head, she pondered what to do. It took her a few minutes to allow herself to accept the inevitable: she had lost her.

Janet went to the nearest bench with an open seat and sat, heavily, her heart still racing. She took in a deep breath to try and slow both her breathing and heart rate. Had it been Molly? *No, that's impossible. . . . But then, who else could it have been?*

She took out her communicator and called Amanda. She left her communicator on voice only.

"This is Amanda. How can I help tell your story?"

"Amanda. This is Janet."

"Janet, hi! How's Jerusalem?"

"Fine. Fine. I have a question for you."

"Is everything OK? You sound out of breath."

"Molly's dress. Have you sold another one?"

"What? Why do you want to know about her dress? Do you want one?"

"No. No. That's not what I'm calling about. I saw someone here with the same dress Molly bought from your boutique—the white one with splotches of color everywhere on it."

"That's impossible. I've only sold one, and that was to Molly."

"So, you didn't produce any more since she was . . . taken?"

"No, the dress is automatically taken out of the selection process for one year. I haven't even thought about changing that policy."

Janet took a few more deep breaths.

"Are you sure it was the same dress?" Amanda asked. There was a pause. "Do you think Molly could have returned?"

"Is that even possible?" Janet asked.

"I . . . I don't know. All I know is I haven't sold another dress like Molly's."

Janet nodded. "OK. OK, Amanda. I believe you. It . . . it was so weird."

"Well, let me know what you find out."

"OK, I will." Janet closed her communicator.

She leaned back and let out a long breath. Most of the crowd had dissipated. When she looked to her right, she couldn't believe her eyes. Next to the bench was a sign that read, "The Overlook." She stood and went to the railing. The water, originating from somewhere under the temple, flowed toward the escarpment and then down onto the rocks below. Spotlights and up-lights highlighted various flowers, shrubs, ferns, and boulders all the way to the bottom. The view was stunning and made her forget why and how she had arrived there . . .

Snapping out of her fog, she remembered she had to get to the ceremony. It would be starting soon.

Janet walked as quickly as possible toward the temple and then turned left to get to the courtyard between the palace and the temple's south gate. Once she reached the courtyard, she could go no farther due to the number of people present. She wondered if she could find Bruce but knew her chances were extremely remote.

She was so far from the temple gate that everyone on the steps above her looked very small from where she stood. A priest stepped forward and the crowd became silent. It was so silent Janet could now hear herself breathing. She willed herself to breathe more slowly so she could hear what the priest was saying.

"Good evening. I am Priest Ya'akov. Welcome to the opening ceremony of Sukkot, the festival which marks the very period of time in which we currently live."

A thunderous applause went up. He waited a few seconds and motioned for the applause to cease.

"Sukkot, sometimes called the Feast of Tabernacles, is the time in the past that looked forward to the time our King would come to earth and reign over us. Today, he does that for us."

Again, more applause, and a few whistles here and there.

"In olden times, this festival was marked with us living in sukkah, or temporary dwellings, to signify God's blessing on his people in times of hardship, and that he would one day dwell with us. Their ceremony incorporated the pouring of water at the altar to signify the gift of Ruach HaKadosh. Today, the Ezekiel River flows from under the temple signifying the life-giving force of Ruach HaKadosh coming from his throne in the temple's Holy of Holies. And their ceremony incorporated a lighting of large menorahs to represent the light our coming Messiah would be to us and to the world." He held up his hands, outstretched. "Today, we don't need those ceremonies. We don't need a visual representation of what is to come. We have the actuality of those ceremonies with us today. We have our King who literally dwells with us. We have Ruach HaKadosh who renews us. And we have our Messiah and King, the true light of our hearts and of the world. Behold. He is with us. He reigns before us today."

A thunderous roar was heard. It then went deathly silent as Priest Ya'akov and everyone in front looked to the palace balcony and then genuflected and bowed before their King. People did so all down the courtyard and into the streets containing the overflow. It looked like a reverse wave coming toward Janet. As did everyone else, she also bowed to the King.

Janet then heard the King speak. His words were clear and distinct. "My subjects, my children, I welcome you this evening. I thank you in advance for all the honor you bestow upon me, and I look forward to seeing all you have brought. Each of you are special to me, and I love each of you very much."

Everyone rose as an angel choir began to sing. Most people stood with eyes closed and swayed to the melodic sounds. No instruments were used, but the sounds and tones produced by the angels were mesmerizing. Others stood with arms raised. For some, the experience and the music were so overwhelming that tears streamed down their cheeks. Janet had to admit the entire experience was extremely moving.

As the sacrificing ceremony began, Janet decided she would at least try to find Bruce. She knew the odds were against her, but she also knew she would not be able to enjoy any of this without him. Periodically, she stopped to bow with the rest of the crowd as the King stood after each person gave their testimony and dedicated their lives to him.

After each one, she heard the King say, "Your sacrifice is pleasing to me, and I accept it wholeheartedly. Please take your animal for sacrifice and present it to the priest who will offer it as a memorial to what you have committed to me this day. Enter the South Gate, exit the North Gate, and wait there." The King would sit, and the people would again stand. This took place several times.

Janet kept weaving in and out among people looking for that special profile that always brought her such solace. *How did I ever live without him?* After she bowed with the crowd for the fifth time, she glanced up at the temple steps. She froze, catching a glimpse of a woman leading a lamb through the gate. It was only a brief second of seeing her disappear into the temple complex, but she wore the white dress with the colorful splotches. *Is that Molly?* Oh, why hadn't she paid attention to the voice when the woman was speaking? Janet closed her eyes and sighed. Another missed opportunity.

"Janet!" She turned. There, in front of her, was the man she loved.

"Bruce!" She put her arms around his neck and squeezed tightly. "Oh, I thought I would never find you."

"Same here."

She looked into his eyes. "That last woman on stage. Who was she?"

Bruce shook his head. "I'm sorry, Janet. I wasn't paying attention. I was looking for you."

Janet nodded. "Yeah, me too."

Bruce took her hand and they weaved their way closer to the front as the angels started singing once more. They stood next to a building where the view was decent. There was a barrel next to the door of the shop. Bruce picked Janet up and helped her sit on it. After standing for so long, sitting was a nice treat for her feet. After a while, almost everyone in the courtyard sat so they could enjoy the presentations that started after the King reappeared in the balcony after talking to each of the ones who pledged themselves to him.

For the next several hours, they saw several singing groups, duets, and solos. They saw skits, both sincere and humorous. There were praise dances, poem recitations, dramatic readings, and even magic presentations with a moral ending. Priest Ya'akov returned to the stage and told the crowd other displays could be seen in the civic center.

"I think that's my cue." Janet hopped off the barrel. "Do you want to go to the civic center, or shall I meet you back at the room?"

Bruce took Janet's hand. "Oh, I'm not letting you out of my sight again."

Janet smiled. "I'm OK with that."

Once in the civic center, Janet found her way to where Edgar and Administrator Billingsley were standing. She introduced Bruce to them, but there wasn't much time for conversation as people came up and began asking questions.

Bruce touched Janet's arm. "I'm going to look around. I'll be back in a little while."

Janet nodded and, for a few moments, watched him head to one of the sculptures. She then got pulled into conversations with others who came by. After just less than two hours, the number of people stopping by had dwindled to only a few. Looking up, she saw Bruce headed her way.

"I have a question," he said to Janet as he walked up.

"Yes, sir. What can I answer for you?"

"When can a beautiful lady walk around and look with me?"

Janet laughed. "Well, I would say about now." She turned to Edgar. "Need me anymore tonight?"

Edgar shook his head. "No, I think we're fine now. Thanks for being here. Those were some tough questions thrown our way."

Janet smiled. "No problem. I'll see you back at the office next week."

Edgar nodded.

Janet took Bruce's hand and walked with him through the civic center looking at various sculptures and other artwork.

Some were very traditional while others were more abstract. After a time, they headed back into the night air toward the Guest House.

"Before we go back," Janet said, "there's a place I want to show you."

"Oh. What's that?"

"A place that puts what we just saw to shame. It's called The Overlook."

CHAPTER 22

"Is it as good as you remember?" Bruce asked her.

Janet finished swallowing and took a sip of tea. "It's tasty."

"But?"

"I remember the falafel being more pungent and flavorful."

Bruce laughed. "Nostalgia never tastes as good as the memory which created it."

Janet shrugged. "Evidently." She put her fork down and leaned back in her chair.

Bruce leaned forward, picked up her fork, and took a bite of her falafel.

"What are you doing?"

Bruce smiled. "Creating a nostalgic moment."

Janet laughed. "Well, get prepared for a letdown next time you eat one." She shook her head. "Who am I kidding? You'd think it was wonderful each and every time."

Bruce put his elbows on the table and his head in his hands. "You OK?"

She gave a weak smile. "I'm just ready to go home."

"Well, we'll be heading home right after the closing ceremony." Bruce looked at his T-band. "In a few hours." Bruce left his head in his left hand and reached his right hand toward her across the table. "Tired of the festivities already?"

Janet leaned forward and took his hand. "It's been interesting." She propped her head in her other hand like Bruce. "Let me ask you: you haven't gotten a self-service vibe from all of these presentations?"

Bruce shifted his head in his hand. "What do you mean?"

Janet looked around to be sure no one was close. "I mean, the King says he loves us, but then everything is about him."

"But he is the King."

"I know, but it still doesn't sit right with me." She put her arm on the table. "None of this bothers you?"

Bruce took her other hand. "I guess I'm not as complicated as you. I mean, everything is going well for me. I like what I do." He intertwined his fingers in hers. "I like who I'm with."

Janet smiled.

"I just don't worry about whether the King started all of this or not. Could something better be coming?" Bruce shrugged. "I know I like the way things are, and I'm happy to be in the moment."

Janet took her hands back from Bruce and took another sip of tea. "I envy you sometimes. I feel I need more control of my life. I can't just live in the moment."

"That's why we're a great couple."

Janet cocked her head.

Bruce smiled. "If you were with someone who loved the King, they wouldn't appreciate you."

Janet raised an eyebrow and nodded.

"If you were with someone who was like you in belief, you would get too wound up creating negative energy and draw the eye of a Shepherd."

Janet chuckled.

Bruce put his hand to his chest. "I, on the other hand, help to even you out. I appreciate you." He shook his head and smiled. "No, I love you. I accept you. I am the yin to your yang."

Janet laughed. "Yes, I guess you are."

Bruce reached over again with his fork. Janet grabbed his arm.

"Well, you're not eating it."

"No. Bruce, look."

"What?"

She nodded toward the other side of the street. "Look in that shop window."

"Is that her?"

"It's the dress."

"You're going over there, aren't you?"

Janet stood. "I have to find out." She headed across the street as quickly as possible, wanting to get there before the woman had time to leave the shop.

Hurrying across the street and looking in the shop window, Janet saw the woman at the counter, so she hurried to the side of the building where the door to the shop was located. As she opened the door, there stood the woman in the white dress with colorful splotches.

Janet froze, staring at her.

She couldn't believe her eyes. It wasn't Molly. No words formed. With her mind blank, all she could do was stare.

"Excuse me."

Janet came out of her trancelike state. "What?"

"May I exit?"

"Oh, yes. I'm sorry." Janet stood to the side as the woman stepped out and walked down the street. Janet stood, unmoving, and watched the woman until she was out of sight.

She trudged back to the bistro table where Bruce was waiting; she plopped into her seat.

"So?"

"It wasn't her."

"Who was it?"

Janet shrugged.

"How did she get the dress?"

"I don't know."

Bruce laughed. "Janet, after all that, you didn't ask her any questions?"

Janet put her hands to her cheeks and shook her head. "I . . . I froze. I guess I expected her to be Molly, and when she wasn't . . . " She shrugged.

Bruce reached out and took her hand. "You may not know the why, but you did get your biggest question answered."

She nodded. Her eyes watered. "She really *is* gone."

Bruce kissed her hand. "I'm really sorry, Janet."

She nodded.

A crowd of people flooded by their table toward the temple.

Bruce stood and held out his hand. "Ready for the finale?"

Janet stood. "I'm ready for it to be over."

They got up, Bruce put his arm around her, and they walked toward the temple with the rest of the crowd.

Janet wanted to be positive like Bruce, but she was finding it hard. When the King took people like Molly, how could she be supportive of him? She looked around at people in the crowd. They were all so happy, even ecstatic. They obviously supported the King, and to what seemed like the nth degree. Should she be like that? Could she ever be like that? She just couldn't see how.

As the sun set, the angel choir began. Everyone was on their feet with hands raised, eyes closed, and most were swaying to the pure, melodic tones.

When the chorus ended, the King stood. Everyone bowed.

"My subjects, my children, I have received much honor from you. I send you forth to prosper. Always remember I am with you. Ruach HaKadosh will guide you. Just because you do not see me doesn't mean I am not there. Go, my children, in peace."

The King sat and the people rose. Priest Ya'akov came to the south gate of the temple. He held his hands wide over his head. "The Lord bless you and keep you. The Lord make his face shine upon you and be gracious to you. The Lord turn his face toward you and give you peace."

The crowd began to file out slowly. It was as if most didn't want the festival to end. Janet couldn't understand why they were not ready to get back to their regular lives. She looked at her T-band. *Two hours.* In about two hours she would be home.

The line at the long-range teleporter was long but dwindled faster than Janet expected. She and Bruce stepped onto the teleporter pad and, in a matter of seconds, were back in Middle America. Janet let out a long sigh and leaned on Bruce's arm. She never thought she would feel this way, but getting back to the farmhouse sounded wonderful.

To the side of the teleporter was everyone's luggage that had come through earlier that day. Bruce grabbed theirs and Janet followed him to their AGA.

"It's so weird. It was late in Jerusalem and all I could think about was getting to bed. Now it's the middle of the afternoon."

Bruce looked at her and smiled. "I know. But it's probably best to push through and go to bed at a regular time. Otherwise you'll be up in the middle of the night."

Once home, Janet unpacked while Bruce went out to catch up on various chores around the farm. Janet went to her office to catch up on e-mail, starting with her Chicago office work. There was not a lot to handle there since both Edgar and Administrator Billingsley had also been in Jerusalem. Happily, most of the mail was congratulatory of her presentation at the Jerusalem Civic Center booth. That helped her feel the trip had been worth the effort.

Next she focused on her encrypted mail. One was in response to her note to the Leader about her conversation with Candis and the potential stele in North Africa. She opened his response with much anticipation but sat back in disbelief at what she was reading.

We need to not be persuaded by myths and hearsay. I am confident we should focus on volcanic activity which was prominent prior to the time described as the Refreshing. That is where I want The Order to concentrate. We still have many places to explore.

Janet stood and paced the office while trying to calm down. How can someone who created such an excellent network be so dimwitted? Yes, where he found his stele was just north of a caldera, but that volcano was much, much earlier in earth's history. How did he get so obsessed with volcanoes, especially when there was other evidence to explore? Shouldn't The Order explore all leads? After all, myth and hearsay usually had foundation in fact even if it later became distorted.

By bedtime, Janet was still upset. Would her physical exhaustion overcome her mental anguish? She snuggled up to Bruce, who put his arm around her. In no time at all, Bruce was asleep and breathing in a regular rhythm. Hearing him breathe was soothing, but Janet's mind was awhirl.

It seemed obvious she would not be able to rely on the Leader's decisions. As she had already done, she would have to move things along. It was clear she had to look for the stele in Africa. The how was unclear, but the need was definite. Maybe she could somehow make the Leader think it was his idea.

Before she could formulate a plan, her exhaustion and Bruce's rhythmic breathing finally overcame her busy thoughts and she drifted to sleep.

CHAPTER 23

The next week, Janet forced herself to focus on the upcoming lodge raising. To keep this in the forefront of everyone's mind and to ensure all went as planned, she decided to come home each night from Chicago. She found it easier than she imagined. Bruce programmed his AGA so it would deliver her to the short-range teleporter in town and return on its own so he could use it during the day. In the afternoon he would send the AGA to the town square so it was waiting for her on her return. This allowed her to prepare each morning for work on her way to the teleporter. She also found, on arriving in Chicago, that her walk to the office was not much farther than her normal walk from the hotel.

Her evenings were full with visiting various women and helping them know their responsibilities for the weekend. Although not her favorite task, it was an important one, for it allowed her to make a positive impression. She got to know each family and hear specific scuttlebutt she could later use to know whom she should focus on regarding their acceptance—or nonacceptance—of the King.

The day before the scheduled building day was the Sabbath. Shepherd Morgan was holding his teaching at the ruins shortly before sundown, so Janet felt she had to attend. Janet didn't always attend Morgan's teaching classes but did come to enough to not raise suspicion. She often came home from Chicago after Sabbath sundown, and this at least appeared to give her a legitimate excuse.

Janet was amazed that all the building materials were already on-site and ready to go. It seemed the whole town had turned out. Everyone settled on the grass while some sat on various building materials. Shepherd Morgan stepped forward.

"It's an exciting day. Our goal is to have this building completed in thirty-six hours. Is everyone ready to make it happen?"

There were various shouts throughout the crowd. "Absolutely!" "You betcha!" "We can do it!"

"The first shift will be at sundown today. We will work in six-hour shifts. At the end of today's lesson, I will pass out the shift schedules. The finishing touches should be completed by 06:30 Monday morning."

Everyone applauded.

"Janet and several women have organized food, water, and snacks." He nodded. "Thank you, ladies." He turned and looked at the men. "So, men, if you struggle with strength, it won't be because of lack of sustenance." There was laughter throughout the crowd.

"Several of the women have also volunteered to help with mixing mortar and various other duties. Again, my thanks." He looked at Janet and waved for her to approach. "This whole idea was actually Janet's, so I think it only fitting she come forward and say a few words."

Janet stiffened. This was unexpected, and she had prepared nothing for a speech. She smiled nervously and went to where Shepherd Morgan stood.

"Well, thank you, Shepherd Morgan—I think."

A few in the crowd chuckled.

"I wasn't expecting to give a speech this evening. All I can say is I was impressed by how many people talked about these ruins. When Bruce showed them to me and told me why they were so special, it occurred to me we could make them even more special by having them become functional once again." She looked at Shepherd Morgan. "When I mentioned it to Shepherd Morgan, he agreed and took it from there." She looked across the crowd. "Through this, I have been able to get to know many of you faster than I ever would have otherwise. That's what makes it special to me."

Janet headed back to stand with Bruce. The crowd applauded. Shepherd Morgan stood and raised his hands to quieten the crowd.

"Thank you, Janet. Although a newcomer, we feel you are already one of us in many ways."

Janet smiled. Bruce put his arm around her and squeezed. She looked at him and smiled in return.

"I want to read a passage today that I think fits what we are doing. It is found in First Samuel chapter seven, verse twelve. It says, 'Then Samuel took a stone and set it up between Mizpah and Shen. He named it Ebenezer, saying, "Thus far has the Lord helped us."' This passage refers to a time when an enemy of Israel was attacking, and God helped them defeat their enemy. The name 'Ebenezer' means 'stone of help.'" Morgan looked across the crowd. "Our Lord, our King, has helped us and has given us a world where everything flourishes. This building, our Ebenezer, marks the turning point of that time—the demarcation of pre-Refreshing to post-Refreshing. The time when it was difficult to make a living as the land was resistant to crops by producing weeds and pestilence compared to now when it is a joy to raise crops, and in much abundance. When we use this building, let us ever remember how great and glorious is our Lord and King."

Several in the crowd applauded.

"The sun is now setting. Let us take time to eat. The first shift will start work after that."

The ladies set the food out and everyone had dinner. Antigravity lanterns were placed around the ruins so people could work through the night. Blueprints on holo-boards were posted in several places around the grounds for people to refer to and contained the order of events so those responsible for electrical, plumbing, and masonry would know what to do and when. Everyone was in high spirits.

Janet looked at one of the schedules. Her goal was to have wives work when their husbands worked. Bruce was on the first, third, and fifth shifts. Cots had been erected both outside and inside the civic center so people could rest. It seemed they would be sleeping here between shifts rather than going home. Janet organized the women so they would know when to have food, snacks, and water ready for the workers, organized the antigravity pallets to take dirt away as they were getting the foundation in place, and helped mix mortar for the stones that would be part of the foundation.

By the end of the first shift, the foundation was completed and both Janet and Bruce were exhausted.

Shepherd Morgan came by and shook their hands. "Well, Janet, the first part of your plan is finished."

Janet nodded. "I feel I'm finished as well and could fall asleep standing up."

Morgan chuckled. "I won't keep you. Just wanted you to know that we decided to make everything look pre-Refreshing but are using today's technology. The mortar we used in the foundation will be cured and ready for building in only a few hours." He smiled. "No need in doing everything old school, eh?"

Janet smiled. "Brilliant. Well, if you'll excuse us." She gave a tired wave to Morgan as she followed Bruce to the nearest cot and collapsed. The ongoing noise from the construction site didn't keep her from immediately falling asleep.

The rising sun woke Janet with the realization that their shift was ready to start again. As she looked over at Bruce, he was already tying his shoes.

Bruce looked over and smiled as she sat up. "Good morning, sleepyhead."

Janet moved and moaned. "I don't think the word 'good' fits the way I feel."

Bruce smiled. "A little sore, are we?"

Janet grunted as she sat up. "You're doing a bad job on your adjectives this morning."

Bruce laughed as he stood. He held out his hand and pulled her up. She moaned again but followed him toward the ruins.

Janet was amazed at how much work had been done while they slept. Half the walls were already erected. After eating a muffin and yogurt, she went back to mixing mortar while Bruce helped lay more stone. She found it intriguing how the plumbers and electricians interwove their work among those who were laying stone. Everyone looked like ants moving here and there. From a distance it looked chaotic, but up close she could see everyone had a designated job and was performing it faithfully.

At noon the next shift started. After she and Bruce got a bite to eat, they sat on the grass under a nearby tree, rested, and watched.

Bruce looked at Janet and smiled. "I'm amazed at what you've done here, Janet. Everyone is so gung-ho. It has really revitalized our town. I'm so proud of you." He reached over and gave her a kiss.

"Get a room."

Bruce looked up. "Mom! I didn't know you were here."

Janet stiffened and prepared for more tension. She hadn't had much interaction with Bruce's mom since their reception.

Mrs. O'Brien sat on the grass facing them. She reached out and put her hand on Janet's arm. "Janet, I owe you an apology."

Janet, stunned, was unable to say anything. She never expected this.

"Forgive an old woman. I was hurt and selfish. So many people have told me about all you have done. It makes me ashamed of my actions."

Janet put her plate down and placed a hand on top of her mother-in-law's. "Mrs. O'Brien . . . "

"Mildred. Call me Mildred."

Janet smiled. "Mildred, first of all, you're beautiful. And second, I do accept your apology and look forward to getting to know you better."

Mildred laughed, her cheeks slightly red. "Now you're just buttering me up."

Janet patted her hand. "No, I really mean it." Janet could see where Bruce got his good looks. She smiled to herself. His easygoing nature must have come from his father. His mother seemed temperamental. Yet she was beautiful, even being at least twice Janet's age but looking not much older than she.

Janet had seen others who claimed to have lived prior to the Refreshing, and most of them appeared much older than anyone born after that time.

"Well, I hope we can start again. I want to be a part of your life," Mildred said.

"Same here."

Mildred stood. "Let me go find John. He's helping out on this shift."

She walked away. Bruce looked at Janet with raised eyebrows. "Miracles still happen."

Janet laughed. "Well, I'm glad that tension has eased."

"For now."

Janet looked at Bruce and slapped his shoulder playfully. "Come on now."

Bruce shrugged. "I'm just saying. She's very temperamental. Who knows how long this truce will last?"

"Let's just savor it while it does."

Bruce put his arm around her. "Agreed."

After eating and resting for a while, they took a walk around the town square and through part of town. When they came back they went to the civic center to try and get a couple hours of sleep before the next shift started.

They ate again just before their shift. Again it amazed Janet how much work was accomplished each shift. They were already working on the roof. By midnight the roof was completed and most of the windows installed. Now it was a matter of hanging a few doors, adding some finishing touches like the fireplace mantel, window boxes, a sidewalk, and some plants around the building. Since this was Bruce's last shift, and Janet had to work the next day, they headed home rather than waiting until the final six-hour shift was finished. Janet's plan was simple: home, shower, bed.

The next morning Bruce drove Janet to the town square. Both were anxious to see the final product. Janet would be at work a little later than normal, but her scheduled meeting with Edgar wasn't until 10:30, so she wasn't too concerned. They arrived at the lodge around 09:15.

"Bruce, it's beautiful." The building sat by itself nestled among the trees. The roof was a red metal and matched some of the reddish hues in the stones making up the lodge walls. The front door was made of clear glass; it was the only modern part of the building. There was a stone sidewalk going up to it from the path, and flowering shrubbery had been planted around the lodge adding to its charm. There was nothing left from the night before. It looked like the lodge had been in place for a long time.

Next to the door was a bronze plaque. It read:

We have raised our Ebenezer (1Sa 7:12). This building demarks the change from pre-Refreshing to our current Refreshing, and from whom our help comes. Let us give glory and honor to our King.

Janet wasn't exactly sure why, but the words on the plaque annoyed her. *Why did everything have to be tied to the King?* Couldn't this simply be a building for the sake of enjoyment and use by the community? Could one not simply think for themselves anymore?

They opened the front door and looked in. While it looked old, the smell was definitely new. Janet gasped when she saw the fireplace. It was huge, and the raised hearth went from wall to wall.

Janet looked at Bruce. "I'm amazed that someone would have something like this inside their house." She shook her head. "An open fire confined within a building? Unbelievable."

"I can't wait to see it in action."

Janet raised her eyebrows. "You mean you plan to use it?"

Bruce chuckled. "It's functional. Why not?"

"Are . . . you sure it's safe?"

"Well, people used these for millennia before the Refreshing."

Janet cocked her head. "Well, you don't see people using them today. Doesn't that tell you we've wised up?"

Bruce chuckled and put his arm around her. "Maybe. Come on. You're going to be late—er."

Janet laughed. "Good point. But you're just trying to avoid a debate you know you can't win."

Bruce laughed and walked her to the teleporter. He kissed her and Janet stepped onto the pad. Once she pressed the button, Bruce went blurry, disappeared, and tall buildings next came into view.

She sighed, took a deep breath, and headed toward the office.

CHAPTER 24

Everything at work seemed back to normal for Janet. The cobalt-colored receptionist desk was replaced. Emily had been hired in Molly's place. She had long, straight jet-black hair and carried a very professional demeanor. Janet had nothing against Emily. But seeing her always brought back bad memories of the day Molly was taken.

Several days after being back, after getting settled in her office one morning, Janet went to see Edgar. He motioned for her to have a seat on the sofa in front of the large window that overlooked her favorite park across the street.

"Janet, being at the honoring ceremony the other week has kept our communicators busy ever since," he said as he walked around the couch to have a seat, coffee in hand.

"Oh? What about?"

Edgar smiled. "I think everyone wants to be on the bandwagon of what you started. Knowing the Jerusalem Science Center is supporting it makes everyone want to be a part of it."

"What do you want me to do? More trips?"

Edgar set his coffee down, stood, and paced.

Uh-oh. This can't be good. Janet looked at him wondering if he had bad news, but Edgar looked too happy for that.

He stopped and turned to her. "I want you to train some-one and have them go on these trips."

Janet's head jerked back slightly. "Why?"

Edgar gestured with open hands while cocking his head. "Janet, you now have a husband. Plus, you can't travel every-where all the time. You need a succession plan so others can do what you do and know what you know."

"And who do you have in mind?"

Edgar sat down again. "Remember James from the satellite office?"

A sandy blond-haired man came to mind. He had always struck Janet as eager and smart. She nodded. "He's definitely someone I think I could work with."

"Good. I'll have him come in next week so you can go over plans with him. When you're working from home, I could have him use your office." He paused. "You OK with that?"

Janet shrugged. "Sure."

Edgar stood. "Wonderful. Thanks, Janet."

Janet headed back to her office, read some of her mail, and sat for a bit in thought. Maybe with James taking on more things she could work more from home and be with Bruce even more. This too came to mind: *What is James's dedication to the King? Could he be another asset?*

Janet went for a late lunch. Although not very hungry, she wanted to get out of the office and think. While eating yogurt and granola, she window-shopped. After about twenty min-utes, she sat at an outside bistro table and did some people watching.

She was almost ready to order some tea but then did a double take of a shop window across the street. Someone in that same white dress with bright colored splotches stood near a jewelry store window. Janet watched in disbelief. So the woman she saw in Jerusalem was from Chicago? What were the odds? She had to know who it was and how she got that dress. Janet hurried across the street.

As Janet opened the door to the shop, there stood the woman in her one-of-a-kind dress. But it wasn't the woman she had seen in Jerusalem!

"*Molly!?*" Janet couldn't believe her eyes.

A bright smile lit up Molly's face. "Janet! Oh, I was hoping I'd get a chance to see you."

Janet stood with mouth open. "How . . . when . . . what . . . ?"

Molly laughed. "I guess seeing me is more of a surprise than I thought it would be." She pointed. "Can we go across the street and talk over tea?"

Janet nodded and followed her. They sat at the same bistro table she was at before the startling discovery. They ordered, and Janet leaned back in her chair, blown away by what she was seeing.

"Molly, I just can't believe you're here." She put her hand to her cheek and shook her head. "How *are* you here?"

Molly laughed. "It's been the most wonderful and surreal experience ever."

"What happened?"

"Let me try and start from the beginning. Do you have time for the story?"

Janet nodded. Actually, she didn't care if she did or didn't. She *had* to hear what Molly had to say.

The waiter came over with tea. Molly took a sip and sat up. "At one of Amanda's meetings, a new person, Jeff, came." She shook her head slightly. "Hearing him tell his story was very upsetting. I'm not sure why it upset me so, but it really did.

The next day, I heard about what happened when you went to China—you know, about the farmer who also got taken by the King."

Janet nodded.

"It seemed like that was the last straw for me. I was so upset I couldn't stay in the office. As I was walking around, I remembered Jeff's grandfather worked at your hotel. I went there to try and find Jeff—and there he was. He was visiting his grandfather. We talked for a while. He was supportive and mentioned what he would like to do to his Administrator."

Janet reached out and put her hand on Molly's arm. "Molly, he wasn't really serious. He was just venting."

Molly smiled. "Yeah, I know. I knew then, too. Yet, as I was walking back, I started thinking: Why not do it and make her understand how upsetting it was to have them take people against their will?" Molly shook her head. "I wasn't really thinking what would happen to me if I did something like that."

Janet took a sip of her tea. So far, Molly's story was just as Jeff had told it.

"On the way back, I remembered some remodeling was being done on the fourteenth floor. I stopped there and found . . . the metal bar. I walked up the stairs, letting anger get the better of me with each stair I climbed. By the time I reached the office, I was literally out of control. For some reason, seeing my desk put me in a rage. I remember hitting and hitting it until it burst into pieces."

Janet leaned in. "What happened next?"

"I remember Administrator Billingsley yelling something like, 'What are you doing?'" Molly shook her head. "For some reason, that made my blood boil. I must have looked like a lunatic because I remember her eyes getting wide as she retreated back into her office. I walked into her office and started doing the same to her desk. She stood there with her hand over her mouth. I think I started laughing."

"Why?"

Molly shook her head. "I don't know. I think I was really losing it. I remember raising the bar and backing the Administrator into the corner. I don't really know if I was going to hurt her or not. I took another step toward her and then . . . I was standing in an empty room. The bar wasn't in my hand."

Janet's eyes widened. "Where were you?"

"At first I didn't know. A door opened and a man came in telling me the King wanted to see me. I was terrified. I remember thinking, *So this is what happens when someone gets taken.* He motioned for me to follow him. I knew this was the end of me."

"But . . . you're here now. How . . . ? I mean, I'm glad. But how did that happen?"

Molly smiled. "I'm getting there." She took another sip of tea. "The man pointed down a hallway. He didn't walk with me. I got to the corner, turned, and froze. There before me were two large angels guarding an even larger door. They were dressed in blue with gold sashes and a large sword sheathed on their backs. I approached them very slowly. One of the angels opened the door and motioned for me to enter."

Janet found herself gripping the edge of the table, knuckles white. She let go and tried to relax.

Molly gave a short laugh. "I half expected the angels to take my head off as I walked through. I was so scared. As I entered, the King was sitting on a throne between two large angel statues bowing toward the throne. The room was square with four large archways on each side exiting to a balcony surrounding the throne room."

"You were in the King's throne room?" Janet found that simply amazing.

Molly nodded. "He approached. I was so nervous. Yet he didn't look mad or angry. He had a calmness about him I couldn't explain. He asked if I knew why I was there. I nodded. He then asked me a series of questions. But he never seemed judgmental."

"Really?" That was not what Janet expected. "So what happened then?"

"At the end of a fairly long talk, he asked if I believed him to be my Lord, King, and hope for my future. At that moment I knew I really did believe that. There was no other hope that made sense. He put his hand on my shoulder. I felt a warmness flood through me. It's hard to explain how that felt. That's when it happened."

Janet turned up her brow. "What?"

"I felt this sense of freedom sweep over me. It came so fast and swift I gasped. The King smiled and said, 'Welcome to the family, Molly.'"

"What did he mean?"

Molly put her hand on Janet's. "Janet, I received Ruach HaKadosh."

Janet pulled her hand away. "What?"

"My future is secure because of my acceptance of the King. After my sacrificing ceremony—"

"So . . . so that *was* you. At the ceremony. I was there. But . . . didn't really get to hear you speak."

Molly nodded. "He told me I was an empathetic person, yet I had never developed my talents in the right way. Now he allows me to help others who are confused about their thoughts concerning the King. I can help counsel them and help them see the truth."

"And what truth are you spreading?"

Molly smiled. "The King is the hope of our eternal future."

"And . . . you're certain of that?" Janet was dumbfounded by everything she was hearing. And saddened she had most likely lost a true friend.

"Absolutely. Others confirmed that for me at our fellowship offering."

Janet squinted.

Molly laughed. "I know. It's all new to me too." She took another sip of tea. "Others there, similar to me, suggested we do a fellowship offering together. The priest manning the temple ovens prepared part of the sacrifice for us and we sat in one of the chambers along the temple wall, ate, talked, told our stories, and talked about what we wanted to do now that we accepted our King."

Janet's eyes widened. "You ate meat?"

Molly put her hand to her mouth and giggled. "I know. I always thought only fish with scales was allowed. But it was good—and symbolic."

Janet shook her head slightly. It was like Molly was a completely different person. She could hardly believe what she was hearing. "Symbolic?"

Molly finished her tea and set her cup to the side. "It was really special, actually. Not what I thought I'd ever be doing. But since our King was our sacrifice long ago, the sacrifices today are symbolic of that. By us partaking of our offering, it is symbolic of us internalizing him into our lives." She sat back with a satisfied smile. "Quite apropos, don't you think?"

"And you're certain of all of this?"

Molly nodded. "How else would I be here today rather than in the place of lost souls?"

Janet was stunned, not really sure of anything. She looked at her T-band. "Oh, my. I really must get going. Sorry, Molly. I wish you all the best."

Molly stood as though she wanted to hug Janet, but then just spoke. "Well, take care, Janet."

Janet stood, took a step, but then turned back. "Oh, wait. Did someone else use your dress while in Jerusalem? I met someone with that same dress on—but it wasn't you."

Molly laughed. "Yes. Another girl just loved my dress, so I let her wear it one day."

Janet nodded, smiled, and walked away, leaving Molly behind, and headed toward the office. *Amanda.* Janet looked at her T-band. She should get back to the office, but this was too important, so she headed toward Amanda's boutique.

Amanda was working behind the counter when she arrived.

Amanda smiled. "Janet, what brings you by?"

"Amanda, do you have a minute?" She looked around. "Are you alone?"

Amanda came from behind the counter. Her tone was now much more serious. "It's just me. What's wrong?"

"I just saw Molly."

Amanda nodded and leaned back on the counter. "She was here not too long ago."

Janet's eyebrows went up. "Really? What did she say?"

"Well, she wanted to know when the next meeting was being held so she could talk to everyone."

Janet's mouth fell open. "What did you say?"

Amanda shrugged. "What could I say? Because of the trauma of her being taken, the meeting place here was disbanded."

"Have you moved where you meet?"

Amanda nodded. "One of the members is a chocolatier, and he has room in the back of his shop. It isn't far from here, so it's really not an inconvenience for anyone."

"That was fast thinking."

Amanda smiled. "Thank you. I thought so." She turned her head. "How could Molly go so quickly from not liking the King to being so pro-King?"

Janet shrugged. "It must be some type of brainwashing. She certainly doesn't sound like the same Molly." Janet paused in thought. "She said when the King put his hand on her shoulder she felt different."

"You think he did something?"

"Maybe." She shook her head. "I don't know. But it would explain a lot of things."

Amanda put her hand on Janet's arm. "Janet, be careful."

Janet nodded. "You too."

Janet left the boutique and headed back to her office. *Could Molly have been right?* But why was there evidence to the contrary? Does the King remove those he can't control and brainwash those he can? Was there any truth to what Molly said? Janet shook her head. No, she needed more evidence to the contrary of what she had already discovered to believe that.

She would stay in Chicago tonight and see what she could find out.

CHAPTER 25

Janet felt badly telling Bruce she was staying in Chicago this night. They both enjoyed being together each night, but she had some thinking to do. She prepared some tea and sat in her favorite chair on the balcony.

How could she know if Molly was right, or if her own intuition was right? It was important to find this next stele. The Overtaker had been prophesied, but what more was prophesied? This had to be a priority. Yet, she reminded herself, The Order Leader would not be supportive of what she felt she needed to do. No matter. Zuri was supportive of the cause, and he already knew of the stele rumor. She would just have to contact him outside The Order.

She needed a plan for that to happen. She couldn't do it directly. *Jeff. He's a geologist.* Not exactly an archaeologist, but a close runner-up, and someone who could engage Zuri with questions without being suspicious. All she had to do was get them connected.

She looked at her T-band. Not too late for a call. She dialed Amanda.

"Hi, Amanda. This is Janet."

Amanda's holographic image came on.

"Janet. Anything wrong?"

"Yes, and no." She laughed. "Sorry. That was cryptic, wasn't it? I wanted to talk with you over breakfast if you don't mind."

"Sounds urgent."

"I need to call someone several time zones ahead, but I'd like your input first."

"OK. Meet me at the coffee shop just around the corner from my office at 08:15."

Janet smiled. "Terrific. I'll see you in the morning."

Janet headed to bed. She always slept better when she had a plan for the issues bothering her.

The next morning, Janet arrived first and ordered tea and a scone both for herself and Amanda.

Amanda arrived only minutes later and sat across from her. "Janet, what's so urgent? I didn't sleep well after your call. I kept fearing it was something ominous."

Janet laughed. "I'm sorry, Amanda. Actually, the reason I called last night was so I could get some sleep."

Amanda looked a little frustrated at that, but laughed. "OK, so spill it."

"First, how's the relationship between you and Jeff?"

Amanda cocked her head. "Fine. Why?"

Janet put her hand on Amanda's. "No, I mean how *is* it?"

Amanda chuckled. "Oh, well, we've gone out a few times. It may be getting serious." She shrugged. "I don't see a ring in my immediate future."

"Well, how about a vacation to enhance that?"

Amanda gave a blank stare. "Wh . . . what are you talking about, Janet?"

"There's a rumor of a stone stele in northeastern Africa. The people we met in Iceland were from the territory south of there and run a safari sightseeing agency. If you go there and engage them in conversation about the stele, perhaps Jeff can see if he can find it." Janet leaned in. "Do you think Jeff would be interested in doing something like that?"

Amanda took a sip of tea as she thought. "Well, I'm sure he would. The real question is, can he take the time to do that?" She looked up at Janet. "How long will it take?"

Janet ran her finger around the lip of her teacup. "Amanda, I can't answer that. He may have to take many trips to find it." She glanced at Amanda. "All I'm saying is, for now, make contact with those that know something and follow up on clues." Janet shrugged. "It could take years, but I'm absolutely not saying to stay there until it's found. Just to continue looking as you can until it's found."

Amanda sighed. "Well, I can certainly ask. I'll let you know what he says."

Janet put her hand on Amanda's. "Thanks, Amanda. This could lead to important information for our cause."

Amanda nodded.

They had some light conversation, finished their scone and tea, and headed to work.

Because of the six-hour time difference, Janet called Zuri shortly after arriving at the office.

"Good afternoon, this is Zuri Turay. May I help you with a safari tour?"

"Yes, please. Do you have a discount from Iceland?"

Zuri activated his holographic display. "Janet! It's so good to see you again. What's up?"

"Hi, Zuri. It's great seeing you again as well. Is business good?"

"Well, we're busy with the Sabbath Year safari right now."

"I have some friends who would like to go on a safari. How soon could they take one?"

Zuri smiled. "If it was anyone else, I would say six months."

Janet's eyebrows went up. "That long?"

"I did say, if anyone else. We state each tour is eight to ten people. We usually keep it at eight as we want to keep them fairly intimate. I can include your friends next month if you, and they, want."

"Thank you, Zuri. You're wonderful."

Zuri laughed. "Well, spread that word. Are your friends married, engaged, or just friends?"

"Does it matter?"

"Well, as I said, these tours make the group tight-knit. If married, we would pair them with other married folks. If just friends, we would put them with other singles." Zuri smiled. "Believe it or not, we've gotten a good success rate for proposals on these trips."

Janet laughed. "Well, they are good friends, but at least one of them would wish it to be more."

Zuri nodded. "OK. I have just the tour for them. I'll forward you some information for them to fill out, and we can take it from there."

"Thanks, Zuri. I really appreciate this. Tell Candis hello for me. And Chika and Afia as well."

"Will do. Expect the information within the next day or two. Take care."

The connection ended.

Janet sat back in her chair and smiled. Her plan was now in motion. It was up to Amanda and Jeff to take it from here.

Edgar stuck his head in. "Have a minute?"

Janet nodded and motioned for him to come in. He sat in the clear Plexiglas chair next to her desk.

"Um, I wasn't expecting you in the office today."

"Oh, well, something came up and I didn't make it home, so I—" A light dawned for Janet. "Oh. Oh, you were going to have James work *here* today."

Edgar nodded. He held up his hands, palms out. "But this is fine. I can talk to both of you together. Mind coming to my office?"

Janet stood. "Sure. No problem."

When they entered Edgar's office, James stood.

James came over and shook her hand. "Hello, Janet. It's good to see you again."

Janet smiled and touched his jaw. "I like the thin beard. It suits you."

James smiled. "Thanks. I thought it a classy look to go with my new hairstyle, don't you think?"

"You were always classy, James." His hair was a buzz cut to just above his ears and then longer on top, giving a contemporary flair.

James laughed. "I've missed you at the satellite office. I'm really looking forward to working with you again."

"Wonderful," Janet said.

Edgar motioned for both to have a seat. They sat in one of the chairs facing Edgar's desk, and he sat behind it.

Edgar spent the next hour going over his expectations of both of them for how they should work together. Janet spent another hour or more going over her findings with James at the small conference table in Edgar's office, her findings projected from the large monitor.

"This is all very interesting," James said, gesturing to the monitor. "This is really impressive work." He looked between Edgar and Janet. "So you want me to take the calls that come in, help address questions, and travel to various places to monitor the progress?"

Edgar nodded. "That summarizes it pretty well."

"And, of course, feel free to discuss any insights you see or find," Janet said. "I'm the first to admit my work can be improved upon."

James laughed. "I don't think anyone believes the Singleton Equation can be improved upon."

Janet's head jerked back slightly. "The what?"

James looked between the two of them. "That's . . . that's what everyone is calling it. The Singleton Equation maximizes the teleporter efficiency between crops and human transport."

"Edgar, did you know about this? I should have been asked before such a name was used."

Edgar shook his head. "I heard someone mention it, but I had no idea it was being widely used."

"Well, I want it stopped. I don't want it to be called that."

James laughed. "Janet, it's way too late for that."

She scrunched her brow. "What do you mean?"

"It's all over the nebula servers. There's no way to retract it now even if you wanted to."

Janet sighed and shook her head between her thumb and first two fingers. "Unbelievable."

Edgar stood and patted her shoulder. He laughed. "You're famous, Janet. Get used to it."

Janet stood. "I'm heading back to my office. James, stop by before you leave today."

James nodded.

For the rest of the day, Janet searched the nebula servers to see where the term "Singleton Equation" originated. She kept reminding herself it wasn't necessarily a bad thing. It could only help her career, but someone had to have started it.

Late in the day, James stuck his head in her office door. "You wanted to see me?"

Janet motioned for him to come in and sit.

"Anything else you want to tell me, James?"

James scrunched his brow. "I'm not following you. About what?"

Janet handed him a piece of paper. As soon as James looked at it, his shoulders slumped. He looked at her sheepishly.

"I'm sorry, Janet. I didn't really mean for this to go viral. I was just trying to get the satellite office some exposure."

"So, you sent a memo to Administrator Billingsley stating the 'Singleton Equation' was really a product of the satellite office?"

James squirmed in his seat. "I didn't know what else to call it. I wasn't trying to coin a phrase. I was trying to put a spotlight on our office."

"Was that it?"

"The Administration has never fairly treated the employees at the satellite office." His eyes widened. "I mean . . . not until you gave it to us."

"And now you."

James smiled nervously and nodded.

Janet breathed deep and left an intended pause. Then she leaned back and slid a piece of paper across the desk toward James. "Well, tell you what. If you ever want to get something nice for someone, check out the Tell Your Story boutique." Janet smiled. "The owner has some unique merchandise."

James looked from the paper to Janet as though unsure if there was a connection, some kind of hidden message. "Thanks. I'll certainly check it out." He stood.

Before he left, Janet said, "I'll send you a work schedule of when you and I can use this office."

James nodded and left.

Janet sat back in her chair. Things were coming together. Hearing James's response, and seeing his strong ambition, may mean he would be receptive to their cause. She only had to let Amanda in on today's doings and see if James would come to one of her meetings. He could be a strong asset if things with Amanda and Jeff worked out.

Janet wanted to call Amanda but decided to leave a little early and stop by on her way to the hotel.

CHAPTER 26

The next several months went according to Janet's plans. James indeed became a regular at Amanda's meetings. He even led the meetings when Amanda and Jeff were away.

Amanda and Jeff were instant hits with Zuri and Candis. Janet received so many pictures from Amanda they made her feel she was almost there with them. As in Iceland, Candis seemed more willing to discuss the African stele than Zuri. Despite the good rapport Jeff had established with him, Zuri seemed to clam up when questioned. When Amanda told Janet about this, Janet knew she likely had to break The Order code of anonymity between core members. One evening while they talked on their communicators, Janet tried to get more direct answers from Amanda.

"Amanda, have you really explored all options with Zuri?"

"Janet, I don't know what else to tell you. One minute, Zuri and Jeff are practically finishing each other's sentences, and then as soon as Jeff asks a question about the stele, it's like a switch has been turned."

"Let me think about this and I'll get back to you," Janet said.

Janet disconnected and sat back in her chair. Was there a way to keep anonymity and still get Zuri to see the steps that must be taken despite the Leader's preference?

One night while staying at her hotel room, Janet looked more closely at the encrypted program the Leader had given her. She remembered that when the Leader called a meeting, he always gave a code for each member to type into the program. There was no electronic address to input. When each of them entered that particular code, they all came onscreen one at a time. Pulling down one of the choices, she saw a place for "input authentication code." So, if she put in a code and only gave that code to Zuri, it should be private between the two of them. She was unsure if that was indeed the case, but believed it worth trying.

Janet called Amanda.

"Hi, Amanda. Are you alone?"

"Hi, Janet. Yes, I'm alone at the moment. Jeff should be along any minute."

"OK. I have a message for you to give to Zuri. Please take it down exactly as I dictate it. That's really important."

"OK, Janet. You're sounding so mysterious."

Janet laughed, then paused. "No, it's just important."

"Ready. Shoot."

Janet spoke slowly. "All capitals here: A-M-A-F, dash, one-zero-one. Time for meeting: nineteen hundred tonight. Give this to who you know needs it for a private conversation." Janet slowly repeated the message.

"What is that supposed to mean?"

"Just give it to Zuri—tomorrow. If he asks where you got it, just state it was given to you to deliver to him, and that's all you know."

Amanda chuckled. "Well, that *is* all I know."

"Thanks, Amanda. Just deliver. No explanation. No names."

"Got it. Don't understand it. But got it."

"Thanks, Amanda."

Janet ended the communication. Well, the message was delivered. Hopefully, Zuri would understand, use the code, and put it into the encrypted program as usual. If she understood correctly, it should establish a link between the two of them. Anonymity would be maintained. At least hers would be.

The next day, Janet left work early. No one asked why, so she didn't volunteer any information. She grabbed a to-go lunch on the way back to the hotel and prepared her tablet for the teleconference with Zuri—or who she believed to be Zuri. It was six hours later where Zuri lived, so she had to be prepared for the conversation at thirteen hundred her time.

She entered the code, sat back, and waited.

At 13:01 her screen split and another silhouette appeared. The word *Africa* appeared below it. It always felt strange talking to a silhouette and going by continent names rather than something personal, but this was what was necessary.

"Good evening, Africa. I'm glad you could join me."

"This is highly irregular. What is this meeting about?" Again, the silhouette looked like Zuri, but voices were also altered. Totally necessary, she knew, but it frustrated her curiosity.

"It has come to my attention a stele may be found in the northeastern African territory."

There was silence. Too much silence for Janet's liking. She started to say something, but the voice from Africa responded.

"Why are you interested in the stele? The Leader was very clear as to our direction."

"And you are comfortable with that decision?"

"Well . . . why wouldn't I be?"

Janet raised an eyebrow. Being hesitant only made it clear he was not one hundred percent convinced the Leader was correct.

"I don't think we have the luxury to explore preferences and not all leads," she answered. "This is a lead we should not ignore."

"Why should I trust you?"

"My dear sir. We are all on the same side, or we wouldn't be so highly invested in being so covert. I haven't included the Leader because we need to provide proof to him to get him to see the truth and the direction we need to go."

"It seems disloyal."

"The Order isn't about loyalty, even though the Leader wants it to be that. It's about being sure everything is prepared for the coming Overtaker. Do you want to tell him you didn't do all you could to prepare for his coming?"

Janet could see him shaking his head.

"We're not in a social club," Janet said. "We are gathering evidence for our cause and to prepare for his coming. Do you want to be part of that?"

"Well, yes." He sounded defensive. "What do you propose?"

"Let's look for that stele. Even myth has its foundation in truth no matter how distorted it gets. We just have to filter through all of that to find it."

"You obviously have a plan, or you wouldn't have called me."

"There is a couple with Zuri Turay. They have asked questions about the stele. I . . . we . . . you . . . should have Zuri be helpful to them in looking for the stele."

"You are connected to this . . . couple?"

"I know of them. Yes. And what they seek."

Again, silence.

Janet went on. "If nothing is found, then the Leader has to know nothing about this." Janet could see a visible relaxation in the man's body posture. "If it is found, then it will, hopefully, put the Leader on the right path to success. Wouldn't he want that?"

The man nodded. "Yes. Your plan does make sense." Janet saw him sit straighter and felt more energy in his voice. "I will speak to Zuri and ask him to be helpful. Just know the stele may not be easy to find."

"Understood. But a trip begins with one step."

The man laughed. "Cliché. But true." There was a pause. "We should stay in touch."

"Agreed. Use the code I provided for private communication. You can leave a message for when to meet and I can do the same."

"Very good. I'll keep you posted."

The communicator went silent, the man's image disappeared, and the split screen went black.

Janet turned off her communicator and sat back. Her plan was in motion. If this proved successful, they all would be closer in preparing for the Overtaker's coming—and understanding the prophecy of his coming even before that.

CHAPTER 27

To Janet's surprise, life turned into a routine. She had seen it happen to her parents and friends and neighbors, but she always swore it would not happen to her. She never wanted mundane. Yet somehow, it had happened. It wasn't a bad mundane, just . . . mundane.

She and James worked out a schedule that worked wonderfully. Amanda and Jeff traveled to Africa periodically to look for the stele, and James helped things run smoothly back home at the chapter meetings, as Amanda now called them. Jeff and Amanda had stayed in Africa for several weeks on their first trip but had to return to America for their jobs. Jeff returned often—on his free time, to avoid suspicion—and Amanda would travel with him whenever she could.

Janet's talks with Zuri (a.k.a. "Africa") increased in frequency. He tried to find additional information to pass to Jeff when he visited, but Zuri also had obligations to fulfill. This was all taking much more time than Janet wished.

The weeks turned into a year.

What scared Janet even more was the routineness developing between she and Bruce. He was as doting as ever, but he too got lost in his farming, and she in both her work in Chicago and with The Order. And she now began to wonder if she had judged the Leader too harshly. She was now as adamant in finding the African stele as he was in searching ancient volcano sites for them. So who really was the more stubborn?

One week, Janet arrived back at the farm in the AGA and planned to work from there for the next couple of days. It was James's turn to work in the Chicago office. She headed to her office to set up for the night's teleconference with The Order.

As she sat at her desk in front of the picture window, she saw Bruce in the field on the antigravity harvester gathering wheat. She knew he would be out there until at least sundown. She tried to understand how he could enjoy farming as much as he did. She had to smile because it was just who Bruce was. After all, she knew that about him when they married. Plus, when he was out late, he always made it up to her. This was the only part that was not mundane in her life now. He always surprised her with a massage, breakfast in bed, or something even more intimate.

Not being a farm girl, she was nevertheless really into this farm guy.

The meeting time came, and Janet entered the Leader's code in the encrypted program. Her monitor divided into six rectangles, and each silhouette appeared in one of them in succession.

"Ah, we're all here." *The Leader's typical response,* Janet thought. "Let's have each of you give an update. North America, perhaps you go first this time."

Janet cleared her throat. "Thank you, sir. We have made some good progress in that we now have small cells in Atlanta, Vancouver, and Tijuana. And one of the members in the larger Chicago cell is proving very solid and developing into a leader in his own right."

"That's excellent to hear," the Leader said. "While we're not growing rapidly, we are growing steadily, even though we lose some along the way."

Molly immediately came to Janet's mind. Many in Amanda's group had some close calls with her. "Yes, sir," Janet said. "It seems a group of individuals called counselors are popping up everywhere creating quite the counterbalance."

Asia chimed in. "They are not only in North America. We have several throughout China as well. It seems the Religion Department of the Jerusalem Science Center has created a new branch of administration under which these people operate and report."

The Leader's tone sounded heavy. "Yes, there is now a department and an Administrator of Reconciliation. I believe that is what they are calling it now."

"No matter," the voice from Africa replied. "We are still more in number than a year ago."

"That is true." The Leader's tone became less somber. "We should capitalize on our successes. Once we find the other steles, more will come to our cause and see the error of the King."

"Any more success?" the voice from Australia asked.

"Not yet, but we still have several leads to follow."

Janet rolled her eyes. *Good thing I'm silhouetted.* She couldn't help herself. This had become the Leader's mantra. How many more times could she hear it without literally groaning? There just had to be a way to increase her chances of finding the African stele.

The others gave updates—mostly routine—and the Leader ended the call as usual. "Until the Overtaker," he said, his usual way of signing off.

They each repeated the phrase, and the individual screens went black.

Janet leaned back in her chair and sighed. She needed to do some thinking, but after hearing the Leader ramble, her brain felt like mush. Upon hearing a light rap on the French doors, she turned in her chair just as Bruce entered.

She smiled and stood. He came over and gave her a hug followed by a kiss. He put his arms around her and led her out of the room.

"Where are we going?"

He smiled. "Just a few rooms over."

He led her to the master bath. She gasped with delight. Bruce had drawn her a bubble bath with candles all around. Soft music played in the background.

She turned and gave him a kiss. "I don't deserve you."

He held her and, with lips only millimeters from hers, replied, "True." He smiled. "But it's all your fault really."

"Oh, is it?"

"Uh-huh. You shouldn't have thrown the gauntlet down that first night in the restaurant."

"Oh, is that what I did?"

"You made winning you a challenge. I always rise to a challenge."

He unzipped her dress as he held her, and she stepped out of it.

"Now take your bath while I fix us some tea."

She didn't let go of him. "Us?"

"Uh-huh. You get a few minutes alone." He got a wicked grin. "Then you're mine."

"Well. Hurry up with that tea, then."

He gave her a quick kiss and left the bathroom.

Janet finished undressing and stepped into the tub. The water was warm and inviting. As she sat she felt the heat go all the way through her, and this elicited a long "ahh" from her lips. As she leaned back in the tub, the bubbles covered her to the neck. There was an aroma of roses as she stirred the water. Every muscle in her body relaxed—one by one. She closed her eyes and let the warm water do its work.

Janet was unsure how long it was before Bruce returned; she must have dosed for a short time. He came back with the tea—delivering it in his birthday suit. With the glow of the candles and his muscular frame, he looked like a Greek god carrying the tray. He sat the tray on the edge of the tiled tub and got in the tub opposite her.

Bruce leaned back and placed his feet next to her head. He took her foot and began to slowly massage it. Another "ahh" unconsciously escaped her lips. "Of all the things you have done, this has to rank as one of the highest," she said.

Bruce laughed. "That's good to know. It was one of the easiest, and cheapest."

Janet kicked water at him with her free foot. "Now, don't go and spoil it. This is too wonderful."

Bruce laughed again. "Yes, ma'am."

Janet was unsure how long they were in the tub, but she didn't care. They didn't talk. She leaned back and enjoyed the music and foot rub and drifted in and out of a dreamlike state. Bruce finally stood, causing her to come back to reality. He stepped out of the tub and, after helping her step out and giving her a towel, raised a terrycloth robe, which Janet slipped into. Bruce donned one as well. He picked her up in his arms and carried her into the bedroom.

"Now you're mine."

Janet wrapped her arms around his neck and put her head on his chest. All she said was, "Yes, sir."

The next morning when Janet awoke, Bruce was no longer in bed. She turned over. On the side table was a tray with tea, hot water, cereal, milk, and a muffin. Apparently Bruce was already out doing chores. She sat up in bed, prepared the tea, and ate about half the cereal. Setting the tray to the side, she grabbed her stomach, feeling nauseous. She whipped back the covers and ran to the bathroom, throwing up the cereal she just ate.

She washed her face and looked at herself in the mirror. Never had she been nauseous before—not truly nauseous. Nausea sometimes came when she teleported, but that was fleeting. This felt different. Being "sick" was ancient terminology no one used anymore. She had never heard of anyone being ill. The only time she had heard of someone being nauseous, truly nauseous, was—

Janet's eyes widened. She put her hand over her mouth, her eyes moistening. Tightening the robe around her waist, she ran to find Bruce. As soon as she flew out the back door, she called to him.

"Bruce! Bruce!"

She looked toward the field but didn't see him. Then, seeing the barn door open, she ran for it with all her might.

"Bruce! Bruce!" She kept repeating his name.

She made it halfway before he stepped out. He threw what was in his hands to the ground and ran toward her. Once they met, he grabbed her.

"Janet, what's wrong? Is everything OK?" His eyes darted over her face looking for any clue as to what was bothering her.

Breathing hard, she tried to speak between gulps of air. "Bruce . . . I . . . I threw . . . up."

Bruce scrunched his brow. "Threw up? You're . . . ill? How is that even possible?"

Janet shook her head. She willed her breathing and pulse to slow. "Bruce, I threw up." She laughed between gulps of air. "I *threw up*."

Bruce looked at her, still perplexed. "You're happy about tha—"

His eyes widened, realization finally sinking in. "Are you sure?" He grabbed her, hugged her, and pulled her back from his embrace, looking into her eyes. Now his eyes were starting to water. "You're sure?"

Janet nodded. "I'm sure. We're pregnant."

Bruce picked her up and swung her around. He stopped and put her down. His tone became somber. "Janet, you're sure you're happy about this? I thought you didn't want kids."

Janet shook her head. "Forget what I said. I'm sure. And I'm happy about it."

Bruce gave her a lingering kiss. He scooped her up in his arms and headed back to the house.

Janet laughed. "What are you doing?"

"You're working for two now. You need to be careful."

"Oh, Bruce. Put me down. I'm pregnant, not helpless."

Bruce laughed and put her back on her feet. They walked hand-in-hand to the house.

CHAPTER 28

As Janet and Bruce approached the house, they saw three people on the front porch.

"Shepherd Morgan! What are you all doing here?" Janet tied her robe tighter as she walked up the front steps.

"Hi, Janet." Shepherd Morgan nodded. "Bruce."

Bruce nodded back.

"You know Administrator Mattathias."

Mattathias held out his hand and shook Janet's and Bruce's hands. "Hello again, Janet."

Janet smiled and nodded but didn't say anything.

Morgan gestured to the third person. "And this is Administrator Chaya."

"It's very nice to meet you both." Chaya shook their hands.

Morgan smiled. "The Administrator's name is very apropos for her profession."

Janet was feeling a little outnumbered and unsure what was going on. "And what profession would that be?"

"I'm a midwife," Chaya said. "I'll be helping you through your pregnancy and delivery. My name means life, so my name is a reflection of my profession of bringing new life into the world."

Janet reached for Bruce's hand. Feeling unnerved, she tried to keep a steady voice, but her next question came out more defensive than she intended. "And . . . just how did you know I'm pregnant?"

Chaya smiled. "From the teleporter. We discovered it when you last used the teleporter."

Mattathias jumped in. "That's one reason Chaya's department is under the teleporter division of the Science Center. We want to be supportive of citizens and be sure they have the best care possible." He paused and then smiled. "I normally send a junior member of our team, but I confess, I wanted to give you my personal congratulations."

Janet smiled back and nodded but was feeling her privacy violated. "Thank you, Administrator. But that sort of spoils the element of surprise."

Chaya raised her hands, palms out. "Oh, don't worry, Janet. No one else knows. We'll certainly let you tell whomever you wish whenever you wish." She came up and put her hand on Janet's shoulder. "We just want you to know you're supported and will receive the best of care."

Janet forced a smile. "So, what happens next?"

"That's why we're here." Chaya pointed to the porch chairs. "Is it OK to sit and go over details?"

Janet nodded and gestured for everyone to find a seat.

"It's really quite simple." Chaya gave a broad smile. "I'll come by every other week just to see how things are going, and I'll be here when you deliver."

"Chaya has done thousands of these, so don't worry about anything," Mattathias said, sitting next to Janet and patting her hand.

"Do you have any questions?" Chaya looked at Janet expectedly.

Janet smiled. "Well, one. Will you announce your arrival ahead of time or just be popping in?" Janet certainly didn't want her just showing up if she happened to be talking to The Order.

"Well, I try to come around the same time of day each time, but we can arrange it however you feel comfortable."

Janet gestured with her hands and gave an affirmative nod with lips pulled in and tightly closed before responding. "As long as I know when you're coming, that is fine with me."

Chaya smiled. "Great. I'll set up a time and try my best to stick to it."

"I have a question." All eyes turned to Bruce. "What can Janet do about nausea?"

"Oh, yes," Janet said. "It came on very suddenly this morning."

Chaya gave a slight chuckle. "We've found saltine crackers are still the best remedy."

Janet nodded.

Chaya went over and patted Janet's shoulder. "Don't worry. It goes by more quickly than you would think."

Everyone said their congratulations and goodbyes and then the three left.

Janet headed with Bruce inside the house.

"Well, that was nice of them coming so quickly," he said.

Janet looked at Bruce with squinted eyes and a smirk.

"What?" he asked.

"You didn't find it a little odd? They actually knew before I did."

Bruce shrugged. "It shows they care and want the best for you—for us."

"I guess." Janet couldn't shake the feeling, though, of a lack of privacy. "Was their visit really for my own good—or for them to keep tabs on me?"

Bruce just gave her a look with the corner of his mouth upturned.

She turned to head to the bedroom. Bruce grabbed her arm, spun her around, and held her in his arms. "Don't get paranoid on me. I want our baby to be stress free." Bruce gave her a quick kiss.

"Oh, so you think our baby is going to be crazy because I doubt the Administrator's true motives?"

"No. The crazy part will probably come from me."

Janet's head jerked back slightly as she turned up her brow.

"Because I'm already crazy about you." He smiled. "It could be genetic."

Janet laughed and put her forehead on his chest. She looked back into his eyes. "That's the kind of crazy I hope the baby develops."

"Inevitable."

Janet gave Bruce another kiss. His in-the-moment attitude was precious and always perked her up. Too bad she couldn't be that way. She was always thinking ahead and working to make things go her way. She always had that drive. Finding someone like Bruce who was willing to let her have that quality without judgment was truly special.

"You get dressed and finish your cereal, and I'll get you more hot tea."

Janet gave a pouty face. "It's all soggy by now."

Bruce laughed. "OK, I'll bring you some more." He turned her around and swatted her backside as she headed to the bedroom. She gave a short yelp and he laughed. "I'll bring it to your office."

Janet dressed and went to her desk to read some of her e-mail and do some work. She also sent a note to Edgar to see if she could develop a schedule that would allow her to work more from home. Once she had children, she wanted to be home as much as possible. She paused, thought about what she was asking, and then laughed to herself.

Bruce came in with tea and more cereal. He sat it on the edge of her desk and then sat on the other side, blocking her view of the monitor.

Janet laughed. "While you're a much better view, I do need to see the monitor."

Bruce smiled. "Name?"

"What?"

"What are we going to name the baby?"

"You want to discuss that now? We have nine months to figure that out."

"I'm putting my vote in now. Peter."

Janet laughed. "You don't even know it's a boy."

Bruce shook his head. "Doesn't matter."

Janet slapped his leg. "Of course it matters. You can't name your daughter Peter."

"Peter." Bruce stood and walked toward the office door.

"You're that sure it's going to be a boy?"

Bruce didn't say anything but kept walking.

Janet yelled after him. "At least think of a girl's name just in case!"

Janet shook her head and smiled, then scrunched her brow. *Why is he so determined about that name?* She sat back in her chair saying the name repeatedly to herself. It did start to grow on her the more she said it. *Stone.* The meaning of the name was stone or rock. She chuckled slightly. Well, she *was* looking for a stone stele, so maybe that wasn't a bad name after all. She hoped it was a boy for Bruce's sake. She had to find out why the name Peter was so important to him. For a guy so easygoing, it surprised her to see him so adamant about this.

Janet turned back to her mail and cereal—which she ate very slowly because of her earlier nausea. After finishing her regular mail, she opened her encrypted messages. There was a message from the Leader. Another failed exploration at a volcano in Norway. *Big surprise there.* She then opened a note from Amanda. She and Jeff had just returned from their fifth trip to Africa. No real success, but they had narrowed down what they believed might be the location for the stele, or at least its original location. They would explore more next time.

Janet drummed her fingers. If only they could look for these steles full time. Could Jeff get a position in the Cairo museum? That would allow Jeff to look more consistently for it. *But what about Amanda?* She couldn't just ignore their relationship. Janet tapped her lips with her forefinger. She definitely had to give that more thought.

Somehow, she had to create a win-win scenario for everyone.

Janet worked until it was late. Bruce came in with a sandwich and set it next to her.

"Hello, workaholic. Ending anytime tonight?"

Janet looked at her T-band. "Oh my. Sorry. I didn't realize the time." She took a bite of sandwich before Bruce pulled her up from her chair and over to the sofa. He leaned back and pulled her onto his chest. "Now isn't that better?"

Janet reached up and kissed him. "Much."

They sat there a while simply enjoying each other's company. Janet glanced up at Bruce and laid her head back on his chest.

"Bruce, why were you so adamant about naming our child Peter?"

Bruce ran his fingers through her hair. "Why? You don't like it?"

"No, that's not it. It's actually starting to grow on me." She looked up at him and smiled. "You seemed so determined. That's all. You've never been so adamant about anything like that before."

Bruce took a deep breath and let it out slowly. "Well, a good while ago, I had a best friend named Peter."

Janet leaned up and put her chin on her hands, still on Bruce's chest, but better able to see his face. "So, where is he now?"

"The place of lost souls, I presume."

Janet sat all the way up. "What happened?"

Bruce pulled her back to his chest. "Well, he was always the cocky one. To be honest, I don't know the whole story. He did something foolish and was taken by the King."

"You don't know what happened?" Janet kept her head on his chest as Bruce continued to run his fingers through her hair.

"I heard it from Shepherd Morgan. He wouldn't tell me all the details, but Peter did something to some of the pieces for an honoring ceremony. I kept thinking Peter would repent and be allowed to come back, but I never saw him again."

"Bruce, I'm . . . so sorry."

"Shepherd Morgan counseled with me for quite some time," he said. "That's when I decided to take things one day at a time and just enjoy life. That's why I can't get too gung-ho about the King. Yet I can't deny what a great life he has provided—or *someone* has provided. So I just live in the here and now."

After a long pause, Bruce added, "I really miss him, though."

Janet glanced up and saw his eyes watering, but no tears came. She reached up and gave him another kiss. "Peter. Our boy's name will definitely be Peter."

CHAPTER 29

Chaya had been right. Time went much faster than Janet imagined—or wanted.

Before she knew it, Peter was born, and it seemed the next time she turned around he was already seven years old.

Janet's work turned more and more into that of a consultant. James eventually became her replacement while she turned full time to that role. This allowed her to work almost exclusively from home to be with Bruce and Peter—as well as spend more time communicating with The Order.

Jeff took Janet's advice and transferred to the Cairo museum. After he started looking for the stele, Amanda would tell her, he became hooked and moped when home until he was able to get back to Africa to start searching again. Amanda, though, moped about when Jeff was gone. Janet also felt an increased tension between herself and Amanda even though Amanda said she understood the need for Jeff to be in Africa.

Janet sat at her desk one morning reading an update from James. She heard the door slam. "Mommy, Mommy!"

Janet shook her head and smiled. "In here, Peter."

Peter ran into the room, his red hair disheveled as ever, his hands clasped together. "Look, Mommy, look!" He ran over and opened his hands. Inside was a fuzzy green caterpillar.

"He's beautiful, Peter."

"Here. You want to hold it?" Peter's eyes sparkled as he pushed the caterpillar toward his mom.

Janet put her hand on his shoulder. "No thank you. It's OK to look at it, Peter. But you need to put it back so it can grow and turn into a butterfly."

"Butterfly?" Peter cocked his head and looked at the caterpillar.

"Uh-huh. Wouldn't it be neat to see that?"

Peter nodded his head enthusiastically.

Janet chuckled. "OK, then. Go put it back."

"OK." He turned and ran out of the room—and straight into Bruce.

"Whoa, bud. What's the hurry?"

"I'm gonna go see my catapillow turn into a butterfly!" He stepped around his father and was off.

Janet heard the door slam.

Bruce laughed. "That boy and animals. He's totally fascinated by them."

Janet pointed her finger at Bruce. "That has to come from you. It certainly doesn't come from me. Remember, I tried to get away from the farm."

Bruce laughed again. "Maybe so."

Bruce headed back to the main part of the house as Janet's communicator beeped. She hit it, and Amanda's holographic image appeared.

"Hi, Amanda."

"Janet, Janet! He finally did it! I can't believe it!"

"What? What are you talking about, Amanda?"

"Jeff. He proposed! And I owe it all to you."

Janet turned up her brow. "I'm happy for you. But what did I have to do with it?"

"Being away from me made him realize he wanted me with him all the time."

"That's great, Amanda! I'm very happy for you. Have you set a date?"

Amanda's grin grew wider. "In two weeks—in Africa."

Janet jerked up straighter in her chair. "Wow. You waste no time."

Amanda laughed. "Yeah, you're one to judge."

Janet chuckled. "Well, you have a point there."

"Afia is helping me put the wedding together. You'll come, won't you?"

"You want me to come to Africa?"

"Please, Janet. Both Jeff and I really want you there. And Bruce and Peter."

"OK. Let me see what I can do. I'll get back to you soon."

They exchanged a few other updates and ended the call. Janet sat back in her chair. She definitely had to think about how to turn this trip into a way to continue looking for the stele . . .

Bruce stuck his head in. "Janet, you've got to come see this."

Bruce took her outside and around to the side of the house. Janet pulled her lips in and put her fist to her mouth to keep from laughing. There was Peter, asleep with his head on Oliver, who was also sound asleep. On Peter's chest was the caterpillar. Around his neck was a snake, and next to him on one side was a rabbit and on the other a baby fox. Somehow all of the animals were asleep as well. He looked so cute, innocent, and peaceful.

Bruce went over and removed—or moved—the animals so he could pick Peter up. As he lifted him, Peter jerked slightly as he woke, but only briefly, and he fell asleep again draped over Bruce's shoulder. Janet rubbed Peter's back as Bruce passed by.

Janet followed them inside the house. Peter was so relaxed his arm dangled over Bruce's shoulder and swayed slightly as Bruce walked. He was so cute Janet couldn't help but smile.

Yet deep inside, she told herself, she also knew this little boy was here for a higher purpose. He already had a keen sense of deductive reasoning and was extremely curious about geography—both traits needed in finding all the steles about the prophecy of the Overtaker.

After Peter's nap and dinner, Janet set him up to view his most favorite thing after animals: geography. His appetite for the subject seemed insatiable. He would look at various maps for hours. He kept looking at older and older maps. This apparently sped up his reading and comprehension; he was already reading at a level twice his age.

As the day of the wedding approached, Bruce bowed out of going as he needed to attend to the farm and his crops. Bruce gave Janet a kiss and Peter a hug and sent them on their way.

"We're going to see Uncle Jeff," Peter told his father.

Bruce patted Peter on his shoulders. "Yes you are, bud. You be good now, OK?"

Peter nodded. "OK. I like Uncle Jeff. He has fun stuff."

Janet laughed. "By 'stuff' you mean rocks?"

Peter nodded. Janet and Bruce laughed.

The AGA took Janet and Peter to the town square. Janet sent it back to the farmhouse, and she and Peter headed to the long-range teleporter.

Waiting for them at the teleporter in Africa were Chika and Jeff.

"Janet, you finally made it to Africa!" Chika said, rushing up. "It is so good to see you again."

Janet smiled and gave Chika a hug. "Yes, it has been a long time."

Jeff approached. "I see Bruce couldn't make it."

Janet shook her head. "The life of a farmer. The crops dictate when they have to be harvested."

"Hi, Uncle Jeff." Peter pulled on Jeff's pant leg.

Jeff reached down and picked up Peter. "Hey, bud! I'm glad you came." He pointed to Chika. "This is my good friend Chika."

Peter waved.

"Hi, Peter. Jeff has told me a lot about you. I hear you like looking at rocks. I do too."

Peter gave an enthusiastic nod.

Chika laughed. "I'm beginning to like them also. Maybe you can help me with some of them."

"Sure!"

Janet turned, looking. "Where's Afia and Amanda?"

"Afia has her trying on various dresses," Jeff said, rolling his eyes. "You know how particular Amanda is about what she wears."

Janet laughed. "I can imagine."

Chika took them all back to his house; that was where everyone was staying until the wedding. That night, Zuri and Candis came over. There was a lot to catch-up to do, and conversations went well beyond dinnertime itself. Peter grew restless, so Jeff let him look at all the maps and charts he was working on in looking for the stele. Chika had let Jeff take over his office while he was there and away from his Cairo museum office.

With Jeff's permission, Janet let Peter look at Jeff's maps in the office. Peter's eyes grew wide when he saw everything in the room.

"Now be careful with Uncle Jeff's stuff," Janet told him. "OK?"

Peter glanced at Janet and nodded, but his attention quickly focused on the maps Jeff was showing him on his electronic tablet. Peter immediately became absorbed. Janet and Jeff went back and joined the adults in conversation.

After several hours, Zuri and Candis left for home. Janet's thoughts turned to Peter.

"Jeff, is Peter still in the office?"

"I guess so. I haven't seen him since we left him there."

Jeff followed Janet into the office. There was Peter in the middle of the floor—sound asleep. All around him were maps he'd been looking at.

Jeff went to one, picked it up, and gasped.

Janet had started to pick up Peter but whipped around at the sound Jeff made.

"What's wrong?"

"I'm sorry, Janet. I can reproduce it, but Peter marked all over my map where I've already explored for the stele."

"What? That's very unlike Peter. Let me see why he did that."

Jeff waved his hand. "No. No need to wake him for that. I can take care of it."

Janet shook her head. "No. I think it's important he apologize before he forgets all about it."

She went over and shook Peter awake. Peter slowly opened his eyes, stretched, and yawned. When he saw Jeff, his eyes lit up. "Like it, Uncle Jeff?"

Jeff gave a grimace. "Well, I wish you had asked before marking on my map, Peter."

"But I found it."

Jeff scrunched his brow. "You found what?"

"The rock you're looking for."

Peter took the map from Jeff and spread it out on the floor. "I found your map of cracks. Your dots aren't on the cracks. All the cracks join here." He pointed to where three fissure lines intersected. "I think your rock is here."

Jeff's jaw dropped. He looked at Janet. "How did he do that?"

Janet shook her head. "Sweetie, what makes you think the rock is there?"

Peter shrugged. "The pictures on the map of cracks showed a lot of hot rocks. Three cracks should have even more hot rocks."

Jeff tousled Peter's hair. "Well, that's very impressive, buddy. Thanks." He glanced at Janet with raised eyebrows. To Janet, he mouthed, "Wow."

Janet smiled. "OK, sweetie. Let's get you ready for bed. It's getting late."

When Janet returned to the others, Jeff was showing Amanda, Chika, and Afia what Peter had done.

"If he has this level of deductive reasoning skills when he's this young," Jeff said, looking up at Janet, "I can't wait to work with him when he gets older."

Janet felt proud of Peter, but gently chided Jeff. "Are you trying to take my son away from me?"

Jeff laughed. "Maybe borrow him every now and then."

Janet smiled. "So, you think he's on the mark?"

Jeff nodded. "I don't know why I never thought of it. Amanda and I were following up on leads Chika and others gave us. I never even thought about how tectonics could fit into the equation."

"Jeff and I have decided to explore this area after our wedding," Amanda said, smiling. "I think I'm getting the archaeology bug myself."

"What about your shop in Chicago?" Janet asked.

"Oh, I'm putting it on hold for now."

Janet raised her eyebrows. "Well, I guess you *have* been bitten."

Amanda laughed. "Jeff, show her what you found—or really, what *Peter* found."

"I was looking at some of the things Peter was looking at on my tablet. The area he found was at one time called the Afar Triangle, where, pre-Refreshing, three continental plates joined. This was likely the beginning of the earthquake that caused the large scarp face around Jerusalem."

"What's a scarp face?" Chika had a puzzled look on his face.

Jeff used his hands to demonstrate. "It's where one side of the earthquake causes the land to go up and the other side to go down. Many times it causes streams to flow out from underground streams or produces caves that didn't exist before."

"Well, there is an area like that in the territory just north of us," Chika said. "Maybe that's it."

Jeff looked at Amanda. "Honeymoon spot identified."

They did a high five.

Afia laughed. "Oh, you two have been bitten bad."

CHAPTER 30

Janet helped Amanda into her dress. "Amanda, I still can't believe you made this. It's one of the most gorgeous dresses I've seen you make."

"Well, it was a little complicated. But once I got the design in my head, it wasn't too hard."

Janet looked at Amanda's creation as she turned and observed herself in the mirror. It was a white strapless full-length dress that had pleats starting from the waist and flaring toward the bottom. Every other pleat was kente cloth made of red, gold, and green. The other pleats were of solid deep purple fabric. The purple matched the top stripe of purple on the bodice while the waist matched the kente cloth within the dress's pleats.

Afia came in with the gelé. "It's finally ready for you, Amanda."

Amanda smiled. "Now, this was all Afia's construction. It was just beyond my capabilities."

Afia placed the gelé, or headdress, on Amanda. It too was of deep purple fabric and looked like fabric wrapped in various angles. It was tall and wide atop her head, but it looked elegant at the same time.

Afia smiled. "Amanda, you look wonderful." She gestured toward the door. "Ready?"

The wedding was on the beach directly behind Afia and Chika's house. A colorfully dressed African band with traditional African instruments was already playing. An arch and altar next to the band was decorated with various colored flowers. Jeff was standing with the local Shepherd wearing a dark purple dashiki shirt trimmed in kente cloth colors.

Afia and Chika walked with Amanda to the altar. Chika then bound the hands of Amanda and Jeff with braided grass and took a seat with Afia.

The Shepherd spoke. "We are pleased Jeff and Amanda have chosen to utilize several African traditions in their wedding ceremony. The braided grass symbolizes their desire to join together in unity. A blade of grass is easily cut; yet, when braided together, they become very strong. So, too, will you become stronger as you are united together."

The Shepherd had Jeff and Amanda say their vows and place rings on each other's fingers. Next to the Shepherd was a small pitcher. The Shepherd then poured the water in the pitcher on the sand.

"The pouring of water has always symbolized the outpouring of Ruach HaKadosh. It is my wish that this couple also receives the King's blessing of such a gift. The kente cloth symbolizes our King and his character. The red symbolizes the blood he has shed for his subjects, the gold symbolizes his divinity, and the green represents the Refreshing he brought to the world. I see you have added deep purple, which is also a representation of his royalty. May the King be a blessing in your marriage."

Janet wondered if Amanda knew of these symbols before the wedding, and, if she had, whether she would have chosen something different.

Next to Amanda was a small table with four small bowls. The Shepherd reached for one of them.

"Within each of these bowls are foods that represent different tastes. Life will bring many challenges and hardships. Some may threaten to sour the marriage . . . " He had each of them taste a piece of lemon. "Or, conflicts may cause bitterness to spring up in your hearts." He had each of them dip their finger in vinegar and put it to their tongue. "Or heated discussions may occur." He had both Jeff and Amanda dip their finger in cayenne and put it to their tongue. "Yet all of these troubles can again lead to sweet union if each looks to the needs of the other and to their King." He then had each dip their finger in the final bowl, which contained honey, and give it to the other person.

The Shepherd then held up a nut. "The kola nut has always represented a symbol of healing." He had each give the other a small piece of the nut. The Shepherd then prayed. "Our King, bless the union of this couple, and may your healing power cause their marriage to prosper and never falter."

Afia came forward and put an elaborately decorated broom behind the couple.

"I now pronounce you husband and wife," the Shepherd said. "Turn around and jump over the broom. This symbolizes you're sweeping away your past and looking forward to a life together with blessing and promise."

Jeff and Amanda turned, took a step, and jumped over the broom. Amanda's foot caught her dress and she nearly fell. Jeff was quick enough that he caught her and made it look intentional by holding her in that position and giving her a kiss. Everyone clapped and cheered.

A reception was held for Amanda and Jeff in Afia and Chika's backyard. The African band relocated there and continued to play. Everyone enjoyed some traditional African food as well as petit fours, finger sandwiches, and wedding cake. Peter was a big hit. It seemed he had the goal of making sure all the petit fours were eaten. He was constantly carrying trays of them to people throughout the crowd.

Once Janet was by herself, Jeff approached. "Janet, can you stay a couple of weeks before you head back?"

Janet scrunched her brow. "Why? I've loved our time here, but I wasn't really planning on staying very long."

"Just give us a couple of weeks to look for the stele. If we don't find it by then, it's likely not there. Some of our leads talked about a cave, but we never found one. If Chika is right about the scarp face, then this could be the big break for us to find the cave."

Janet sighed and nodded. "OK. Two weeks. And then I have to get back."

"Thank you, Janet." He picked up her hand and kissed it.

Janet laughed and playfully pushed him away.

After a couple of hours, Amanda and Jeff changed clothes and prepared to leave. Their honeymoon would be a rustic one as they were headed to where the Afar Triangle used to be. Chika helped Jeff prepare the camping gear they would need. Although far from civilization, an AGA would get them there well enough.

When Chika found out how much Peter loved animals, he took him on one of his safari trips. Janet spent her time with both Afia and Candis. When Peter returned at the end of the week, he talked almost nonstop about all he had seen. He was still talking when he fell asleep that night.

Janet was laughing with the others after she put him to bed. "Chika, you are definitely his new best friend. He's a talkative kid, but I've never heard him talk so much before." She pointed her finger at him. "I may be complaining to you in the near future because he may never stop talking about this week."

Chika laughed. "He was a pleasure to have around. And those on the safari loved him as he told them all about the different animals. I was basically just a chaperone."

Janet chuckled and yawned. "I think all of his talking wore me out." She said her goodnights and headed to bed.

The next morning she awoke to the beeping of her communicator. She answered but kept the holographic display off. "This is Janet," she said drowsily.

An excited voice made Janet jerk awake instinctively. "Janet, you have to get here as soon as possible."

"Amanda? Is that you?"

"Your son is a genius! We found it! Janet, we found it."

Adrenaline kicked in. Janet sat up, wide awake. "You're kidding."

"No. No, it's true. Get here as fast as you can."

"OK. I'll call you when I'm on my way."

Janet dressed quickly. Afia and Chika were more than willing to watch Peter. Chika was sitting with Peter who was showing him something on the tablet. Chika looked up and laughed. "Hey, by the time you get back, I may know as much about rocks as Peter," he told Janet.

Janet laughed. "Thank you so much for this."

Once Janet took the short-range teleporter to the north-eastern African territory, she obtained an AGA, entered the geographic coordinates where Amanda and Jeff were located, and sat back while the AGA drove. This gave her time to think. She was definitely excited about this find—for several reasons. First, it would likely give more evidence to the legitimacy of the coming Overtaker. Second, it should finally get the Leader off his obsession of looking at ancient volcano sites and move him to start looking at other leads. And third, of course, it should provide needed additional information to lead to more clues to find the other steles. There wasn't much time left to find the other steles. She was just glad to be part of this find. It made her extremely proud that Peter had a big part in it as well.

As the AGA pulled up, Amanda came running over.

"We haven't moved it. We wanted you to see it as we found it."

Janet laughed. "Amanda, I used to think you got excited over clothes. This has taken your excitement to a new level."

Amanda giggled. "I just find this so exciting."

"Where's Jeff?"

"In the cave." She pulled on Janet's arm. "Come on. I'll show you."

Janet looked around. The area was lush with vegetation that grew up to the rocky cliff in front of them and even continued to grow all the way up the cliff face. Janet couldn't see a cave but followed Amanda, who was walking with determination toward a large grouping of ferns. Once there, they went through the ferns, and this led them to the mouth of the cave, where Amanda handed Janet a flashlight. Once inside they followed a corridor to their right and Janet found herself standing in a large opening. Jeff stood near the middle waving his flashlight. "It's over here," he yelled.

As Janet headed over, there on a large flat rock was a glass box with a stone stele inside. She couldn't help but have a sense of awe as she gazed upon it. "Wow. It's been here all this time."

"Take a look at this." Jeff shined his light around the flat rock. There were other, smaller flat rocks around this larger rock. "It looks like this was some type of meeting place."

"That sounds like one of the stories Candis talked about," Amanda said.

Janet turned toward Amanda. "What did she say?"

"She wasn't very specific but talked about secret meetings being held."

Janet took Jeff's flashlight. "OK, let's take it into the light and see it better."

The glass case was hollow on bottom and simply lifted off the stele. Jeff carefully picked up the stele, and Janet walked slowly in front of him showing the way. Once out of the cave, Jeff set the stele on a small table at their campsite. The stele was roughly square and had variations of gray- and emerald-colored streaks throughout.

"It's beautiful," both Janet and Amanda said at the same time.

Janet reached out and touched it. It felt smooth except where broken. "There seems to be four types of writing here."

Jeff nodded. "It's pretty obvious the first is Egyptian."

Janet pointed to the last line. "I believe this is Arabic."

"What about the other two?" Amanda looked from Jeff to Janet.

Both shook their heads. Janet looked at Jeff. "This third one." She pointed to it. "Do you think it looks similar to Hebrew?"

Jeff shifted his head back and forth. "Well, sort of. Maybe it's some language akin to Hebrew."

"Maybe." Janet continued to stare at the stele. "Jeff, does your time at the Cairo museum give you any insight into an interpretation of the first line?"

Jeff held his chin in thought. He pointed at the last Egyptian symbol. "I think this is a rising sun and therefore can mean rising or coming to power."

Janet nodded. "Well, that would make sense."

Jeff sat down in one of the camp chairs. "So, what do we do from here?"

Amanda sat in Jeff's lap as Janet sat in the other chair. She ran her forefinger and thumb around the corners of her mouth in thought.

"I don't think we should say anything until we know what these lines of text mean," Janet finally said.

Amanda shifted on Jeff's lap. "What do you propose?"

"Amanda, can you take a picture of this stele?"

Amanda nodded and ducked into their tent.

"Jeff, maybe you can find something at the Cairo museum to help decipher these meanings," Janet said.

Jeff shrugged. "I'll try. It may take quite some time since, I assume, you don't want me to alert anyone about our find here."

Janet shook her head. "No, we can't afford that."

Amanda walked over and took a holographic picture.

"I'm going to take the stele back with me," Janet said. "You two use the picture as a reference and see what you can find out. But you need to be secretive about this."

Amanda turned to Janet. "And what are you going to do with the stele?"

Janet shook her head. "Nothing for now. But I'll see if Peter can learn these languages. I'll be sure he doesn't know about their true meaning. At least not until he's much older."

Amanda looked at Jeff and then back to Janet. "Uh, Janet. No disrespect to Peter. Heaven knows he's smarter than all of us put together, but why not get a linguist to decipher these? Wouldn't that be faster?"

Jeff nodded. "Isn't time critical here?"

Janet gave them a stare. *They just don't understand.* "Jeff, yes, time is important, but the more people we bring in, the more our exposure is at risk. We must stay under the radar about this. Not an inkling of this can get out. We can't let King lovers get any wind of this. My way is longer, but much safer. Plus, I have great confidence in Peter's ability."

"So, how long will it take to decipher all of this?"

"I don't know, Amanda." She stood. "But Peter's pretty bright. You've both witnessed his deductive reasoning skills."

Both nodded.

"Let's keep in touch. We'll figure this out together."

Janet carefully packaged the stele, and they exchanged hugs and said goodbyes. Janet left in the AGA.

Heading back, she was deep in thought: *Maybe Peter is a bigger key with all of this than I ever thought.*

Before she informed the Leader, she needed to know the meaning on the stele. Otherwise, the Leader would take the stele and she would be in the dark.

Before she left Africa, she had to be sure Zuri was on her side about this decision.

CHAPTER 31

Before heading back to Afia's house, Janet went to see Zuri, who was at work. Chika was there too, but she tried to get Zuri's attention without Chika seeing her. Zuri saw her and headed over.

"Hi, Janet. Everything OK?"

"Do you have a minute? Can you come out to my AGA?"

Zuri's eyebrows raised, but he followed her.

Once they were in the AGA, Zuri looked at Janet. "So, what's with all the cloak and dagger?"

Janet laughed. "Well, that's being a little overdramatic, perhaps." She took out the cloth bag in which she had placed the stele. "But I have something to show you."

Janet carefully pulled the stele out of the bag and handed it to Zuri. His eyes widened and his jaw went slack. He looked from the stele to Janet, then responded in whispered tones. "You found it?"

Janet nodded. "Any idea what the writings are, or what they say?"

Zuri ran his hand over the stele as his eyes darted over the various symbols. He finally shook his head. "I'm pretty sure the first line is Egyptian and the last Arabic. But I have no idea what it actually says." He looked back at Janet. "Sorry."

Janet's shoulders drooped a little. She hoped Zuri would have known more. "Well, that's as far as we got as well."

Zuri put the stele back in the bag and looked over at Janet. "What do you plan to do?"

"My bigger concern is: what are you going to do?"

Zuri turned his head slightly. "What do you mean?"

Janet placed her hand on his arm. "Zuri, we can't let anyone know about this until we have it deciphered."

Zuri's brow furrowed. "Why?"

"Think about it, Zuri. If we tell anyone, it will get taken from us before we know its true meaning and value." Janet's tone turned a little defiant. "I don't know about you, but I don't want to be in the dark. This is our chance to provide a huge find. But we can't present it until we can also deliver its meaning."

Zuri stared at Janet for a few seconds. Janet was afraid he was going to disagree. But slowly, he began to nod. "Yes. I can see the truth in what you're saying." As if coming out of a fog, he perked up again. "How long do you think it will take?"

Janet shook her head. "I don't know." She gave a slight shrug. "It could take a couple of years."

Zuri's head jerked back a bit. "That long?"

"Well, think about it. We only have ourselves, as well as Jeff and Amanda, to figure this out. Currently, we know very little. Jeff can hopefully find out more at the museum, but he has to do that with stealth and not bring anyone else into the picture. We can't afford anyone else knowing."

Zuri nodded. "Yeah, that's true." He sat up straighter. "What about Peter?"

"What *about* Peter?"

"Well, I heard how he found the potential—well, I guess it's now the *actual*—spot for this stele. Maybe he could help Jeff at the museum."

This time Janet turned her head. "What do you mean? I was going to try and get Peter to learn these languages—"

Zuri put his hand on Janet's arm. "Think about it, Janet. If Jeff asks questions, it will raise suspicion. But if Peter asks the same questions they will appear an innocent curiosity. The way your son processes information, he would pick it up much faster in the museum environment."

Janet leaned back in her seat and let out a breath while looking back at Zuri. "Well, he certainly wouldn't think it tedious being in that environment, and he loves being with Jeff."

"Janet, I know it's a sacrifice. But you could visit often."

Janet sighed. She knew Zuri was right. This would be the fastest way to get Peter to learn these languages. But her other concern was this: how would she convince Bruce to go along with it?

Janet slowly nodded her head. "Yes, I think you're right. I'll tell Bruce he's staying for a few weeks. Let's see how it goes and then determine how long he needs to stay."

Zuri patted Janet's hand. "We'll stay in touch."

Janet nodded. "Definitely."

Zuri left the AGA and headed back inside the building.

Janet directed the AGA back to Afia's.

Bruce isn't going to like this one bit, she thought to herself while traveling. Hopefully Peter's curiosity would be in high gear. Once he had the interest, he could continue his learning at home. *Well, that's all wishful thinking right now.* She had to take this one step at a time. First, she had to convince Bruce that Peter was staying a couple of weeks to be with Jeff. Well, that part wasn't a lie.

Not full disclosure, but not a lie.

That evening she decided to call Bruce while alone in her bedroom. She took a deep breath, put on her best smile, and dialed. Bruce answered almost immediately.

"Hi there," he said on answering. "I was hoping to hear from you. How's it going, and when will you be coming home? I miss you—both of you."

Janet smiled. "Things are going well. Amanda and Jeff's wedding was beautiful. Peter made a mission of getting everyone to eat the petit fours. I think he was in cahoots with the caterer."

Bruce laughed. "Sounds like he had a great time."

"Oh, he has been enthralled this whole time. Chika took him on a safari. He hasn't stopped talking about it. He, Chika, and Jeff have been talking about rocks nonstop as well."

"Well, I'm glad he's having a good time. I miss him. Coming home soon?"

Janet grimaced. "I need to talk to you about that."

"What do you mean?"

"He really wants to stay with Jeff and Amanda for a couple of weeks and see what Jeff does at the museum."

"You mean I won't see him for a whole month? What if you both come home for a couple of weeks and then he goes back?"

"I'm sorry, Bruce. He's really excited about it right now, so I don't want to disappoint him. It's only a couple more weeks."

Bruce looked crestfallen.

"I'll be coming home, though."

Bruce smiled. "Well, I'm glad I get one of you back. Can I talk to him at least?"

Janet smiled. "Of course. Let me get him."

Janet found Peter and put him on the call. Talking nearly nonstop, Peter went into a long explanation of all he had done. Bruce smiled, laughed, and was able to occasionally get a question in when Peter took a needed breath.

"Do you really want to stay with Uncle Jeff for a few weeks?"

"Uh-huh, Daddy. He works at the museum." Peter placed a heavy emphasis on the second and third syllables and drew them out, making it sound like a place of wonder.

Bruce laughed. "I guess that sounds more fun than being on a farm."

Peter suddenly looked very serious. "No, Daddy. The farm is your museum. I like your museum, too."

Bruce's eyes watered. "Thanks, buddy. That's exactly how I feel about it. You have a good time, OK?"

"OK, Daddy. Bye."

Peter hopped down from the bed and ran back to the other room where he had been reading.

"What a kid we made, Janet."

Janet smiled. "Indeed. I'll see you in a couple of days."

Bruce nodded. They said a few more words then ended the call.

Janet let out a long breath. That went better than she expected. Now she had to be sure Jeff was OK with her idea. If not, she would have to convince him somehow. This was really important. Hoping he would see it that way too, she dialed.

Jeff answered. "Janet, hi. Everything OK?"

Janet nodded. "Yes, everything's great. I talked to Zuri. He agrees with us to keep it all hush-hush for now."

"Great. Anything else? You still look apprehensive."

"Well, I have a favor to ask. When do you plan to go back to Cairo, and when back to work?"

"We're actually heading back to Cairo tomorrow. I'll be back at work Monday."

"Would you like to have Peter with you for a couple of weeks?"

"Uh, well . . . sure. But, uh . . . why? Why now?"

"I know the timing isn't perfect for you, but Zuri and I were talking. Rather than you asking questions, Peter could ask the questions and they would appear more as a child being curious than something suspicious."

Jeff's eyebrows went up. "That's . . . a great idea. That would certainly speed things up a lot."

"OK. I'll drop him by at the end of Sabbath. Will that be all right? Will Amanda mind?"

"Oh, she'll be thrilled."

Janet smiled. "Great. Just remember. Peter needs to be totally enthralled by the end of the two weeks so he'll be anxious to continue once he's back home."

Jeff nodded. "Got it. My mind is already turning as to how to work through all of this and who he should see and talk to next week."

"If Amanda has a problem with this, have her call me."

"Sure, but I know she'll be fine." Jeff waved and terminated the communication.

Janet let out another long breath. Well, the plan was in motion. She smiled to herself. If all of this came together as she hoped, it would put her in very good standing with The Order. Her prominence would increase.

Maybe she could even have more influence with the Leader.

CHAPTER 32

Janet called Jeff and Amanda every night. Jeff usually had high accolades to pass along. Apparently, everyone at the museum adored Peter. He got answers to any and every question he asked. Most were thrilled that someone so young was interested in such ancient things as languages and artifacts. Peter seemed to absorb and retain everything.

He had been there only a week when Jeff told Janet that Peter was already starting to make the right connections and form words from the Egyptian and Phoenician symbols. Peter would then tell Janet and Bruce all the things he was learning. He couldn't stop talking about the mummies the curator allowed him to see.

The first night of the following week, Janet made her usual call. Jeff looked way too somber for a routine call.

"Jeff, what's wrong?"

Jeff paused as if trying to find the right words for something he didn't want to say.

"Jeff? Is it Peter? Is something wrong with Peter?"

Jeff held up his hands. "Calm down, Janet. Peter's fine."

Janet let out a big breath; she realized she'd been holding it and not breathing.

"It's just that the museum administrator, Professor Akhem, has him in custody."

Janet's eyes went wide. "In *custody*? What happened?"

Jeff shook his head. "No, no. Bad choice of words. It's just that Peter is with the professor."

Janet quickly did the math in her head knowing there was a six-hour difference between them. "Jeff, it's twenty hundred there right now. How could Peter not be with you?"

Jeff gave a sheepish grin. "Professor Akhem asked Peter to spend the night at his place."

"What?" Janet leaned forward, her nostrils flaring. "Why on earth did you allow that?"

Jeff held out his hands, palms up, and shrugged. "Janet, he's the museum administrator. I thought it would create a bigger scene and raise more suspicion if I didn't agree to it."

Amanda came into view. "Janet, I know his wife. She's very sweet. He's perfectly safe."

Janet shook her head. "I'm not worried about his safety. What will he tell this administrator? He knows about the stele. He's very bright, but also too trusting at this age." Janet fanned herself; she was feeling very warm. Sweat was starting to bead on her forehead. "Why did this administrator want Peter to stay the night?"

"He said he had more information at his home that Peter would be interested in."

"I'm coming over tonight." She looked at her T-band. "Can you meet me at the teleporter in an hour?"

Jeff raised his hands again. "Janet, I really think you're overreacting."

Janet shook her head. "Oh, really? And what will you tell your administrator in the morning if Peter tells him about the stele?"

"But he really doesn't know about the stele, Janet. He hasn't seen it. He still calls it a rock. Even if he talks about it, no one will be able to picture what he's referring to, and he hasn't seen the writing. We've only been asking about the different types of writing—not *why* we're asking about it."

"All the same. There's no way I can rest knowing he's there with this man. What if he tries to brainwash Peter and turn him into one of those 'connected with the king' people?"

"OK, OK. I'll meet you at the teleporter. I do think you're overreacting, but I can understand your concern."

Janet disconnected, quickly threw some things in a travel bag, and went to tell Bruce.

"What's the big deal, Janet?" Bruce said, looking at her with some surprise. "The administrator is going to teach him more about these languages that he's now so into. Isn't that a good thing?"

She didn't—couldn't—tell Bruce what she was really concerned about. "I just want to be there, that's all."

Bruce shrugged. "I think you're overreacting, but if that's what you want to do, go ahead."

"Thanks, Bruce." She reached up and gave him a quick kiss. "I know I'm being silly, but it's something I just have to do."

Bruce reached down and gave her another kiss. "Give me a call tomorrow night, OK?"

Janet nodded, and she was off.

Jeff was waiting for her at the Cairo long-range teleporter. The aromas reminded her of her earlier trip to Jerusalem even though most of the shops were closed at such a late hour.

Amanda had tea ready when they arrived. She poured Janet a cup so they could talk.

Jeff came over and put some cards with symbols on them in front of her. "See, I broke the stele writing up into what we think are individual words. Therefore, he only sees them as words and not sentences." He sat down next to her. "That's why I said even if he talks about the stele, he doesn't really know enough in context to make the administrator suspicious."

Janet looked at the cards. Her eyes widened. "Some of these are already interpreted?" Having these words decoded so quickly, Janet thought, was remarkable. One card had an Egyptian symbol she already knew: *rise*, or *come to power*. Another had an Akkadian symbol translated as the word *false*. The next card she picked up had a Phoenician symbol translated as *woman* (*she*). And another card had Arabic words translated as *unity*.

Jeff nodded. "It's amazing what Peter has already done. He identified the two languages we didn't know, and what he has already interpreted gives us a good gist of the meaning." Jeff altered his cadence as though now reading. "'The Overtaker comes to power overthrowing a false government with the help of some woman, and thereby brings unity.'"

Janet slowly moved her head back and forth. "Yes, but that's filled with a lot of conjecture on our part." She glanced at Jeff. "But it's certainly a good start. We just need to verify things."

Jeff nodded. "Yeah, you're right."

Janet put the cards down. "Now, tell me what the administrator wanted to show Peter."

Jeff shrugged. "I'm not completely sure. Administrator Akhem came in just as Peter was stating that some of the symbols of one language reminded him of those of another. Apparently, that got his attention, and he wanted to show Peter something about how they are connected."

"What if he starts telling Peter about the king and gets him too curious?"

Jeff shrugged. "Peter's bright. I know he's still young, but he's not going to just take someone's word for it. Especially someone he hardly knows."

"Maybe you're right." Janet tapped the table with her fore-finger several times. "I hope so."

Amanda walked over and put her hand on Janet's shoulder. "I know you may not sleep well, but I've prepared a place for you in Peter's room where he's been sleeping. It's small and has his things everywhere, but there's plenty of room to lie down."

Janet smiled. "Thanks, Amanda. I'll try and get some rest."

Janet followed Amanda and said goodnight. There were rocks, maps, and papers everywhere. She picked up a paper. Peter had lines drawn from symbols of one language to those of another. It seemed he was already trying to make the connection between them. Janet thought back to when she was seven years of age. While bright, she knew she didn't function at anywhere near this level of deductive reasoning at his age. Bruce was right. Peter was simply amazing.

Janet had some fitful sleep but rose early; she wanted to be at the museum when the administrator arrived.

When Jeff told everyone that Janet was Peter's mother, they gave her free access to any area of the museum. About an hour after she and Jeff arrived, Administrator Akhem arrived with Peter. Peter's eyes suddenly grew huge when he saw his mother.

"Mommy!" Peter let go of Akhem's hand, ran, and jumped into Janet's arms.

Janet gave him a big hug with a squeeze. "I'm so glad to see you." She released the hug and asked, "Did you have fun last night?"

Peter nodded enthusiastically.

Janet smiled. "I bet you did! What did you and the professor talk about?"

Peter's eyes lit up. "Oh, lots of things. Semtic languages."

Akhem laughed. "Semitic, Peter, remember?"

Peter nodded. "Yes, Sem-it-tic languages."

"Mrs. O'Brien. I'm Professor Akhem, the museum curator. I must say you have a remarkable son."

Janet gave the professor a nod. "Thank you. He certainly keeps us busy."

Akhem laughed. "I can see why. He certainly kept me on my toes last night." He gestured toward a hallway. They all followed him to his office.

Jeff tousled Peter's hair. "What did you like most about last night, bud?"

Peter looked up and smiled. "Mummy ice cream."

Jeff laughed. "What's that?"

Akhem chuckled. "Peter and my wife had fun in the kitchen after our session together. They took graham crackers, crushed them, mixed them with white chocolate and ice cream, shaped them into strips, and before they got totally hard, wrapped them around a human-shaped milk chocolate mold. My wife makes them many times for our museum benefits."

Janet smiled. "Sounds complicated—and messy."

Akhem nodded. "It is. But my wife has made them so many times it's easy for her." He looked at Peter. "But cleanup was the best part, huh Peter?"

Peter nodded enthusiastically. "I like chocolate."

Everyone laughed. Akhem motioned to his assistant. "Can you take Peter to the holo-show and let him watch that while we talk?" He looked at Janet. "Is that OK with you?"

Janet nodded.

Akhem motioned for Janet and Jeff to have a seat.

"As I stated, Ms. O'Brien, I find Peter quite fascinating. And his interest remarkable. I was amazed someone so young would have any interest in languages that have been dead for millennia. I only know of them because of my time as a museum curator before the Refreshing."

Janet was starting to feel she was being put into justification mode; she began to grow defensive. "Well, geography has always come naturally to him. Second to animals, of course."

Akhem laughed. "Yes, he told me some interesting stories about his safari trip."

"Peter has always adored Jeff and his rocks. So I guess this is just an extension of that."

Akhem looked at Jeff. "He called you Uncle Jeff. I thought you had no siblings."

Jeff smiled. "My wife, Amanda, and Janet were good friends even before I knew Amanda."

Janet jumped in. "Yes, since we see them so often, Peter needed to call them something. Mr. Starling seemed too formal and, well, just Jeff seems too . . . informal. Uncle Jeff and Aunt Amanda seem more appropriate. Don't you think?"

Akhem smiled. "Certainly." He paused. "Peter also talked about a rock with writing."

Jeff readjusted in his seat but smiled. "Well, I dabble a little in archaeology. Sort of a hobby."

"Are you looking for anything in particular?"

Jeff shook his head. "No, just following up on leads and things I hear people say."

"Oh? And what have you heard?"

Janet gave Jeff a quick glance in a furtive attempt to warn him to be careful.

"Oh, just a few rumors. Amanda and I spent our honeymoon south of here exploring an escarpment. We had a good time together being outdoors."

"Well, I want to caution you about such rumors."

Janet jumped in. "Are they false rumors?" She knew she shouldn't have said anything but couldn't resist pushing just a little. "I've found that even myth has some remnant of truth somewhere."

Akhem nodded. "That is likely true. But a true myth may not provide a true message."

"I see." Janet sat back in her chair. It sounded like more of a cover-up to her. Yet she couldn't deny the truth of Akhem's statement either. But if there were seven messages with similar evidence, wouldn't that provide evidence of being on the side of truth?

Akhem continued. "The languages Peter has been asking about are Semitic in origin and were at some point in earth's history spoken in this part of the world. It seems a little too coincidental they are also the ones rumored to be on a stone tablet supposedly somewhere in this area of Africa."

Janet tried to remain nonchalant. "Oh, I thought Peter's questions came from things he had seen here at the museum. Jeff mentioned that many of your staff kept giving him information, and that led to more of his questions." She shrugged. "Maybe coincidence is sometimes coincidence."

"Hmm. Maybe." He smiled. "At any rate, I just wanted to say be careful about following rumors. And to tell you I find Peter remarkable." He stood. "If his interests continue in this direction as he gets older, I'm more than willing to have him work for us."

Janet stood. "Thank you, Professor. I'll certainly keep that in mind."

Once Janet gathered Peter and they stepped outside the museum, she let out an exaggerated breath.

"Are you OK, Mommy?"

Janet nodded and smiled. "Fine, Peter. Mommy is perfectly fine."

Peter looked around. "Where's Uncle Jeff?"

"Oh, he has to work today, sweetie. We'll see him at dinnertime."

That evening, Janet called Zuri. She told him all that Peter had translated.

"It isn't everything," she said, "but I think we have the overall gist of the translation even if we don't have it all translated."

"So, you think we should go ahead and tell our contacts in The Order?" Zuri's face showed worry.

"Well, we're no longer in the complete dark about it. Also, If Administrator Akhem feels suspicious, it's only a matter of time before The Order gets wind of it. This is the best time to bring our results forward."

Zuri nodded. "I guess you're right. You tell your contacts. I'll tell mine."

After ending the call, Janet sat back, contented for now. This could be excellent leverage with The Order; it would show her understanding of how to find such steles. The thought of telling the Leader her asset—as well as Africa's—had found the stele, and that they had already translated some of it, made her smile.

The Leader would not be able to ignore it—or her—this time. She could feel her rise to prominence within The Order.

Maybe now she could be in much greater control of her destiny.

CHAPTER 33

Jubilee Calendar
19:3:3

Janet sat at her desk while Peter worked at the table nearby. Pausing, she looked at him and smiled, impressed at what a young man he was becoming and amazed he was already nineteen years of age. His interest in animals had never waned. That was likely why he helped Bruce so often; it afforded him the opportunity to see many of the animals in the area.

His appetite for geography and languages, however, became even more insatiable. He would visit Jeff often, and Jeff had become somewhat of a second father to him. Peter loved Bruce but shared so many interests with Jeff. He had worked off and on over the last decade deciphering the message of the stele.

Peter wasn't satisfied with the substance of the message. It became an obsession for him to understand it exactly. Meanwhile, Janet couldn't have been prouder of him and his keen interest in translating the stele. She tried to flame his interest but let Jeff be the one to spur him on to complete the message.

Peter turned in his chair. "Mom, I think I finally got it."

"You mean, all of it? Did you figure out the Phoenician section?"

Peter smiled. "I think so." He came over to her desk. "Only after getting it all translated was I able to put it in a more understandable form." He pulled up a chair and sat next to her. "Look. It actually forms a poem." He pointed to the first line. "I originally had

The one to conquer must come to power
The world of false now free
A woman from [some type of bird]
Is the key to unity.

"But I found the part in brackets to be the word 'starling.' You see, the phonetic sound of this word, if I spell it in Hebrew, is the word for starling. So I think this is the Phoenician spelling of the same thing. In the second line, I know the word 'free' is the key word, so the word 'key' must be the key word in the last line. I think a more correct translation is this:

The Overtaker must rise
A false-world to free
She of the starlings
From their unity is the key."

Janet looked from the translation to Peter. "Peter, I think this is really it." She grabbed his hand. "The way it reads, it has a rhythm that the original writer would want it to have. This . . . this must be it."

Peter beamed. "See what I can do in ten years?" He laughed. "I feel like this huge weight is off my shoulders." He straightened and stretched. "It was like having a giant jigsaw puzzle where you could never get the last few pieces to fit." He kissed his mother on the cheek. "I feel like I defeated the jigsaw."

Janet smiled. "Yes, I think you did."

"I'm hungry. Want a sandwich?"

"Sure."

He turned before he walked out. "And I think I have some ideas for where another stele could be." He waved his hands. "But I want to talk to Uncle Jeff before I speculate." He smiled and did a shadow boxing routine. He laughed as he walked out. "We're on a roll."

Janet picked up the paper with the translation, stood, and paced as she read it again. Yes, this really sounded like a correct translation. The first two lines made sense, but what did the last two lines mean? Maybe they needed all the steles before it would all come together.

She looked at herself in the mirror. Her life was a very good one. So why did she have this insatiable appetite to have more control over it? She wasn't sure. All she knew was that she couldn't be satisfied with being under the control of someone else. She read the second line again. Yes, freedom was something she desperately wanted.

Her stomach felt funny. Maybe she was hungrier than she realized. No. That wasn't hunger . . . it was nausea. She looked into the mirror, eyes widening.

Oh no.

She heard the doorbell ring.

When she turned into the hallway to answer the door, she saw Administrator Chaya's face through the glass.

EPILOGUE

Jubilee Calendar
19:4:5

Nine years later

J anet stood next to her desk, arms folded, looking out the picture window. Kalem, her eight-year-old, was playing with several of his friends in the backyard. In the distance, Bruce was at work on the anti-gravity harvester—his most favorite place in the world, it seemed. The doorbell chimed. She looked at the kids a brief second longer and stepped from her office.

Opening the door, she stood there for several seconds with mouth slightly open. Before her was a tall black man, someone she hadn't seen since Peter was little.

The man displayed a huge grin and held his arms wide. "Janet! It is so good to see you after all of these years."

"Zuri?" They embraced. "What . . . what on earth are you doing here?" Janet slightly shook her head. "I mean . . . please, please come in."

"Janet, I was so sorry to hear about Peter." He turned and waited until his gaze caught her eye. "I know he was your asset."

283

Janet's eyes widened, and she quickly put her hand on Zuri's shoulder to stop him as she glanced down the hallway to make sure no one had come in. She motioned to him. "Please, come into my study."

After Janet gestured for Zuri to have a seat on the sofa, she closed the French doors to her office. She sat on the other end of the sofa facing Zuri.

"Zuri, I'm grateful for your visit. But I'm not sure of your implications."

Zuri gave a sly smile and bended his head down slightly, looking at her. "Come on, Janet. We both know you recruited me for The Order."

Before Janet could say anything, he added, "You can't deny it, Janet."

Janet sighed. "OK, yes. After we first met in Iceland all those years ago, I referred you to the Leader and felt sure you were the one leading The Order from Africa after that." She cocked her head. "But how did you know I was the one leading The Order from North America?"

Zuri chuckled. "I didn't at first. But when I heard you had an asset who seemed to be a whiz at translating the stele, that really got my mind to thinking. After all, I heard from Chika about Peter identifying the Afar Triangle, where the three continental plates converge, as the place for one of the steles."

Janet shook her head. "I knew he wouldn't be able to keep that to himself." She looked back at Zuri, eyes wide. "Who else knows about that?"

Zuri smiled. He reached over and patted Janet's hand. "Relax, Janet. Just me."

Janet let out a long breath. "This secret stuff gets so complicated sometimes."

Zuri raised his eyebrows. "You're telling me. It's hard to keep all of this from Chika, as well as from Candice. How do you keep it from Bruce?"

Janet gave a slight smile. "Bruce knows—and doesn't know."

Zuri furrowed his brow. "And that means?"

Janet's smile widened. "It means he has always known I haven't seen eye-to-eye with the King. Yet he hasn't tried to interfere with, or know, anything I've been doing. He's pretty laid-back."

"Lucky for you."

"Well, it has been." Janet's throat constricted, her voice low. "Until . . . recently." Janet's eyes got teary.

Zuri drew closer. "Janet, what happened to Peter?"

Janet's gaze darted between Zuri's eyes. The concern she saw there broke down her defenses. Tears trickled down her cheeks. "It was such a mix-up. I . . . I should have been in more control of the situation."

"What do you mean?"

Janet stood, walked to the picture window, and looked out. She turned back to Zuri. "Peter moved to the next territory north of here." She shook her head. "I really didn't want him to, but . . . " She gave a quick shrug. "He wanted to raise animals, and most of Bruce's land is for crops."

Zuri came over and put his hand on her shoulder.

She glanced into his eyes and looked out the window again. "My father always had a farm waiting for my return. He was glad when Peter wanted to use it." She gave a short laugh and looked back at Zuri. "He wanted a petting zoo."

Zuri smiled. "That would have been unique."

Janet nodded, but her smile faded. "He became infatuated with one of the local girls, Raina." She folded her arms across her midsection. "I can't really blame him. She's quite beautiful." She pointed to a silver filigree-framed picture on her desk with a happy couple looking back.

Zuri picked up the silver-framed picture and studied it. "They look so happy."

Janet nodded. "But she got him so confused. Shortly before their wedding, she was selected for one of the Sabbath Year safaris with the king. When she returned, she was one of his followers."

Zuri sucked in a short breath. "No!"

Janet nodded. "Yes, and it certainly complicated matters."

Zuri set the picture on the desk as Janet began to pace. "He, being my asset . . . I had to stay in the background. So I had Jeff and Amanda stay in contact with him. But they got excited about the stele prophecy as they became convinced the prophecy that talked about 'the unity of starlings' was talking about *them* specifically, that being their last name. They became . . . obsessed. I tried to temper their enthusiasm, but after their daughter Angela was born, they became more and more uncontrollable." Tears formed again. "Jeff worked with Peter in finding the third stele." She smiled. "He had such a knack for finding them." She took in a deep breath and tried to keep from crying. "He told me the next time he visited he would have an idea about where to find the others."

Zuri took a step forward. "Really? What did he say?"

Janet shook her head. In spite of herself, tears came again. "He never made it home before . . . the incident."

Zuri put his hand on her shoulder. "What happened, Janet?"

She looked into his eyes; they looked so sympathetic. "Jeff and Amanda had been having meetings in the town near Peter's farm. They got this stupid plan in their heads to spoil the King's next honoring ceremony." Janet started pacing again. "Their zeal got a few others caught up in their enthusiasm—including Peter."

She turned and looked at Zuri. "Get this. They went to the town civic center and demolished several of the items Shepherd Randall had been collecting for the upcoming honoring ceremony. They . . . " Janet's voice trailed off. She put her hand to her mouth, slightly shaking her head, as tears came again.

Zuri led her to the desk chair near the picture window and had Janet sit. He knelt next to her. "What did they do?"

"Ya'akov was there from Jerusalem."

"You mean the priest gathering the items for the honoring ceremony?"

Janet nodded. "Jeff and Amanda lost it. Can you believe it? They took Ya'akov to the roof of the civic center, stabbed him, and tried to throw him off." Janet stood and paced again. "Unbelievable." She threw her arms in the air. "I have no idea what they were even thinking. I hear they were spouting something like, 'Our daughter will guide the Overtaker' and 'The device must succeed.'"

Janet shrugged. "But then . . . they were taken. They disappeared—including Peter." Janet put her face in her hands. Her whole body shook. She looked up again. Her face was tear-stained. "If only I had known. I could have put a stop to such a foolish plan."

Zuri came over and embraced her. "Oh, Janet. I am so very sorry."

After a few seconds, Janet let go of the embrace and patted Zuri on his shoulder. "Thank you." She walked over to a small table. "Care for some tea?" Her hands were shaking as she picked up a cup.

Zuri came over and took it from her. "Please, allow me. You sit and I'll prepare it for us."

Janet smiled and headed back to the sofa. "Thanks, Zuri. I guess I'm a little frazzled."

"That's totally understandable." He brought her tea and sat on the opposite end of the sofa.

Janet took a few sips and felt the warmth go all the way down. It did seem to calm her nerves.

"Do you think the girl is the key to the prophecy?"

Janet shrugged. "I don't know. But I heard Shepherd Randall had Raina, Peter's wife, take guardianship of the girl."

"Why would he do that? Where are they now?"

Janet shook her head. "Unsure on both questions. Although I heard Raina did attend the honoring ceremony, but she hasn't returned yet to my knowledge."

Zuri nodded. "I did hear Isabelle say something the other day."

Janet's eyes widened. "And?"

"And she said she was glad Angela was in Jerusalem, near the Prince."

"What does that mean?"

Zuri shrugged. "I don't know, and I couldn't ask since I wasn't supposed to hear it in the first place."

"Very curious. Do you think they're holding back on us?"

Zuri cocked his head slightly and gave a quick shrug. "Maybe. I don't know."

"Whatever it is, I hope it isn't as unfounded as her husband's volcano theory."

Zuri chuckled. There was silence between them for several seconds.

"How did Bruce take all of this?"

"Pretty hard. He's more withdrawn. Not his lively self. Although he tries not to, I think he blames me." She set her cup down. "I think even I blame me."

"No. You can't think that. How could you?"

Janet sat back on the sofa and looked down at her lap for a few seconds while smoothing some wrinkles in her clothing. She looked back at Zuri. "You may think this makes me a bad person, but we were so close to getting things ready for the Overtaker. This puts us significantly behind."

Zuri shook his head. "No, it's understandable you would feel bad on both counts."

"You and I know we can't be unprepared for the Overtaker's coming. It's not that far away. We must speed up the process. I was very hopeful since Peter was a quick study and had a passion for linguistics, geology, and geography."

"And animals."

Janet smiled. "Oh, most definitely animals. He was gifted in so many areas. Now, I'm—well, we're—at a loss. I don't even know what he was going to tell me about his idea of where to find the other steles." She paused but kept looking at Zuri.

"You have a plan, don't you?" He smiled. "You're always thinking, Janet."

"We need the Jerusalem Science Center."

Zuri's smiled faded. "What? No. I mean . . . yes, that would be nice. But . . . how is that even possible?"

Janet stood and strolled back to the picture window. "I have another son, Zuri."

Zuri walked over and stood next to Janet. "He's so young." He looked at her. "What will you do?"

"Oh, it will take several years to prepare him. But when he's ready, I'll give him all Peter's work and the steles."

Zuri's eyebrows raised. "You want him to follow in his brother's footsteps?"

Janet shook her head. "No. Although I'm sure he would want to. Kalem and Peter were very tight despite their age difference. Kalem is gifted—just not in the same areas Peter was."

"You want to teach him what Peter knew?"

"I think Kalem will make a fine archaeologist. He's very curious and likes to solve puzzles. Yet geography and linguistics—I don't think those will ever be his strong suits."

"So, what is your plan?"

"I want him to be taken."

Zuri's face paled. He took a step back. His voice was a hushed whisper. "Janet, surely not!"

Janet shook her head. "This will be planned and calculated."

"But . . . how?"

She looked out the window at the children playing. "He has several friends. I'll watch each of them over the next several years and see which of them will also be receptive to my influence. Before he can be considered rebellious, I'll let Shepherd Morgan know of the possibility of his actions—discretely, of course. Once he is taken with the steles, Professor Tiberius, head of the Science Center, won't be able to resist getting his team involved in interpreting them."

Zuri's eyes had been widening with each sentence, his lower jaw becoming slack. "Janet, that is so very dangerous."

Janet nodded and again looked out the window. "I know. But I think I know my son. With the right training and setting the right expectations, I know he can do it. He can be taken and not be converted." She looked back at Zuri. "It's a calculated risk, but a necessary one. Do you agree?"

"What will the Leader think?"

Janet gave a look of annoyance. "I don't really care, actually."

Zuri raised his eyebrows.

"Oh Zuri, really! Look at his obsession in looking all these centuries in the wrong places for these steles. It was you and me who convinced him he was wrong. Yet, has he changed his tactics? No. We still need to guide him. Granted, he started something wonderful, but it's up to us to finish it correctly." She paused and looked at him. "Are you with me on this?"

Zuri gave a slight smile. "Janet, you're the shrewdest person I know. I would be foolish not to follow your lead. You haven't steered me wrong yet."

Janet smiled and put her hand on his shoulder. "Thanks, Zuri. The Overtaker, I'm sure, will reward you greatly."

"Me following you is easier than you following you. What if Bruce finds out about this?"

Janet didn't hesitate. "He would probably hate me forever. But hard decisions must be made for the greater good of the coming Overtaker."

Zuri nodded and then burst into laughter.

Janet squinted but then turned to follow where Zuri was looking.

She chuckled. There stood Kalem with his face plastered to the glass in the French doors to her study. His nose was upturned against the glass, and he was making it go up and down. Once Kalem realized his mother saw him, he called her name.

Janet went over and opened the door.

"Mom, can me and the guys have some ice cream?"

"Sure. But first come in and meet someone. Kalem, this is Mr. Turay. He came all the way from Africa to extend his condolences to us regarding Peter."

Kalem shook his hand. "You knew my brother, Peter?"

Zuri smiled. "Yes I did, Kalem. It's great to meet you, also."

"Thank you." Kalem went over to the desk and looked at the picture. He looked at Janet. "I miss him, Mom."

Janet walked up behind Kalem and put her hands on his shoulders. She kissed the top of his head. "I know, sweetie. I do too."

Another boy walked in and stood next to Kalem.

"Zuri, this is Kalem's friend, Dillon."

"Hi, Dillon. I'm pleased to meet you."

Dillon shook his hand. "How do you do?"

Zuri smiled and looked at Janet, who smiled back in his direction.

Dillon pointed to the picture. "Where is she, Mrs. O'Brien?"

Kalem quickly wiped a tear from his cheek with the back of his hand. "Yeah, Mom. Where is she?"

Janet looked at the picture and frowned seeing Raina looking back at her. "I don't know, sweetie. I guess we're on our own to grieve." She patted his shoulders. "Let's go get that ice cream, huh?"

Janet motioned for Zuri to follow. "Care for some ice cream, Zuri?"

Zuri smiled. "Sounds good. I haven't had any in a long time."

As Janet reached the door of the study, she turned to close it but saw Dillon still at the desk gazing blankly at the picture.

"Coming, Dillon?"

"Do you blame the King, Mrs. O'Brien?" Dillon looked from the picture to her.

Janet walked over and put her hand on Dillon's shoulder. As she looked at the picture, she realized it wasn't just Raina at fault.

The King also was to blame.

"I do. Indeed, I do." She took his hand. "Let's go get that ice cream."

I hope you've enjoyed this book. Letting others know of your enjoyment of *Iron in the Scepter* is a way to help them share your experience. Please consider posting an honest review. You can post a review at Amazon, Barnes & Noble, Goodreads, or other places you choose.

Reviews can also be posted at more than one site!

This author, and other readers, appreciate your engagement. Also, check out my next book coming soon!

—Randy Dockens

The Facts Are Likely Different from Our Traditions!

And tell us what you think at randydockens.com

**Advance orders available at
Amazon and Barnes & Noble
October 2020**

Do the biblical facts match our fondest traditions?

Some people have difficulty understanding how the Old and New Testaments can gel into a cohesive whole. Yet, if the fact is accepted that the authors of Scripture were Jewish, and their point of view is considered, then many Scriptures typically overlooked or considered boring actually come to life and yield deeper meanings with rich nuances to these otherwise ignored passages. In addition, with the biblical view of humans divided into Jews and Gentiles, another layer of understanding comes alive. While it is known that the Jews are considered God's chosen people, we see that God entrusts them with the great responsibility of being his ambassadors. Yet we also find that God had the idea of inclusion for both groups from the very beginning. All these things shape our worldview, how we interact with others, and even how we view God.

So come read and expand your biblical horizon. How God views the world may actually help you change how you view *your* world. And it may just change how you celebrate your most precious biblical traditions.

You may even start some new traditions from a different perspective.

Also, please check out:
https://randydockens.com/news/

THE STELE PENTALOGY

Do you know *your future*?

Come see the possibilities in a world God creates and how an apocalypse leads to promised wonders beyond imagination.

Read how some experience mercy, some hope, and some embrace their destiny—while others try to reshape theirs. And how some, unfortunately, see perfection and the divine as only ordinary and expected.

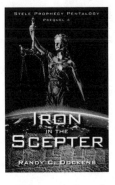

All five books of this exciting series from Randy C. Dockens are available now.

THE CODED MESSAGE TRILOGY

Come read this fast-paced trilogy, where an astrophysicist accidently stumbles upon a world secret that plunges him and his friends into an adventure of discovery and intrigue . . .

What Luke Loughton and his friends discover could possibly be the answer to a question you've been wondering all along.

This series is available now!

Erabon Prophecy Trilogy

Come read this exciting trilogy where an astronaut, working on an interstellar gate, is accidently thrown so deep into the universe that there is no way for him to get home.

He does, however, find life on a nearby planet, one in which the citizens look very different from him. Although tense at first, he finds these aliens think he is the forerunner to the return of their deity and charge him with reuniting the clans living on six different planets.

What is stranger to him still is that while everything seems so foreign from anything he has ever experienced, there is an element that also feels extremely familiar.

This series will be available in 2021.